All characters in this book are ...
persons, living or dead, is entirely coincidental. The names, incidents, dialogue, and opinions expressed within are products of the author's imagination and are not meant to be construed as real. Nothing is intended or should be interpreted as expressing, or representing, the views of DARPA, or any other department or agency of any government body. Nothing is intended or should be interpreted as expressing, or representing, the views of MIT, Sapienza University, or any institution of higher learning.

Copyright © 2021 by Rod P. Couser

All rights reserved. No part of this book may be reproduced or used in any manner without written permission of the copyright owner except for the use of quotations in a book review. For more information, address: rpcouser@gmail.com

First paperback edition December 2021

Book design by Rod P. Couser
Cover Photo by 19234655 © Leach | Dreamstime.com

ISBN 978-1-7376917-7-8 (Hardcover)
ISBN 978-1-7376917-3-0 (Paperback)
ISBN 978-1-7376917-4-7 (eBook)

Dedication

To Barbara, my bashert, for always allowing me the freedom to do the things I love and enjoy. I am blessed to have you in my life.

Prologue

Halifax, Nova Scotia

Bridget Drummond stepped out of the dark blue Mercedes S600 sedan and gave a polite nod to the driver as she turned and walked toward the doors leading into the Granville Hotel in downtown Halifax, Nova Scotia. A chilly wind roared down Hollis Street, as she quickly entered the revolving doors rather than pull on her overcoat. Once inside the lobby, she adjusted her demeanor to let others know she intended to be left alone, heading straight for the lobby bar and her preferred seat in the corner.

The observant bartender saw her coming, and familiar with this look, quickly placed a 'reserved sign' in front of the stool to the right of the corner. He then placed a glass of 2009 Sancerre Sauvignon Blanc down on the bar. The mysterious Ms. Drummond was an excellent tipper for outstanding service and Sancerre was her usual drink of choice, although it was not on the bar's wine list. She had previously complained their wine selections needed repair, although hotel manager, Pierre D'Entremont had no intention of changing them. The taste of Ms. Drummond highly outperformed his clientele, so it made more sense to stock a few special bottles just for her.

Bridget sat, placing her phone and tablet in front of her before taking a sip, allowing it to roll into her mouth for a moment as she thought about the events of the day. Her dark blue and cream pant suit was flawless as she wiped down a crease in her slacks to avoid a wrinkle. In fashionable heels, she was over six feet tall, which when added to her exotic features, and shoulder-length blond hair, created a memorable, if not intoxicating appearance; hence her bitch face. She enjoyed many things, but being hit on by unworthy business executives was not one of them.

She glanced at the bartender and tipped her glass to him as a sign of thanks before jotting several fresh notes on her tablet. It wasn't long before her thoughts drifted to her deceased brother, Maximillian. Six months earlier, Maximillian Drummond, then CEO of MDE Enterprises, had been self-exiled on an island in the Southern Sea. It is unclear what happened, but within just days of arriving, the head of his security detail and Maximillian were both dead.

The searchable information on the matter was highly scripted, but said the Royal Marines had stormed the island and killed them in a subsequent gun battle, but Bridget thought this suspicious. Head of security, yes, but Maximilian? No. He would never have placed himself in such a situation, so she had made it her mission to understand exactly what really happened. To assist with this effort, she had spoken to her senior analyst, Angus Adair who was directing a team of hackers to uncover the truth. He had concluded they needed an eyewitness and further surmised that on the day of his death, only two persons might have been with Maximillian. One was his acting head of security, Bruce Morgan, and the other, a physicist, Dr. Christopher Berniece, who often worked with him on special projects.

Morgan and Berniece were at that moment, incarcerated, having been arrested during that same raid, but Angus speculated Morgan had most likely been with his men as the attack was beginning. That would leave Berniece as the likely candidate. With this lead, Bridget had contacted her solicitor to pay him a visit.

Solicitor Hasina Andrianasolo was one of many in the vast army of the MDE Enterprises legal team, but he wasn't just any solicitor. He was one of a few used for projects, rough projects, that required more than just a sharp legal mind. And so, here he was, at Her Majesty's Prison (HMP), Edinburgh, waiting for access to Dr. Christopher Berniece.

Berniece was awaiting a transfer to HMP Glenochil to serve the rest of his eight-year sentence. Because of special circumstances arranged by the Secret Intelligence Service (SIS), formerly known as MI6 of James Bond fame, he could be eligible for release in just two years.

The guard buzzed Andrianasolo in and he walked down the various corridors and security stops before being led into a small room with a steel wall and a plexiglass shield in the center. Andrianasolo sat and waited for them to bring in the prisoner and after several minutes, the door opened and Berniece entered and went to the chair, and sat. The guards walked out and left them alone.

Looking at each other, Dr. Berniece spoke first. "They said you were a solicitor; you don't look it."

Andrianasolo replied, "Funny. You don't look like a criminal, but here we are."

Bernice did not react. "What can I do for you?"

"I need some information."

"About what?"

"The events leading to the death of Maximillian Drummond. My client wants to know who killed him, and I think you were there."

"Sir, I cannot help you."

"I think you can."

"I can't and I won't. They based my sentence on my limited participation and absolute silence, but I know why you're here. I cannot say anything about that day to anyone, including what I assume is a solicitor to Bridget Drummond."

"Doctor, I just need to know who did it. Was it someone from his own security? Was it Royal Marines? I'm told the US Navy Seals were there. Was it one of them? You?"

"Me? What about me?"

"Maybe you killed him?"

"That is absurd and for your information, although I have a doctorate in physics, it is socially incorrect to call me *Doctor*. I'm sorry, but as I have said, I cannot help you."

"When do they transfer you to Glenochil?"

Surprised he would know this, Berniece replied, "I don't know, but expect it will be soon."

"What if I told you that won't happen?"

"Are you threatening me?"

"Of course not. I just know how dangerous prisons can be."

"And what? If I don't tell you, I'll be a recipient of this danger?"

"Your words, Doctor, not mine." Andrianasolo replied with a smirk.

"Please… I honestly cannot tell you."

"Okay. Be very careful the rest of the week." Andrianasolo replied as he stood and gave one last look to Berniece. His expression told Berniece all he needed to know. They were going to kill him, and he knew all too well the powers within this company. Wishing he had never agreed to work for Maximillian Drummond, he motioned for Andrianasolo to sit, and he did.

He looked about as if someone could hear him, placed his hand over his mouth and said, "It was the young Italian girl, Sara Ricci," he mumbled, shaking his head.

Surprised, Andrianasolo looked at him and said, "You're joking, right?"

"No. Maximillian and I were off to one side in a small room with the girl. Maximillian became highly agitated after Grant Aiken, his head of security, was killed and demanded, forcefully, answers from her. One minute she was looking for papers needed to reveal a secret that Maximillian insisted was there, and the next she shot several times. I don't recall how many shots, but one hit Maximillian in the head and another hit me in the side. I awoke twenty-four hours later in the infirmary aboard the HMS *Dauntless* under heavy guard and didn't realize Maximilian had perished until they questioned me in London."

"Well, Doctor, I gotta tell you, I was not expecting that. You helped me, so I will help you."

"With all due respect, sir, I will be fine on my own. Thank you."

"Let's cross that bridge when you get out." Andrianasolo pounded on the table twice and then stood as a guard opened his door to let him out. As he retraced his steps out of the prison, he decided not to meet with Bridget Drummond face-to-face. He would do this over the phone. It would be safer.

Bridget was still at the bar with a fresh glass of Sancerre as the thoughts of her brother entwined with thoughts of revenge. At issue were those that called for the raid on their residence on the Isle of Skye in the Scottish highlands weeks before the subsequent raid on the island. That single act had started everything. It had forced Maximillian to flee, and that ultimately led to his death, regardless of who killed him.

Maximillian was no saint, and Bridget knew he had crossed many lines with his government and various intelligence agencies during the year prior, but someone killed him. Murdered him. And Bridget felt compelled to avenge him. It is certainly what he would have done.

On the flip side, her current situation was powerful. As the newly appointed CEO of MDE Enterprises, Bridget was no longer in his shadow. Under her leadership, the businesses were doing very well, and she wasn't yet convinced it made sense to risk everything to prove a point that would not change the outcome of what had happened. The buzzing of her phone interrupted that thought. She took a quick sip of her wine and noted it was her solicitor, Andrianasolo. "What do you have for me?"

"Your intel was correct; Dr. Berniece was there."

"And?"

He explained the exact words that Berniece had used and left nothing out. When he finished, he waited for a response, which came quickly.

"So, after all Maximillian's efforts to get to her… she got to him. How ironic."

"That's what he said, and I believe him. I left him no doubt of his predicament."

"Yes, I can imagine. I would never have thought of her."

"Will there be anything else, Ms. Drummond?"

"No, not yet. I need to think. Thank you." As she hung up, she took a sip and thought, *perhaps she would avenge Maximillian. If nothing else, Sara Ricci had to die. It was only fair.*

1

Rome, Italy

Sara Ricci walked briskly out of the three-story building where her flat was located, just a few hundred meters from the campus of Sapienza University, a medieval university in the heart of Rome. Sara had transferred here the year before from Massachusetts Institute of Technology (MIT), where she had started her PhD in physics. This short walk to campus was a gift from her father, Giovanni, who had purchased the flat as an investment, or so he said.

Bounding down the stairs, she turned out of her parking lot before crossing the busy Viale Regina Elena motorway. Once across, she was effectively on campus and headed toward the Department of Physics building. She was meeting with her thesis chair, Dr. Emilio Ferrera.

As she came into the foyer, she said hello and asked if he was available. He was, and the assistant took her in. He looked up from the desk as she entered, smiled as he put down a small stack of papers. "Sara, pleasant afternoon. How is your dissertation coming along?"

"Very well, Dr. Ferrera. All chapters are complete in draft form. I was wondering if you could recommend a scientific editor."

"As your chairperson, I cannot do this, but we do have a list of candidates you may choose from."

"Okay, I understand. Please send it to me when you have a chance." She was hoping she could have just gotten a name and number as she waited for him to locate it.

"Hold on, it's right here." He opened a file cabinet, searched briefly, and pulled out a single page and handed it to her. "There you are. If I might ask, when do you intend to submit?" He was referring to her completed dissertation and subsequent presentation.

"I'm just months away. I still have many citations to verify, and need time for the editor, but to be honest, I'm struggling right now. It's all becoming a blur, and I think I need to step back for a bit."

"Sara, please know you are not alone. Many PhD candidates feel this way, although few, if any have gone through your journey." He nodded with respect, knowing much of her problems both in America and here in Italy the year before. This young woman was tough, that was for sure. "Perhaps you might consider a few days off. A mental holiday, if you will."

"I just might. Thank you, Dr. Ferrera." As she waved the editor list and left.

Born in Horsforth, England twenty-seven years before, Sara Ricci was the only child of Italian parents, Giovanna and Annini Ricci. They had moved back to Milan, Italy in late 2003, when Sara was just thirteen.

Fortunately, she was fluent in Italian since her parents, immersed in English at work, usually spoke Italian at home. Her father, a pension administrator, and mother, a writer of children's books, nurtured their intelligent and dedicated daughter toward higher education. Sara had completed her master's two years earlier and when it came time to consider her doctorate, she had chosen the Massachusetts Institute of Technology (MIT). Life in America was wonderful when, literally, all hell broke loose in her third year, bringing her back to Italy and to Sapienza University.

Heading now to her office on campus, her cell buzzed. She glanced at her watch and noted an incoming text from Jason Sykes in America. Jason was the closest thing Sara had ever had to a boyfriend, even though they were thousands of miles apart and, frankly, not much of a couple. They had never been intimate but were close and romance seemed at least plausible.

Part of the issue was that Sara was a scientist, an honest to god nerd to the extent, her old roommate at MIT nicknamed her Robot Girl. Not that Jason was much better. He was a former soldier from an all-military family and worked for the Defense Advanced Research Projects Agency (DARPA), which meant, that collectively; they sucked at personal communication.

Curious, Sara pulled the phone out of her hobo bag and read the text with some amusement as she walked: "Hey Sara. Well, I did it. I quit DARPA and I'm driving to Seattle to work for Dann De Vires at Versilant

Nanotechnologies. Sorry I didn't tell you, but it all happened kind of fast. I'm driving to Seattle now. It will take three days. Call anytime."

When Sara first met Jason two years before, she didn't really care for him. He was the liaison for DARPA to scientists they had under grant at Harvard and MIT, and his role was not the science. He was there to protect the scientists from harm, and the year before, he had certainly saved her. More than once, in fact.

Those close encounters brought them closer together, and given Jason was strong and unintimidated, it made Sara feel safe. Which was kind of sad. Until the year before, she had always felt safe. Now she rarely did.

Once she got to her office, she called him.

Jason was nearing Kansas City after driving for almost seventeen hours and had just hung up with Sara. The following day, he would continue west on Highway 70 before heading north at Denver, then west again toward Seattle. He occasionally patted his dashboard, hoping his late model Toyota 4-Runner would make it there in one piece.

After two more long days and an unhealthy amount of truck stop coffee, he pulled onto South Alaska Street just off Fifty-Fourth street. This was in Seward Park in the town of Lakewood, Washington, about ten miles south of downtown Seattle. The one-acre property had a principal house and a smaller rear guest house with a small workshop in the rear, which was for rent. Only minutes from Versilant

Nanotechnologies, his new employer, Jason jumped on it based solely on online pictures. Looking at it now in person, it was perfect.

The next morning, he drove to Versilant and met with his former roommate and friend, Dann De Vires, president, and owner. "Jason, great to see you. How was the drive?"

"Beautiful. I'm all settled in and glad to be here."

"Yeah, let's talk about that." As they sat down in his office. "Jason, our nanostructures are impressive, but our capabilities have limits. To expand them, we recently started working with a company out of Montreal, Cadieux Medical Technologies, or Cadieux MT for short. Unlike us, they are a true medical company, and they make a variety of surgical robots and cellular bots that can actually enter the body. Together, we want to expand and create an entire family of nanobots, but many will need a skeletal frame, which we do very well. I bring this up because I want you to head up a team to work with them. Our goal is to create a family of intravenous nanobots, and Susan and I are thinking of financially partnering with them. A company within a company, so to speak."

"Wow, I'm honored, but you have far better talent here than me. Why not tap into one of your own, rather than the new guy? And a consultant at that."

Dann laughed. "Well, you're not wrong, but first, this might not work. Second, we are really busy, and my two top designers are already leading projects equally, if not more important. The real reason I want you to head this up is because some of these nanobots need to drive, like a car. The locomotion power would likely be magnetics and I thought with Sara in your back pocket, we could get there faster than otherwise. She's almost done with her PhD, right?"

"Yes, actually." Jason paused as he thought about this, *how cool would it be for Sara to be here in Seattle and the two of them working on the same project...*

"So, questions, thoughts?"

"It's a great idea and I'm in. I'll call Sara in the morning."

"Great, I'll have the Cadieux MT guys get hold of you."

"So, this company within a company, how would that work?"

"We haven't actually figured it out, but conceptually, we, Versilant, would supply labor and technology and act as the manufacturer and Cadieux MT, would provide early and live trials, marketing, and sales. They would buy into the joint venture with their company stock as the balance of their side of the venture."

"Sounds simple."

"It's actually not. I haven't accepted their offer because we need cash to weather the R&D phase. Obviously, I can't allow Versilant to fail because of this venture."

"And they're only offering stock?"

"Yes, but here is the problem. Although we would get about ten-million dollars of in Cadieux MT shares, they are restricted. We couldn't sell for six-months and that is precisely when we'll be spending the most cash."

"Okay. Well, good luck. I'll let you know what Sara says. I know she loves a challenge."

2

Montreal, Canada

The brutal cold was coming to Montreal, as Remy Cadieux stepped out of the helicopter that had just brought him to the Cadieux MT headquarters from the Montréal/Saint-Hubert Heli-Inter Heliport. He had been to an offsite sales meeting to discuss strategies for the next year. As he glanced from the rooftop helipad, the city views of Montreal were stunning in this four-season metropolis with a Parisian look and feel.

Remy, a third generation Chief Executive Officer (CEO) for the hundred-year-old company, hurried into the elevator that took him down to the fifth floor and his office. His four-year stint as the CEO was outwardly a tremendous success. The Company had gone from a private, to a public concern, revenues had tripled, and they were a leader in medical robots, related supplies, and service contracts. Financially, the company stock was ten times higher than their initial public offering, although it was down from its high two years before.

Such rapid growth gave him some leeway with the board of directors, but his father, Gustave Cadieux, the former CEO, now the Chairman of the Board, was always a threat. Gustave was privately proud of his son, but the amount of debt Remy had placed on the business alarmed his highly conservative nature. So, while the board was kind to Remy, Gustave, with his long-term relationships with the board members, could sway them his way if needed. For now, he considered that his little secret, although everyone, including Remy, knew it.

Remy said a quick hello to his assistant and headed down the hall to the office of his Chief Financial Officer (CFO), Jenesse Tremblay. "Jenesse, love, what do you have for me?"

"Good morning, Remy and I am certainly not your love. How was the meeting?"

"Overall, good. They have some great ideas for next year. Any thoughts on the Versilant deal?"

"Well, as we have discussed, this shouldn't be a big deal. Our estimate of the joint venture valuation is thirty million dollars. When you remove the intellectual capital from both sides, it suggests our portion requires a buy-in of ten million. Given the board will not allow you to create debt; our only option is cash or an all-stock purchase. My advice is to create a separate entity in your name, and fund it yourself with your own money."

"I don't have that kind of cash and can't sell my own shares because I would have to get family approval, so here we go again. Another epic battle with Dad and the family over my own fucking money."

"Remy, surely you can raise ten million using your own assets as collateral."

Gears turning in his head, he asked, "Not without lifestyle changes I do not wish to consider. How about private money?"

"Expensive but possible."

"How much return would they require?"

"Fifteen to twenty percent. The problem there is the endgame. If they give you the money on a five-year note, at fifteen percent, you will get ten million up front, and five years later, owe them just over twenty million. It's certainly possible for the new product family to raise that much profit in five years, but it's also a risk."

"Jenesse, you have not been helpful. Find me ten million dollars that my father doesn't know about," as he turned and walked out, slamming the door.

Jenesse knew Remy was frustrated, but seriously, here was the CEO of a billion-dollar company with a personal net worth of at least one hundred million, but had almost no cash of his own. Of course, she would never say it out loud, but Remy simply spent money like it was water. She would have to make a few calls.

Sara Ricci sat cross-legged on a small outdoor couch on her terrace with the sounds of Rome's infamous traffic congestion in the background. Dressed in leggings and an extra-large Sapienza University sweatshirt to ward off the cool breeze, she read the paragraph within her dissertation for the third time. And for the third time, it made no sense. She considered that a sign her brain had gone into protection mode and wisely turned away from her tablet computer. As she did so, she tilted her head back and momentarily closed her eyes as the melodic piano of Yanni, *One Man's Dream*, played softly in the background.

A PhD dissertation is a written account of one's entire effort. Usually produced as a book with six chapters, the first is an introduction to your thesis; what are you trying to prove? Following that is an abstract, or an executive summary of the entire process. The next four to five sections are separated, and explain how the researcher conducted the experiments and then how they verified and validated their thesis to be correct. That is following by conclusions, and occasionally, suggestions for future work.

As Sara opened her eyes, she wisely elected to stop for the day and as she went to turn off her tablet, her cell phone rang. She looked at her watch and again; it was Jason. She picked up her phone and answered, "Ciao, Jason. How are you?"

"Good, just checking in to see how you're doing. Are you done for the day?"

"I literally just finished. My brain actually hurts. How is Versilant?"

"Really well. We are working on a new line of medical nanobots. Some with nanostructures, others biological, but here is the amazing part and the reason for my call. Some of these nanobots will be transporters of medicine, healthy cells, or as repair devices. They're called nanobot cars, and doctors will drive them from outside the body. We don't have a complete design specification, but I'm leading the project and thought you might help."

"Jason, that sounds fun, but I know very little about nanotechnology or biology."

"Yeah, I got that, but here's the fun part. We're considering electromagnetics as the primary method to move them."

"Okay, interesting, but wow, I have almost no downtime as it is."

"I know and wasn't even going to call, but Dann De Vires, you remember him from your sensors, right? Well, he was asking if perhaps you had an interest in being a paid consultant to Versilant on this. At least for the design specification."

"Jason, I know you want me there, which is very sweet, but I still have a job here and need to see this through. I am so close to the end."

"I know. Sorry to bug you, but at least think about it. I suspect you can do both." They talked for several minutes before hanging up. As Sara did, she thought a bit about what he said and reached over and turned her tablet back on.

In Seattle, looking at the boats on Lake Washington from an Adirondack chair he had made in his small workshop, Jason smiled as he took a sip of his beer. He knew Sara and would bet anyone that right that second; she was already looking into this.

3

Three hours later, Sara was still on the terrace in the dark researching nanobots and their medical applications; truly amazing and innovative stuff. There were devices to diagnose, analyze, deliver drugs, and even repair. Built on a nanoscale, meaning billionths of a meter, they were making nanobots using human cells, organic/inorganic systems, acids, bacteria, and even DNA strands. Sara, knowing she was way over her head, had earlier sent a quick text to meet with a fellow PhD student and friend, Amy Keningburg. Amy was a biologist and could save Sara hours of research.

The following afternoon, Sara and Amy met and discussed the basics. As expected, Amy was all over this, and they talked about the possibility of using ultrasound, radio waves or magnetics to move the cellular based nanobots and concluded that all could provide guidance. Magnetics provided an easy source of movement, but ultrasound signals could not only provide movement, but also give signals. Signals that told the nanobot to perform functions such as repair, dumping or providing drugs to a specific area to lessen the side-effects from therapies such as chemotherapy.

As they were finishing up, Sara realized this was really cool stuff, and Jason was her boyfriend, right? She felt a sense of obligation to help him, but seriously, what did that mean for her? She was just months away from completing a five-year journey towards her PhD. Now was probably not the time to get distracted.

Amy sensed her interest and was excited for her. "So, what are you going to do?"

"I don't know."

"But you'll need at least four weeks for the editor right and then another two just to complete the edits. That's six weeks."

"I thought of that as well."

"You seem apprehensive. Is it about being with Jason?"

"No, not at all. It's about America."

"I have never been but heard it's great."

"A year ago, I would have agreed. That was before everything changed for me."

Amy looked down, not sure if she should say anything, but replied, "There was some talk going around that someone tried to kill you. Is that what you meant?"

Sara had not really told anyone at the university about the events that led up to her enrolling in Sapienza or after. Dr. Ferrera knew because he was part of the Carbonari inquest and faint news of her abduction was out to the public, but not much else. After a brief pause, she gave Amy a synopsis of what happened.

"I actually started my PhD at MIT in Boston, and all was fine until the beginning of my third year. I had just finished my prelims when my original thesis was disproven. Not three weeks later, my mom died. When I returned to Milan for her funeral, I was so emotionally broken, I decided to not come back."

"Oh Sara, I'm so sorry, I had no idea."

"Well, that's not the half of it. My dad was highly concerned, since to him, getting a PhD was my destiny. My great-great-grandfather was a physicist and taught at Padua University. He died in 1943 and it turns out his son secretly held onto his private work papers that eventually ended up with my dad. He had no idea what the papers were about, but thought if I read through them, it might revive my interest."

"Did you read them? Were there any secrets?"

"I did and yes there were, but I can't discuss that. I can tell you the Nazis wanted to weaponize his research. He refused and hid his papers before taking his own life. One hypothesis resonated with me, and I ended up going back to MIT and revising my thesis to his. Unfortunately, when I applied at MIT, during my background check, American intelligence tied me, Sara Ricci, to him, Gilberti Ricci, and immediately DARPA became interested in me and my work. That is actually how I met Jason."

"DARPA, how cool is that? They do amazing research."

"Yes. The problem was someone else had made the same connection. A rich industrialist out of Scotland, and within three months, someone hacked my data on the MIT server, searched my office, and even tried to abduct me. Jason saved my life. That was the first time. When I took my backup data offline to a private security company, gunman using a helicopter shot the owner and stole all my detailed research. We would find out later it was all related to this industrialist. He wanted to commercialize my inventions."

"So, you came here to Sapienza to get away from him?"

"No. While at MIT, I eventually accepted a grant from DARPA for proper security. Turns out the assistant director that gave me the grant was working with the industrialist as a spy. They believe he was also involved with a terrorist organization and was ultimately killed, but not before the terrorists leaked information on the dark web from my stolen work. I made it look like I was involved, and MIT suspended me pending an investigation. In time I was exonerated, but the fact they thought I could align myself with a terrorist was humiliating and I immediately resigned from their program and severed my grant with DARPA."

"Sara, I had no idea. That is just baffling and downright scary. I can't believe you went through all of that."

"Sadly, it didn't stop here. The industrialist had his security team kidnap me from Rome and took me to an island off the coast of Antarctica. I can't discuss what happened there, but he thought within Gilberti's papers, was a design for a weapon of mass destruction and threatened to kill me if I didn't locate it for him. There was no such secret, and he was killed before he could kill me. Jason and others rescued me. That was just eight months ago."

Amy, with a look of horror on her face, was speechless and immediately hugged Sara. Sara wasn't sure what to do, but hugged her back. As they separated, Sara said, "So that is my story and the reason I am afraid to go back to America."

"But the crazy bastard is dead right, it's over regardless of country you're in."

"The corporation he ran is still there, and the sister is now the CEO. Although I have never met her, I'm told she is as ruthless as he, but you're right in one respect, Versilant has nothing to do with her."

As she said that, she realized she had decided. This had nothing to do with MDE Enterprises and there was no reason for her to be afraid and besides, she would have her favorite bodyguard with her the entire time. Jason Sykes.

4

The dark blue AS365 Dauphin helicopter with the MDE Enterprises logo banked left as it slowed and hovered downward to the heliport. Located atop the joint headquarters building of MDE Aerospace and MDE Defense, it touched down in an icy drizzle on the same grounds as Gatwick Airport, forty-five minutes outside of London. Bridget Drummond looked out of the window and waited for her assistant, Giselle Brodeur, to come out from under the protective cover with an umbrella.

Giselle had been the executive assistant to Maximillian prior to his death, although Bridget didn't care for her. In time, she would replace her, but right now, Giselle knew where the bodies were buried, and less than a month officially into the job, Bridget needed some help with whom to trust.

Out of the rain, Giselle and Bridget went directly to her new office. They entered, and Giselle spoke first. "Ms. Drummond, welcome and again, congratulations."

"Thank you Giselle," knowing that she was referring to the board of directors' recent decision to remove Bridget's Acting CEO position and appoint her the CEO. Bridget had long been second in command at MDE Enterprises, the corporation she and her brother had built on the remnants of her father's original business, a textile manufacturing company in Leigh, Scotland.

Giselle continued, "You have meetings for much of the day, most of which are routine for you. The exception is meeting with your solicitors regarding continued disclosures and documents as they continue to unravel the holdings of Maximillian to yourself. Is there anything I can do to assist you in preparation?"

"Yes,… make sure there is a cold bottle of Rombauer Sauvignon Blanc in the fridge. I cannot handle his solicitors cold sober."

"Already taken care of."

"Very well." As she looked through various phone messages on her tablet, she paused at one and asked, "Giselle, who is Ms. Jenesse Tremblay?"

"She is the CFO of a medical robotics company in Montreal. I believe they received our inquiry regarding MDE Defense, but rather than talk with Alexandre Arnaud, she wishes to talk directly with you."

"I shouldn't, but I'll hear her out. Arrange for a call whenever you can fit it in."

"Yes, no problem. If that is all?" Giselle rose and left without waiting for a response.

Bridge walked over to the window, which looked over the south runway at Gatwick, thinking of her empire. The holdings of MDE Enterprises included MDE Aerospace, MDE Defense, MDE

Commodities, the newest company in the portfolio, MDE Trust. With Maximillian's death and a firm hand on his solicitors, Bridget now owned thirty-nine percent of the company stock, with an estimated net worth of four billion euros. Offshore and hidden away, she had at least half that amount more.

It was late afternoon when Bridget received the call from Jenesse Tremblay in Montreal. Her accent was hard to understand, but Bridget's French was limited, so they spoke in English.

"Ms. Tremblay, I'm told you would only talk to me and not the Managing Director of MDE Defense, Alexandre Arnaud, who sent you the original prospectus. I assume there is reason."

"Ms. Drummond, I know he is capable. I am calling on behalf of Remy Cadieux, the CEO of Cadieux Medical Technologies. The opportunity we have is approximately ten million dollars. Because of investments monsieur Cadieux has already made, and the debt related to our explosive growth, the board is not allowing him to raise funds through debt until they achieve certain debt coverage ratios. Such information is sensitive for a man in his position."

"Ms. Tremblay, that seems positively ridicules, given your size, but I am not here to judge you. Tell Mr. Cadieux I can meet him at his convenience."

"Thank you, Ms. Drummond. I wish you a pleasant evening." She hung up as Bridget did the same, thinking there just might be an interesting opportunity here. Bridget loved people in power that didn't understand it, and Remy Cadieux sounded like just the sort she could own.

5

Seattle, Washington

Alitalia flight 7614 landed in Seattle after a long layover in New York. Jason was there at the airport to pick Sara up, and, after a quick hug, they headed to his guest house. They had both eaten prior to her arrival, but he pulled out some crackers and cheese and they walked across the street. There he set up two lawn chairs off to the side of Lake Washington Blvd, allowing them to watch the water just as the moon was showing over the clouds, offering some natural light.

"So, were you able to get an editor?" Jason asked.

"I did, and he has the manuscript. He's estimating four weeks to completion."

"Excellent. What about your citations?" Jason was referring to the fact that Sara could use any published research within her own as long as she gave credit to the actual person or entity that did the original research. In Sara's case, she had just under three-hundred citations, and each had to be verified.

"No problem. I hired a former assistant to help cite my research material."

"I can imagine your dad wasn't too happy about you coming out here?"

"No, and neither was Dr. Ferrera. I told them I needed a break, but it wasn't a defection. I even allowed Dr. Ferrera to schedule my presentation; eighty-four days from today. But let's forget all that. I'm here."

This was only the second time they had been together following Sara's rescue on Heard island the year before. When Sara finally returned to Italy, Jason had spent a week with her. Sitting now by the water's edge, drinking wine, and talking of everything under the rare partial moonlight, you would think they had always been together.

The next morning, after the weakest cup of coffee Sara had ever tasted, they headed over to Versilant. Jason walked her in, and they headed straight for Dann De Vires' office.

Jason introduced Sara to Dann. "Sara, it is so great to meet you face-to-face."

"Yes, thank you. I'm happy to be here and would love to meet the team that helped Jason with the sensors. It was a big deal, and I have the details on what we accomplished."

"Of course. That would be outstanding. We rarely get direct feedback, and the engineers will appreciate it. Has Jason brought you up to speed on the nanobot family we are working on with Cadieux MT out of Canada?"

"He has, and that is why I am here," as she handed him the signed consultant agreement and NDA. "I have six weeks before my dissertation is back from the editor and will use that time to work with you. I already have a lot of information and have been working with a fellow biologist in Italy to understand the interactions I am less familiar with."

"Excellent." Dann replied.

Sara and Jason worked the rest of the week with the Versilant team, and quickly meshed to where several commented it was as if they had always worked there. Not much later, they had a rough design specification for six different products and at some point, they would share this Cadieux MT.

As the day ended and the members dispersed, Jason and Sara headed to his truck. Driving back to the guest house, Sara asked casually, "Jason. Perhaps it's time I considered getting a place of my own."

Jason held the steering wheel a little tighter. Although he expected this, it didn't make it feel any better hearing it. "I know. God forbid we spend too much time together. By all means, do whatever you want." He didn't mean it to come out so childishly, but it was already out.

"Jason please. It is wonderful to be with you, but in less than five weeks, I'm off again. You are starting a new life here and I am going back to Italy. How will that be any easier if we are together like a married couple the whole time?"

"Yeah, just imagine. One of us might even get feelings during that time strong enough to question if we really want to be apart."

"You are saying I have no feelings?" Sara shouted.

Sensing her anger, he softened. "Sara, I didn't say that. Really, it's no problem. If you have a place in mind, we can drive over tomorrow and check it out." He pulled into the driveway, and they went inside in silence.

The next morning, they drove over to a tiny house Sara had found. The term "Tiny House" was a sound bite for television to describe what was actually a two-hundred-eighty square foot prefabricated home. This one had a partial view of the lake, and it was just minutes from Jason's house. Not ten minutes later; Sara was already signing the paperwork and Jason's first thought was perhaps they just weren't meant to be.

Later that evening, sitting in her new place, Sara was reading about hollow nano-objects that could trap viruses to render them harmless. She reached over and hit play on her old but relevant MP3 player and soon, *Atlantis,* by Richard Kastle, filled the small space. Her mind drifted to Jason and while she enjoyed being with him, she needed to protect herself. There was just no way she could live full time in America, not even for him.

By Thursday, the following week, the Versilant team had completed the six preliminary design specifications, plus the virus trap version Sara and Amy had considered. These seven designs would be shared with the CEO of Cadieux MT who was arriving the next day.

When Remy Cadieux arrived, it was raining as a limo pulled up and two people stepped out. When they entered the building, Jason recognized Remy and mentioned it to Sara. She smiled, thinking he was an attractive man. The other was the Chief Operating Officer, (COO), Henri Cadieux, Remy's brother, and a skilled scientist himself. They all met in the conference room and Dann started the meeting. Jason rose and walked over to the front and introduced himself and then the key members of his team. When he introduced Sara, Remy seemed to recognize her name, but said nothing.

One by one, Jason went through each general design specification and both Remy and Henri asked many questions, in fact, more than seemed reasonable. Jason answered what he could and occasionally asked Sara or other engineers for input. In most of the verbal exchanges, all was fine, but when he asked Sara, her answers were very succinct and vague.

In one exchange, Henri asked, "And would this nanobot include an embedded chemical biosensor and, if so, what type?"

"Yes, and as yet undetermined." Sara said.

"But if you were going to use one, what do you think it would it be?"

"I cannot answer this until we determine if this is an actual design candidate."

It was obvious he wanted to know, and she would not say. Frustrated, he dropped it. In the next exchange, Remy asked a question as they discussed the mechanisms for propulsion.

"Ms. Ricci, besides ultrasound, which is your preferred source of locomotion, I have a note from my team that you were considering a non-radiated version of electromagnetism. Can you explain this, please?"

"Monsieur, since we have not elected to use it, the method does not matter."

"Yes, that is true, but I'm interested."

"Until we start a project that uses this, I cannot discuss this further."

Remy rose, looked at Dann, and then back to Sara. "Ms. Ricci, have Henri or I offended you." The entire room was silent now.

Sara answered, "No, monsieur, not at all."

"Then why do you refuse to answer any of our questions?"

Sara looked bewildered, but noticed everyone was looking at her, including Dann. "Monsieur, I meant no disrespect. I am merely a consultant to Versilant, and my NDA does not allow me to reveal anything that is deemed to be our intellectual property. Until I am instructed otherwise, I have offered only a general description, but not the crux of any design. This is most appropriate given that to my knowledge, no formal agreement exists between the two companies."

Dann, mortified, looked over at Remy and thankfully, he was actually smiling as he replied, "But of course, Ms. Ricci. I understand." With that, he rose and said they had enjoyed the day and would return to Canada, motioning for Henri to rise as well, and shortly after, they walked out to an awaiting car. The team continued to look at Sara. There were looks of agreement, admiration, and a few of disdain. One engineer actually said, "Nice work robot girl, you just cost us our chance at millions." Jason actually agreed, but said nothing.

Moments later, Dann stood and said, "Sara, Jason, my office. The rest of you, well done." He turned and went to his office as Sara and Jason followed him. He sat and asked Sara to close the door before he said highly agitated, "Sara, I will remind you, I own this company. Please do not speak for me again."

Sara, hardly a wallflower, immediately responded, "I did no such thing. They asked me the question, not you. I answered the truth. Do you deny the legal documents you made me sign? If they were for show, why have me sign them? And if you do not agree with my response, why did you then not instruct me to tell them whatever they wanted?"

"Sara, we were meeting with the CEO. This was our chance to show them why they need us and although I think we did, we could have really wowed them. Instead, they are likely questioning the deal itself and I would never call out one of my employees in public."

"Mr. De Vires, I apologize for any misunderstanding. If the outcome of today was to give them all our secrets so they might proceed without us, you should have told me that was your intention. The amount of questioning today was not just because it was simply interesting."

Dann looked down embarrassed and for a split second realized he never looked at it that way and further, she might be right. They were asking a lot of very detailed questions. He could have calmed the situation right then, but rather than agree, he simply reaffirmed his previous comments. Sara excused herself, silently fuming, and immediately left Versilant, taking an Uber home.

Jason, who was still in Dann's office, didn't even know she left.

As the limousine pulled into the executive jet terminal, Remy said to his brother, "The designs are even better than I imagined. Versilant has a great team and wow, that Italian gal is smart as a whip." As he looked out the window, he added, "And easy on the eyes."

Henri rolled his eyes at yet another sexist remark and replied, "I have a lot to work with, but we'll have to see how far we can get. Much of the information was simply too general to complete the design. We need this team, Remy. Find a way to make it work."

Jason left that evening at his normal time. The team had told him Sara left hours before and he stopped at a local store and got a nice bottle of wine before heading for her house; they needed to talk. It was raining as he drove into the dusk light. As he parked, he found Sara sitting on a wooden log in the rain, soaking wet, looking out over the water. She didn't acknowledge him as he walked over to her.

"You're going to catch a cold out here. Let's go inside." He held out his hand and after a minute, she grabbed his hand and he helped her up. Her hands were cold as ice.

Inside, he helped her out of her wet clothes, making no advances, although that was the hardest thing he had ever done. She then took a warm but not hot shower before pulling on a fresh pair of yoga pants and a large sweatshirt. Jason poured the wine as she silently pulled a comb through her wet hair. He handed her a glass as she mumbled. "I'm sorry if I got you in trouble today. Even though I try to do the right thing, somehow, I always mess it up."

"Sara, I'm not in trouble. Dann got the team back together, and many felt the same as you. We have been giving these guys everything, and you basically called Dann out, and it was a bit of a gut kick for him. In retrospect, he agrees with you and he's sorry. He's calling Remy Cadieux tomorrow to tell him we're done if we can't get a deal."

"Jason, it is probably best if I just leave. The team might agree outwardly, but they aren't businesspeople and will only think I screwed this up for them if it doesn't happen."

"Sara, please don't go there. We need you. It's just that we have been so euphoric we didn't realize the dangers. I don't think there is any animosity towards you. We're just a little embarrassed, me included."

Sara looked at Jason directly, "Jason, it is highly possible they already have what they need. I watched Henri Cadieux, and he was literally taking it all in with purpose."

"I guess we'll find out tomorrow when Dann calls Mr. Cadieux. Maybe we'll both be out of work," as he raised his glass to toast her. Sara allowed a slight smile.

6

Montreal, Canada

Remy walked into Jenesse Tremblay's office. Determined, he skipped any pleasantries and asked, "So, what do you have for me? I have to make this work."

Knowing he was talking about Versilant, she replied, "Remy, there are no choices other than what I have suggested. Either you consider lifestyle changes to allow you to fund this yourself or get an outside investor."

"Do you have a single investor good for the entire amount?"

"The precise valuation is unknown, but yes. I have found someone. The CEO of MDE Enterprises out of Scotland wants to talk with you or meet you. I explained the circumstance, and she has no problem."

"She? The CEO, is a 'she'?"

"Be serious, Remy, it's a modern world, but my advice is to listen to her and not try to get in bed with her." Jenesse rolled her eyes and added, "This is a powerful woman, and if she is anything like her brother, the late Maximillian Drummond, she could be downright dangerous."

"She's Maximillian Drummond's sister? Wait, that's why that name was familiar?"

"What name?"

"Sara Ricci, the Italian gal that works for Versilant. The story I read was that Maximillian Drummond kidnapped her to get secrets from her. The Royal Marines killed him and rescued her. It has to be the same girl."

"That sounds positively horrible. Are you sure you want to meet with Bridget Drummond?"

"Yes, set it up. I'll get the money and maybe have some fun doing it." Jenesse rolled her eyes again as Remy left, smiling his way down the hall. If she wasn't making so much money, this would be a sexual harassment suit in the making.

The weather in Paris was mild, but at least the rain had stopped when a hired car came onto the tarmac to pick up Bridget Drummond from the latest addition to the MDE fleet. A dark-blue Gulfstream G500 with the MDE logo affixed to the tail. She exited and got into the hired car as it left the Paris Le Bourget airport, heading into the heart of Paris. There she would meet Remy Cadieux of Cadieux MT at a restaurant he had suggested.

As the driver pulled in front of the restaurant on rue Beethoven, the doorman quickly opened the car door and, under his generous umbrella, led her inside. Remy had seated himself facing the door, not sure what to expect when Bridget entered. His heart skipped a beat as a tall, stunning woman was being led toward him.

Bridget noticed him right away, having had her team thoroughly vet him. She knew all about his womanizing and, while he was no doubt attractive; she was there to win, not be won over.

Remy stood and ignored that she was at least half a foot taller than he, as he kissed the hand she had extended. They both said hello and sat. He said, "Thank you for meeting me, mademoiselle. I am excited to discuss this opportunity with you and hope you might find it attractive. It is a small investment, but one that might suit you. Ms. Tremblay did not mention the reason for your interest."

"That is because I did not tell her, monsieur. I'm still not sure I understand why you seek private funding for this. You run a large public concern and I would think ten million is of no consequence."

"Yes, of course, it is an embarrassment. Growing the company as I have, we have taken on much debt, although we easily cover the expense. My father, chairman of the board, is old-fashioned however, and while the board is favorable to me, he controls it. I assure you, there is nothing a foul here, just the politics of a large company behaving as a small one."

"Well, I don't envy your position and assume you have researched the holdings of MDE Enterprises?"

"Not me personally, but Jenesse and others have."

Bridget rolled her eyes at his lack of interest in details. "It is my defense company that plays into my interest. Despite the name, MDE Defense does not make weapons of any kind. We make highly profitable subsystems to hold them, control them, and store them. I wish to expand the company to make tools for war, but not conventional variants.

Alexandre Arnaud, the Managing Director, and I wish to make field level nanobots, capable of helping or hurting. I am told you have such capabilities."

"That, of course, is the exact purpose of the joint venture I propose."

"Joint Venture? So, Cadieux MT would supply all the technology and MDE would be a financial partner with a supply agreement from Cadieux MT? That sounds complicated for such a small product family."

"That was not my thinking. Cadieux MT has the cellular technology and ability to make devices that can enter the human body. We have been working on an agreement with another company to assist us in the nano skeletons for the more robust delivery and repair nanobots. I propose using MDE supplied funds to create a joint venture with them. They would be the manufacturer and through Cadieux MT, MDE would receive a favorable supply agreement."

"So, without this third party, Cadieux cannot create this technology?"

"We could, over time, but they already have it. They'll even make it for us. The beauty is they are not a medical device company, so it is the perfect joint venture. We each have something the other needs."

"And your endgame?"

"Well, profits, of course."

Bridget shook her head. "A joint venture cannot live on forever. It is a concept created by today's knowledge. In time, both concerns strengthen and weaken as markets change. It becomes a game of survival of the fittest. The joint venture must evolve to the strength of the strongest partner. Is it your intention to one day own this company, Versilant?"

"I have not thought out all scenarios but you are correct, it would develop, but Cadieux MT is clearly the stronger partner and always will be. It is a bridge I would cross at a later time."

"I see," realizing he had no idea what she had just said. Enough business then, she thought. "French food is not my first love, but perhaps we should order."

Bridget knew much about Remy Cadieux. He was flashy and acting the role of CEO, but was a bit out of his league. The father apparently knew this as well, which is why he had financially handcuffed him.

7

Industrial District, Washington

Dann pulled his Range Rover into the visitor parking spot in front of Cerium Scientific Compounds (CSC). This company specialized in grinding, mixing, and curing rare and common metals to bond onto various surfaces. Some were used to make metals harder, softer, self-lubricated, or impervious to corrosion or oxidization. When De Vires had just started Versilant, his parents died within months of each other and, rather than plow the inheritance solely into Versilant, he paused.

It wasn't but a few months later when Lillian Masters, a member of Dann and Jason's study group in college, married a PhD from Harvard, Liam Boylan. Liam had started CSC, and he was raising capital from friends and family. The technology impressed Dann, and he gave them two-hundred-fifty thousand dollars of his inheritance for a fifteen percent stake in the company when it still had no revenues. Boylan had since tried unsuccessfully to buy Dann out several times, but Dann saw an opportunity for Versilant and CSC to collaborate. Now, seven years later, with CSC worth around forty million dollars, his fifteen percent was too rich for Boylan to buy him out.

Dann walked in and headed straight for his office. He knocked and Liam turned, smiled, and asked him in. "Dann, you're looking well."

"Same to you Liam. How are things?"

"Well, thanks, and Versilant?"

"Same. We are working on an opportunity with a company in Canada on medical nanobot devices. Groundbreaking stuff and could be a lucrative business."

"Is this the joint venture I heard about?"

"Where did you hear that?"

"I don't recall who mentioned it, but you have never been one to keep secrets. I presume the entire community knows. Close to a deal?"

"Close, but I need cash and they are only offering controlled stock. Given we'll have to fund this from scratch, and I can't have let Versilant's working capital suffer."

"And they won't budge?"

"Not as yet. They have grown enormously in five years, much through debt. The CEO's father is the chairman and won't let him near cash."

"Sounds like you need a new partner."

"That will be the case if we can't get closer. Anyway, the reason I came by is we have Sara Ricci, the MIT gal from last year, working for us as a consultant. She has been a great asset, but with her here, it brought me back to her abduction, and the demand from the Scottish guy, Drummond, to understand the coating process for her conversion dish.

Although he is dead, I suspect others in the company likely still want her invention."

"And we'll gladly do the work for them. Dann, we discussed this. Unlike you, everything about CSC is on a need-to-know basis. No one has the recipe except for Lillian or me. They could break in and camp here for a month and never put it together. There is nothing to worry about."

"Well, Sara thought the same thing, and they abducted and almost killed her. They could do the same to you or Lillian."

"Dann, please."

"I'm just saying watch your back." With that warning he left to go back to Versilant, and Liam sat wondering what the hell he was going to do.

The second year after Liam and Lillian Boylan started CSC, investor money began pouring in, much faster than the highly controlled Boylan could spend it. At the same time, he heard about a project involving a nanobot that could stop bleeding in the field on wounded soldiers. Boylan got a call from an army doctor, Dr. McMillan, who told him he was going to partner with Cadieux MT out of Canada to create the nanobot that DARPA had abandoned. Boylan eventually met the then CEO of Cadieux MT, at a seminar in Boston and as Boylan was leaving, McMillan mentioned that the company was considering going public. Those that invested now could be millionaires overnight.

When he returned to Seattle, impressed by the company and its technology, he invested half-million dollars into Cadieux MT using the investor funds he hadn't yet spent. The company did, in fact, go public, and twelve months later, his shares were worth over one-point-two million. He promptly sold some of the stock to return the original half-million dollars back into the business. As the stock continued to rise, he sold more shares to pay off early investors, and occasionally buying more shares. Only De Vires refused to take the money, which infuriated Boylan. Not that he wasn't thankful for the initial funds, but he never wanted long-term investors.

Today, Boylan's shares were worth over five million, which made him ecstatic, but there was just one problem. Somebody was blackmailing him.

It had started a week before when he got a call from a computer-generated voice saying they knew of his shares and how he got them. Technically, everyone made out, no harm done, but he essentially stole the money, even if momentarily. Even though he paid it all back, this would look terrible, and he might be open to insider trading laws. It might not ruin the business, but it was a worthy scandal; one that his wife Lillian would not likely understand or agree with. She had no idea he had used the company money.

The blackmailer had yet to make a demand, but it was coming. And now, fucking De Vires was trying to get into bed with the same company. How in the hell could this have happened?

8

South Beacon Hill, Washington

Sara sat with a bioengineer in Versilant explaining how Amy Keningburg, her PhD friend at Sapienza University, had theorized a nanobot that could use magnetics to regenerate damaged blood vessels in weakened veins. It might also be used in reverse to slow down blood vessel growth to limit the expansion of cancer cells. They didn't really need additional ideas, but if the deal with Cadieux MT fell through, the more ideas, the more funding they might get. They wrapped things up, and Sara went to find Jason. As she walked by the conference room, they were there, not talking, just thinking. Sara walked in and asked, "Hey. What's up? You guys look deep in thought."

Dann replied, "The lead engineer at Cadieux keeps calling Jason and they're wondering what's up with our silence."

"So, no new conversation with their CEO?"

"No. I told him what we require, and the ball is in his court, but apparently, he hasn't told his own team."

"So, how do we break the tie?" Sara asked.

"That is that we are trying to consider."

Until that point, Jason had only listened when he shook his head and said, "I would do nothing. Wait for him to call you. Meanwhile, we'll move forward as usual." He looked over at Sara. "On that note, are you ready to call it quits for the day?"

"Give me a few minutes to grab my stuff. I want to have some of this material handy while we're away." Although they worked less than ten miles from downtown Seattle, Sara had never been, so Jason was taking her to a hotel downtown. Their train left in an hour and for the next few days, they would walk the city and be tourists.

Waking up the next morning in the hotel, they dressed and went down to the fourth floor, where the complimentary breakfast bar was located. They also had an expresso machine. Sara rarely ever drank American style drip coffee and was so used to expresso, or coffee mud, as Jason called it, anything else wasn't right. Unfortunately, neither she, nor Jason, nor Versilant owned an expresso machine.

It was close to eleven when they finished and ventured out. They headed for Discovery Park where they went up the Space Needle, saw Chihuly's glass garden and the Museum of Pop Culture. From there, they walked southwest to the equally famous Pike Place Market and had a beer during a bout of drizzle. They held off eating so they could indulge at Von's 1000 Spirits, a trendy restaurant and bar on 1ˢᵗ street. Tired but happy, they made it there in time for their reservation and Jason ordered a nice bottle of wine, planning to make it a long and relaxing dinner.

Jason raised his glass to toast and said, "So I know you're leaving soon and just wanted us to have a few nights to ourselves. Hope that's okay."

"Absolutely. Today was fun, what a great city. That is the farthest I've walked in a long while. My hip flexors are going to be killing me in the morning."

"So, when do you leave?"

"Well, that depends on Dann. Without Cadieux MT, I'm not sure what else I can do. I have nine days left before I need to be back."

"Can't you work on your dissertation from here?"

"Well, maybe a little, but the heavy lifting is all there. We'll get together once I'm done. Are you coming to my dissertation presentation?"

"I planned to. Dann said it would be fine."

The server came, and they ordered their meals as he poured them each another glass of wine and ordered another bottle. Two hours later, meals done, and two desserts consumed, Jason poured the last of the second bottle. They were talking about some art they had seen earlier in the day when the server finally walked over and said they were getting ready to close. Jason paid without paying much attention to the bill and they both downed their wine. Jason stood first and realized he was a tad wobbly. Sara laughed, but when she stood up, she was hardly better. They laughed together as they did the drunk walk to the door. At least Jason had the mind to realize the long walk back was not in the cards and ordered an Uber. When they arrived back at the hotel, they made it back to the room, where Jason opened a half-bottle from the minibar, an astronomical price for an inferior wine. Sara giggled and the next thing they knew, they were drinking again.

The clocked showed 7:30 a.m. and with all the blinds wide open and no clouds, the sun glared into the corner suite on the sixteenth floor of the hotel in Pioneer Square without hesitation. The two occupants in the one of the two queen-size beds lay spooned in the middle, the other bed full of yesterday's clothes. On the conversation table in the room overlooking Elliott Bay sat a half-consumed bottle of wine and two glasses, one empty and one partially full. The hotel itself had begun to stir. Doors were opening and closing, people walking down the hallway talking, elevators chiming, and housekeepers were starting their busy day.

The occupants of the bed didn't notice. They were still asleep until Jason blinked at the sunlight and came back to his senses as the fog in his mind slowly lifted. Where was he? How had he gotten here?

He rolled over to avoid the heat to his left, opened his eyes and mouthed an "Oh Shit," as he noted Sara's naked form cuddled where he had just been. His brain was spinning, and he felt unwell, but not enough to resist lifting the covers a bit. They were both naked, and he did a double take at Sara's backside, but he was too hungover to get aroused. He momentarily panicked. *Oh my god, what the hell did we do?*

Just as he smiled, Sara stirred and rolled towards him. He froze, but it was too late as she opened her eyes. "Jason?"

"Good morning." Was all he could think of.

It took Sara a few minutes to realize she was naked, but she, too, was hungover and flopped over and went back to sleep. Jason got up and fought his way to the bathroom. He used the toilet and took three Advil, hoping it might ease the pounding in his head. He made it as far as the couch in the front room where he laid down and fell back asleep.

A pounding on the door hours later woke them. Jason, still naked and still feeling like shit, got up and opened the door, standing to one side. The housekeeper was standing there with a look, *why you are here?* Jason realized it was check-out time and muttered, "We're spending one more night," and closed the door. Walking back, Sara, barely able to hold herself up, admired his naked body for a moment and then realized the implication as she asked, "Oh crap, what the hell did we do?" Jason smiled and tried to be a stud, saying with a swagger, "You don't remember?" even though he was contemplating throwing up.

"No. Nothing after the restaurant, but wow, I guess we…"

"I'm just messing with you. I remember the Uber and coming back here, but that's about it."

"What do we do now?" Sara asked. Knowing this was a tipping point in their relationship.

"We're going to go back to bed and hope we wake up feeling better." Jason then called reception and added another night to the room before going back to the sofa, wondering what had happened. He couldn't believe his dream had finally come true, but he was too drunk to remember it.

9

Antananarivo, Madagascar

Senior analyst Angus Adair stood and looked out of his small office as he gazed out over his team of eight, all armed with computers, multiple monitors, and a month's supply of Red Bull. All were hacking away with wild abandon. This had once been the main offices for MDE Commodities, a company under MDE Enterprises that ran mines in Madagascar, Heard Island, and a new company in the desert of California that produced Lithium. With that recent acquisition, MDE Commodities needed more space, but Angus did as well, so he stayed while MDE Commodities moved several kilometers east to a larger, more modern office complex.

Adair relied on very expensive chairs to ease the toll that sitting for hours did to his short, pudgy frame. With flaming red hair, white porcelain skin, and rosy, red cheeks, he wasn't much to look at, but he was wicked smart with a computer and had an eidetic memory. He had joined MDE Enterprises ten years before, just out of high school. Constantly in trouble with authorities for hacking into things just to prove he could, his reputation earned him a job offer working directly from the CEO and founder, Maximillian Drummond. At just seventeen, he made more money than his entire family combined, although he told no one and had little time to spend it. Ten years later, that was still the case.

MDE Enterprises may have run its headquarters in West Sussex, England, but they also operated a private company on the lower floors of a spectacular residence on the Isle of Skye in Scotland.

This private company comprised three groups. One group was a legitimate research team. They worked within the laws of Scotland and the host location gathering intelligence, collecting published news, rumors. This was essentially public information on topics Maximillian or his sister Bridget thought important. The second group was a covert research team led by Adair. They had free rein to hack any source and even use MDE's private security force to get news that was insider information or secrets. The last group, ran by Bridget, was the integration team. They took these various forms of information to the businesses within MDE Enterprises to improve them, offer competitive advantage, and sometimes create acquisitions or aid in new product development.

Maximillian had an insatiable appetite for data and, besides simply gathering it, Adair eventually expanded this knowledge base by building a private digital library. Within five years, instead of working topic to topic as doled out by Maximillian, his team, armed with that database, and his quantum computers, were creating the topics and giving them to Maximillian.

That digital library had helped MDE Enterprises grow into a thriving success, but that all changed when Police Scotland launched a poorly executed raid on their residence a year earlier. When it was over, many were dead, and Bridget was severely wounded.

Without an extradition treaty with the UK, Maximillian, Grant, and Angus were exiled to Madagascar, leaving Bridget in Scotland to convalesce. Although subsequent actions would kill Grant and Maximillian, Adair spent his days rebuilding the enormous private library, and soon thereafter, the covert team. Someday, they would all would return to the Isle of Skye.

Meanwhile, Bridget had recovered from her injury and although she used the information and his team differently up to this point, she was still his new boss and today; he was updating her on a Canadian company, Cadieux MT.

The video came on and Angus nodded to Bridget before saying good morning. She responded with a nod as well, asking, "What do you have for me?"

"Some of this you likely know, but based on our findings, the company has trending revenues of one-point-six billion Canadian dollars and net margins near fifteen percent. At present, the Chairman and former CEO, Gustave Cadieux, has control over the board and the finances of the company, although it had not been that way just a few years ago. His youngest son, Remy Cadieux, became CEO four years ago and according to notes and emails, they intended him to be a modern, hipper figurehead. They had hired a PR firm prior to their initial public offering, and this was one of their recommendations, as Gustave had just become an octogenarian."

Angus continued, "Just months after the announcement, Gustave fell seriously ill and took a medical leave of absence. It was almost deadly. Before he would return on a day-to-day basis, the son proved quite aggressive and mounted an enormous growth campaign that caught everyone by surprise. The market loved the growth, stock prices soared, and the board rubber stamped his agenda with no one to reel him in and seemingly no reason to do so. The father regained his health two years later and has held a firm grasp on the purse strings since."

"So, Remy Cadieux made poor decisions?" Bridget asked, as if not surprised.

"Not necessarily. In fact, the company is worth considerably more thanks to the son's moves at a time the general market was stagnant. His consolidation strategy put the entire industry on the map. No, their problem is cash flow. With the rapid growth, their balance sheet was constantly in flux because for sixteen months, they were buying a new company nearly every month. They did this primarily through debt, but nobody cared as long as they kept growing. When the father returned, he enjoyed the stock appreciation, but not the debt. As I understand it, Gustave in that same week sacked the CFO and replaced two board members for not holding Remy more accountable. He then, for reasons unknown, put the shares of the entire family and all officers under a special clause; they could only buy or sell shares if the board of directors agreed. His actions stopped all non-organic growth, and that eventually exposed their balance sheet for what it was; heavily indebted. Between the drop in stock price and having to meet bank covenants on their debt, it wiped out their cash reserves, and they have been struggling to bring the down their debt ever since."

"So, Dad blames the son. The son blames Dad, and nothing changes."

"That's about it."

"What about Versilant?"

"Remy wants to grow the nanotechnology side of the company. In his view, surgical robots are great but can only perform certain procedures which limit growth. While they already have a small line of cellular and bacterial nanobots for monitoring and diagnostics, he wants to develop delivery and repair systems. Nanobots and nanobot cars that drive inside the body to bring medicine or repair bots to a specific area. These need a skeletal frame and that is what Versilant provides."

"So, he was honest when he said he does not have the money and the father, Gustave, won't let him spend a penny outside until their debt ratio drops. Thank you for the update, although I'm not sure this helps me. Remy Cadieux is mine for the asking but his father sounds unreasonably stubborn and is perhaps living in the past. I was going to invest directly in Cadieux shares. But what good is that if his father controls the board?" Angus did not answer, assuming it was a rhetorical question.

In Montreal, Jenesse Tremblay sat with Remy in his office as they discussed the possibility of working with MDE Enterprises. Tremblay thought it was a good idea, considering all others. Remy agreed, but Bridget concerned him.

"Jenesse, there is ice in that woman's veins. She knew everything about me and the company. Not all of which is public information."

"That is hardly a surprise. I have heard her brother had at his disposal an entire team to hack all sources possible to assure he knew exactly what competition was doing before they did it. It seems logical that she has access to the same."

"Yes, I understand being prepared, but for a ten million dollar deal. It sounds excessive."

"What do you care as long as you get the money?"

"It's her look, Jenesse. She seriously seemed a thousand miles ahead of me. Like she is thinking of something much grander, far bolder. It's unnerving."

"Well, okay. Bottom line, do I contact her?"

"Yes, I have no alternatives."

Dann De Vires was sitting at his desk when the phone rang. He picked it up, and it was Remy Cadieux. "Were your ears burning? We were just talking about you." De Vires said causally.

"All good I hope."

"Perhaps that is a matter of opinion. Remy, I assumed we would be partners by now and frankly, my team has given you far more information than we should have. You know my concerns; you know my situation. Without a deal, I think there is nothing more for us to discuss."

There was a pause when Remy said, "Dann, you are correct. I know of your situation, but I have my own. I'm trying to find alternatives, but these take time. As to your demand, consider this. The two leads on your side, while gifted, are simply consultants. How about I give them a million each to work for me directly and do all this without you? Only Cadieux MT can complete the live trials and take the final products to market." He paused, allowing De Vires to consider the words, and hung up the phone before De Vires could respond.

Dann hung up slowly and realized he was out of his league. These school yard bully tactics were tools of the trade to such people. When Dann was young, such personalities bullied him regularly. It always hurt and here he was at thirty-five years-old, putting up with the same shit. Fuck Remy Cadieux and Cadieux MT. Dann would get the money and do it himself. All he needed was to raise the money and find a company who he could pay to do the trials. With a huff, he rose from his desk and headed out the doors to drive home and talk this over with his wife, Susan.

The meeting with Bridget was all set, and she would fly to Montreal and visit the Cadieux MT headquarters. At breakfast, Remy prepped his family, reiterating that he wanted to expand their nanotechnology line and that he had located a company in Seattle to help them. They had little to concern themselves with, as this would be a joint venture of sorts. The Seattle based company would do all manufacturing and take the day-to-day risks. For the Cadieux MT ownership, he intended to use third party funds, hopefully from Ms. Bridget Drummond, CEO of MDE Enterprises, out of Scotland. She would arrive for a visit, and he was asking them, and especially his dad, to assure she received a warm welcome.

Given the small size of the investment, it raised few eyebrows, but a few members silently waited for Gustave to counter, although he didn't. He just smiled and said nothing. Privately, Gustave met with a few of the board members at his club in Quebec City to explain, this might be a good lesson for Remy. Gustave knew of the Drummonds and Remy would soon realize he was out of his league.

The dark blue MDE Gulfstream touched down at Montreal's Saint-Hubert Longueuil Airport and taxied to flight services. Rex Williams, Bridget's head of security, surveyed the surroundings, including the car and driver he had hired. With nothing amiss, he returned to the plane and helped Bridget into the car. The driver then promptly took them to the company headquarters, twenty minutes away on the corner of Av Dollard and Boul De La Verendrye. Once inside the building, Remy Cadieux and his father Gustave were there to meet her at the grand parkway.

Bridget offered her hand, which Remy held while introducing his father. Gustave nodded softly and replied, "Mademoiselle. It is an honor to meet you and our profound condolences for your brother."

"Thank you monsieur, did you know Maximillian?"

"Mostly by reputation, although we had met several times years ago."

"Such a waste." Bridget replied coldly. They proceeded on a tour of the facility before going back to the lobby and up to what she assumed was Remy's office, given the bright and modern décor. After exchanging verbal pleasantries, Remy asked outright, "Have you given thought to our previous conversations?"

"Why would I be here if I had not?" Bridget replied.

"But it seems to be overly complicated, yes, mademoiselle?" Gustave interjected before Remy could answer.

Remy immediately said to Bridget, "What my father is trying to say is that…"

"Remy, I understand exactly what he is saying and agree with him. For such an insignificant investment, a venture within a venture makes no sense to me. I trust my visit will stimulate a more direct method of investment."

Remy, wishing he had kept his father out of this thought through his response and replied, "And by that, you are referring to the purchase of Cadieux shares?"

"Perhaps it is the easiest way to arrive at the cash you need to partner the technology without debt."

Gustave added, "Ah yes, but as you know, equity is a distant cousin to debt."

Bridget got their attention as she rose and held out her hand to Gustave. He seemed to understand and shook it firmly. She moved toward Remy, who was clueless but held her hand as she said, "When you are perhaps more serious, call me. Thank you for the tour." Before Remy could say a word, Bridget was halfway to the door with Rex Williams more or less blocking Remy and Gustave to assure Ms. Drummond's exit was uninterrupted. He himself then departed and closed the double doors behind him.

As soon as the door closed, Remy unleashed on Gustave. "What the hell was that about? This is nothing to her, and I had her right where I wanted her. Instead of closing the deal, we are back to game playing."

"My poor Remy. You never had her, and you never will. She is looking for something much bigger and I fear you may have just invited the lion to the feast." Gustave was very concerned and realized even he may have underestimated her.

10

Harley Sykes lifted both trash barrels with ease and carried them over the rock garden as to not leave tire marks before he wheeled them across the decomposed granite driveway to the curb. Still remarkably fit, the recently retired Sergeant Major and former army ranger worked out every day at 5:30 a.m., rain or shine. He didn't have to prove himself to anyone anymore, but he was still a ranger and still a threat. His wife of over forty-years, Annabel, was inside. She was probably cooking, her favorite pastime, as Harley walked into the large garage and sat down overlooking a 1956 Ford truck in various stages of disrepair. It had belonged to his father and for years he had slowly been restoring it back to the image he had of it as a boy.

A third-generation soldier, like his grandfather, his dad, and his brothers before him, they all enlisted in the infantry and the expectation was, at some point, you applied to ranger school. Not all of them made it through ranger training, quite the opposite. Harley could count fewer that did as than those who didn't, but nobody cared. It was the process and courage to attempt it that mattered.

Harley met Annabel when he was nineteen. Shortly after his first year in the army, he applied for ranger training at Fort Benning, Georgia. Annabel was a waitress at a local coffee shop, and on his occasional passes into town, he would always go there to see her. Not a drinker, nor a smoker, he jokes he was in AA, as in *Army and Annabel* and they married after he completed his ranger training.

Once attached to a battalion, Harley was rarely home, always deployed somewhere, but coinciding with his rare leaves home, they had two children. The oldest, Jason, got a sister two years later, and Annabel named her Rachael after her mom. Proud to have a son, Jason Sykes was the focus of Harley's life until Jason turned eighteen. That was when the boy betrayed him and refused to enter the infantry.

Apparently, he thought he was too good for that, wanting to be an engineer or something and justified it as he would join the army as an officer. Harley had only spoken to him twice since, and didn't much care if he ever did. It didn't matter he got a college degree or joined the army as a first lieutenant. Tradition was a birthright, dammit. No man simply changed it for his own desires.

To Harley's surprise, his daughter Rachael, the one he rarely paid any mind to, not only followed tradition, but even applied to ranger school. A girl, no less, and she made it all the way into the Ranger Assessment Selection Program (RASP). Rachael pushed herself so hard she collapsed and had to spend a week in the base infirmary. Had she made it, she would have been the first women in history to become a ranger. As it was, she made it farther than any women previously and Harley was damn proud of that girl.

As he grabbed a sanding block and began lightly sanding the truck hood, he wasn't thinking of Annabel or his kids. He was thinking of his current situation that had started several years before. Harley had been working with DARPA on a way to stop bleeding in the field, with a nanobot that could target areas of internal bleeding. He was not a scientist, far from it, but having a Sergeant Major on the team helped visibility and hopefully funding. The initial concept came from an army doctor named Miles McMillan. In time, Dr. McMillan pitched DARPA the concept, but they rejected it. They favored a compression tourniquet device that could save a good percentage of lives but could be field ready in a third of the time. McMillan told Sykes he was going to move forward, using a Canadian company called Cadieux MT. McMillan also mentioned to Harley that the company was considering going public. Those that invested now could become millionaires.

Sykes was a very conservative guy, but after giving it some thought, he took some of his savings and used a home equity loan on their house to invest two-hundred-fifty thousand into Cadieux MT stock. In less than twelve months, his investment had doubled to over five-hundred thousand and was now, almost four years later, two-point-seven million dollars. He couldn't believe his luck… until recently. Somebody was blackmailing him.

Two weeks before, he got a call from a computer-generated voice saying they knew of his shares and that he had used insider information to get them. The blackmailer had yet to make a demand, but it was coming, and Harley wasn't sure what to do.

11

South Beacon Hill, Washington

In the large conference room within Versilant, Dann De Vires pulled the team together. With Susan, Sara and Jason front and center, he looked about the room and said, "Team, the deal with Cadieux MT has fallen through." Faces fell around the room, and several voices ejected sighs as the words sunk in. "Rest assured, this is not the fault of Versilant, but the inability of Cadieux to provide us with enough cash to fund the startup. If I were to accept their terms, they would own half of this new product family, but we would have to go out and immediately borrow millions of dollars. While we have no debt and could likely afford this, Susan and I view this as a major liability with no additional financial return. In fact, it could risk the current Versilant pipeline. I just couldn't do that."

At that moment, Dann regained their attention. "Having said that, I think we have something here. Do you agree?" The team was passive at first, but then several yelled and cheered, signaling they agreed. "I thought you might feel that way, so here is what we're going to do. We're going to do this ourselves."

The room erupted in cheers and high-fives before Dann continued. "I'll put up some initial funds and if any of you want to invest, you may do so. Meanwhile, I'll raise additional money through minor investors. Along with product development, we'll have to find a medical company that can take this into trials, but I already have been looking into this. We'll find something."

Weeks later, the teams, all of whom were already going down this path even before Dann's announcement, had prototypes to do basic proof of concept testing. Early on, the Cadieux MT team had supplied several cellular and biochemical bots and although they didn't have many, they had enough and used them to create the nanometal skeletons. Four of the seven teams were already drafting the information to derive provisional patents. Their patent attorney would be there in just three days, so it was crunch time.

Sara was winding things down since the teams had working designs and she called her dad from Versilant since it had been weeks since they last spoke. "Hi Dad. Is this a good time?"

"Of course, my special girl. When are you coming home?"

Sara let out a sigh. "Soon Dad. How are things?"

"Things are fine here. Same old stuff. Some of us have responsibilities."

"Dad, seriously? Since I don't have patience for such conversation, I'll just say the project is going fine. I even invested in the new startup. I'll be home next week. Love you and I'll talk to you later." Sara just hung up. On the other end of the phone, Giovanni realized without intending to, he had upset her. He reflected further and realized that perhaps it was just that he couldn't get over all that had happened to her and yet she could. And she was coming home in a few weeks, just like she said she would. He sent her a text telling her he loved her and to call when she was heading home.

The next morning, it wasn't bitterly cold as Sara jogged down the street towards the water of Lake Washington. She had called off this morning mainly because her mind was being consumed by her dissertation. She hadn't even looked at it once since arriving in Seattle five weeks earlier, hoping the forced time away would allow a refresh or, perhaps better said, a reset. Three days ago, she had received the manuscript back from her scientific editor, but still hadn't opened it. Until last night.

Over a glass of wine, she opened the file and saw page after page of suggested edits and changes. She had expected some, but it looked like there were hundreds, if not thousands. Argh, that meant work. Lots of work!

No longer jogging, she was running now, her legs used to the new daily routine. In fact, she had pushed herself from her normal ten-minute per mile pace when she first arrived to now under nine minutes. Once she got back to Italy, she would run every mile between under eight, her new target zone. Arriving at the end of Andrews Bay, she turned around and headed back. With the wind now behind her, she poured it on as the sound of *Our Destiny*, by Epica, blared into her earbuds. By the time she got to her tiny house, she was sweating something fierce having just covered six miles. After a shower, she made a coffee from a French press, her affordable alternative to an expresso machine, and opened her computer.

Slowly going through each chapter, she realized it was not as bad as she presumed the night before. The edits were less about what she said than how she wrote it. It would take time, but she could do this. After four hours straight, she stopped, had some juice and a granola bar, and called her dissertation assistant, Hernan De Costa. Hernan was a master's student from Brazil, and Sara had hired him before she left for Seattle, to verify that every citation in the document matched to the actual article or person.

In research, the entire collection of everyone's previous research is available to you. While you will always have new research, it was acceptable and a standard practice to refer to prior research when applicable to avoid recreating experiments similar or the same as what you would have done. But you have to acknowledge this and in her dissertation document, she had referenced over two-hundred-seventy-five other scientists or technical papers. Sara had taken meticulous notes to keep track of them, but once published, this was an area that needed to be flawless. Hernan answered on the third ring, "Ciao Sara, how is America?"

"It is good. I'll be home soon and was wondering how the citations were doing."

"Very good. I'm able to give this at least an hour each day and as of yesterday, I have verified and validated just over two-hundred, so twenty-five percent left to go. I can complete them in two weeks. Is this okay, or do you need them faster?"

"Two weeks is fine. Ten days is even better. I have hundreds of edits, mostly for punctuation or grammar, but it will take time to clear them. Scientific writing does not always follow the same conventions as conversational English."

"When do you give your dissertation presentation?"

"It's scheduled six weeks from yesterday, and I'll need at least ten days to get the printed copies back from the publisher."

"Okay. I'll aim for ten days. Travel safe and we'll see you soon."

"Thanks Hernan." Sara hung up and went back to it for an hour before she came to a section she wasn't sure how to answer. Rather than research it, she grabbed her phone again and called her old roommate at MIT in Boston, Lisa Payne. Lisa was in the last year of her masters in geology and had helped Sara work out elements to consider in her initial testing of what would become the Ricci Gamma Ray Conversion Dish. Sara found her contact and rang her.

"Sara, hi. How are you?" Lisa squealed.

"Hi Lisa, I'm good. And you?"

"Good as well. How is Italy and your dissertation?"

"Coming along, but I'm actually in Seattle with Jason. We are working on a nanobot design."

"What the hell? You quit?"

"Relax, I just took a six-week break. It was getting impossible to stay focused, and this was a really interesting opportunity."

"To be with Jason, you mean?"

Sara rolled her eyes at the inference. Lisa was boy-crazy, at least to Sara. "No, I have my own place. We see each other every day and get together a lot, but you know me, I need my space."

"OMG, such a robot girl!"

"Thanks, you're a real comfort." Sara switched gears and explained the problem with how she had described the metal she ultimately used in her experiments. It was a contaminated version of the element Thorium, which in the periodic tables, was an found in the Actinide series, but it contained traces of Lutetium, which was from the Lanthanide series. "So, the editor has suggested I refer to it as a lower purity Thorium to avoid confusion. I think if I say that, it's takes away from the uniqueness of the metal." Sara suggested.

"Sara, I agree with the editor. It just doesn't matter, as the purity of the Thorium is still close to ninety-five percent. You can always add a footnote that it contains a trace amount of Lutetium, but I assure you, that trace amount is not what made your experiment work, it's solely the density of the Thorium."

"Okay, that makes sense. Glad I called," Sara replied.

"So how is Jason?"

"I'm not really sure. We have fun together and got so drunk the other night, I think we had sex but neither of us remembers. We just woke up naked next to each other."

"Can't say I haven't been there. That's a big step for you two, right?"

"I know he wants more from me, but I don't know how to bridge this. I like him, I really do, but Seattle is not home. Italy is home, but not to him."

"Have you guys talked about it?"

"Not really. When we try, I clam up and he gets defensive."

"Listen robot girl, I like Jason. He is a good guy, but still a solider at heart. And you, well your robot girl, especially when stressed. I think you need a softer guy to deal with your own emotional issues… just saying."

"Maybe I can change?"

"Sara, Jason is your first boyfriend? And nearing twenty-eight, I think you are who you are."

"Great, you mean I'll be alone for the rest of my life?"

"Sara, get your PhD and put it behind you. Perhaps then life can, for once, just be life. I just tease you with the whole robot girl thing, but seriously, when was the last time you weren't in school?"

"I always have been, maybe that's the issue."

"Maybe. Hey, I gotta go but text when you're back in Italy."

"Thanks Lisa."

12

The wind was up as Harley Sykes walked out onto the small pier and climbed down into his twelve-foot Lowes aluminum boat. He needed to think, and fishing in the center of the lake, away from everyone, was the best place to do that. His wife, Annabel, had packed him a small lunch, and he had plenty of water as he expertly untied the stern mooring line and grabbed the oars. The small lake allowed gas motors on permit during the season, but Harley preferred rowing.

The Sykes had bought the property on Farmway Road as close to the shore as any on Lake Lowell, in Caldwell, Idaho, fifteen years prior, and Harley thanked his lucky stars every day. They built the house nine years before and with the influx of former city dwellers from California to New York, his modest investment was now worth over a million dollars. Had he ever put serious money into the moderate-sized house, it could be worth more, but his needs were simple. Bought as their retirement home, he and Annabel loved it here, or at least he did.

As he neared the deeper part of Lake Lowell, he brought the oars into the boat and dropped his anchor. It was about thirty-five feet deep here and regardless of what he caught, he only kept bluegills or a rare trout.

The real prize was a tiger muskie, but he had never caught one, but they were there, somewhere.

But today wasn't about fishing. Today was confession time. Harley had never told Annabel about the money he took out of an equity line he, that he alone created. It was easy enough to make the payments. Harley controlled all finances. He also didn't tell her of the hit to their savings account, which had almost recovered. He might have become a Sergeant Major, a big deal in the army as the highest enlisted rank, but the pay was nothing to write home about compared to the civilian world. That said, his E-9 salary, with allowances for housing, food, and hazard pay for deployment in hostile places, made for a comfortable living, with measured frugality.

He was less concerned about the money. After all, with the house and the Cadieux MT stock, they were millionaires. The issue was the insider trading. Harley was a rules-based guy. He was a pillar on which nobody questioned, and he feared that if this blew up, Annabel would lose respect for him, and his recruits and peers would see him as a fraud. That would truly kill him.

And Jason, fucking Jason. Harley might never talk to his son, but he followed his career. He was working with his old friend Dann De Vires at Versilant, The very company that was in cahoots with Cadieux MT. He hoped he and the boy would never meet over this.

His first thought, perhaps deep down, was that he actually cared how people would react, but then knew that was just bullshit. His reputation, honed through forty years of sacrifice, created an image of pure discipline for others to follow. Shit, all that tarnished over money.

Harley had enough. This wasn't helping. He reeled in his line and then pulled the anchor and started rowing for shore. As he was leaving, he decided he would just come clean with Annabel. He had to, but as he rowed, he became agitated. The harder he pulled, the angrier he got, when halfway to shore, a light came on in his crewcut topped, chiseled head and he stopped rowing.

He was a former army ranger. A recently retired Sergeant Major. This situation was unacceptable, but he didn't have a problem. This fucking low life piece of shit blackmailing him did. He started rowing again and by the time he was almost at his dock; he had a new plan. Somebody was going to die, and it wasn't him.

Thousands of miles east, similar thoughts were in the mind of Jessica Estrada as she sipped a glass of 2008 Veuve Clicquot La Grande dame. Looking out over the Balearic Sea in the Mediterranean off the coast of Spain, Jessica was founder and CEO of the PR firm, Imagen International. They were based in Barcelona and had satellite agencies around the world. The firm netted her millions, and this house was the epitome of success as very few people in the world would ever call this view as their own. She had all she ever wanted and even got rid of her leach of a husband who took everything and gave nothing. Despite that success, she was still human and subject to shitty days. This had been a shitty month.

She had been in her Barcelona office late one night when she received a computer-generated call. She would have hung up immediately, but the voice started with, "We know about your Cadieux stock. We know you bought it using insider information."

As her heart slowed back down, she recalled the investment. Her agency had been working with Gustave Cadieux, a gentleman if there ever was one, to prep them to go public. While she was involved, an army doctor working with them suggested she invest because before they went public. Anyone who did would be millionaires and with little thought, she made a one-point-five million investment. Today, those shares were worth eighteen million. Not that she needed the money, but not bad for a hunch.

The blackmailer said they were determining the value of this information, but did not offer details. Jessica suggested they negotiate when the call abruptly ended.

Afterward, Jessica did a PR campaign for herself, just as she might advise any client who faced a similar crisis. Blackmail happens more often than one might think. In Estrada's case, the result was not pretty. This could hurt her and the company, but she still assumed she could negotiate the situation, so she simply waited for the next call.

13

Jason pulled his 4-Runner into the drive-thru window at Starbucks. Sara, sitting in the passenger seat, was the coffee snob being pampered by the experience as Jason was far from a four-dollar coffee guy. While some people didn't care for the acidity of Starbucks coffee, its roots were in Italian style roasting and that is how they started, roasting beans, and selling them. No drip coffee, frou-frou drinks, or pastries. That all came after they were bought out and taken public. Why Sara had not done this, the first day she arrived, she didn't know, but for the last several days, this was how their morning started.

Once they arrived in Versilant, they had about two hours to prepare for a former Microsoft employee and multimillionaire who Dann was bringing in to review the seven designs. The hope was to raise the rest of the cash they needed and to avoid overpowering him, Jason and Sara would give the presentation instead of the seven teams.

The investor, not much older than Jason, arrived a few minutes early. He asked them to call him Elliot, and he was clearly an informal guy. That was based on his cargo shorts, a non-matching Hawaiian shirt, flip-flops, and a man bun that Sara thought was ridiculous but would never say so. Dann kicked it off, and then Jason took over.

"Elliot, we have developed an entire family of medical devices, all built using nanotechnology. To not bore you on details, how familiar are you with the technology?"

"Zero knowledge. I know of it, but nothing about it."

"Okay, fine. We'll keep it at a cliff notes level. First off, when we say Nano, we mean we're using the microscopic scale of a nanometer, one-billionth of a meter. Using that as a reference, this family of seven bots range from one-hundred times smaller than the cross-section of one piece of human hair to as big as ten times smaller." Jason said with confidence.

"Wow, you can't even see that, right?"

"Not with the naked eye, no."

"And you make these?" Elliot asked.

"Well, no. You can't exactly build these in a conventional sense. Versilant is using tried-and-true methods. Some are biochip based, a blend of nanotechnology, photolithography, and new biomaterials. These are best suited for diagnosis and drug delivery. Three of our teams are using Nubot technology, an acronym for nucleic acid robots. Man-made, these fabrications are DNA origami. Using single and double strands, bioengineers can design these robots to walk and carry things using DNA strands as arms and legs. There is also one design that Sara here came up with that is hollow and can basically eat viruses. Last, we have two teams using bacteria or biological microorganisms as the basis for their bots.

These use flagellums to move. It's like a tail-like whip that snaps for propulsion. We control them using electromagnetism."

"That is amazing. So, all movements use electromagnetism?" Elliot asked. Jason motioned to Sara.

Sara answered, "Yes. Most use ultrasound waves, and we prefer this because those same waves can create action, like opening, closing, moving right, moving left."

"And the market for these products is all medical?"

Jason jumped back in. "Applications are in surgery to diagnose and correct lesions. Some are best suited for diagnosis and testing, like getting vitals from different parts of the body. There are several manufacturers already in the space of cancer detection and treatment. For new markets, there are three. One is gene therapy for vascular repair and cell repair. A second with Sara's design is virus detection and elimination. Last, a market that can benefit, is dentistry. The sky is the limit here. Our engineers sense applications for desensitizing teeth, oral anesthesia, teeth straightening, and improvement of appearance."

"How big is the overall and addressable market?" Elliot asked.

Dann answered. "Elliot, we estimate using preliminary data the overall market in five years at over eight billion dollars, with positioning nanobots like these holding the largest share. Healthcare is driving that roughly eleven percent year-over-year increase. The United States and Europe are seventy percent of the overall market and our addressable market, the one we can sell directly into, is about two billion."

"How many companies are in this addressable space?"

"Few companies say this is what they do, as most are doing such work out of their R&D budgets, but I suspect it's crowded. We know of sixteen companies equal to or larger than Versilant, in the US, Japan, Germany and Israel. We are one of the very few that is a dedicated business." Dann replied.

Jason asked if Elliot would like a tour of the facility, and he did. All of them spent an hour as he reviewed the various products they already made and the actual designs of the new ones before heading back to the conference room.

Elliot took a sip of coffee from his now freshened glass. "I think I understand these basics, but how do you create the skeleton itself? You said this can't be manufactured, right?"

Jason replied, "That is correct. By using nanomaterials, the atoms of metals, and catalysts, we can fabricate the structure to strengthen the biological forms and even add biosensors."

Eliot faced Dann. "How much have you invested to date?"

"The design team has invested just under two million to get us designs capable of obtaining provisional patents. I have raised an addition million through friends and family, leaving about five million to buy testing equipment and find a medical device company to enter trials."

"Okay," Elliot said, but did not elaborate.

A minute passed before Dann asked, "I'm sorry, Elliot. Okay what?"

"Okay, to the five million. My investment guy will be in touch with you. I really like the vibe here, and I like these two," as he looked over to Sara and Jason. "I have to go, but he'll call you later today. Sound good?"

Dann was so stunned he wasn't sure what to do as Sara and Jason looked on with their mouths still open. "It sounds very good, Elliot. You won't regret this."

Three days later, as the week ended, the team was having a party in the company courtyard with beer and wine flowing faster than Seattle rain. They had their funding, which was more than anyone had imagined possible.

During the party, several made speeches, praised fellow workers, thanked Dann for keeping the dream alive. They also thanked Jason for doing a better job at leading the teams than they had imagined when Dann brought him in. When all eyes landed on Sara, she turned red, but thanked everyone for being so kind to her and letting her in on such a fun project. They all cheered and toasted her. It was then that she told them it was time for her to return to Italy to complete her PhD. They cheered her again, and she promised to stay connected.

The party went on, and everyone was having a blast. Everyone but Jason. He knew this had been coming and didn't want Sara to leave, but he just smiled, not saying anything.

The next morning, Jason helped Sara pack up, and she bid goodbye to her tiny house. She really loved that little place. Jason drove her to the airport, and they barely spoke on the short drive there. When he pulled up to the Delta terminal, the code share partner for Alitalia, they gave each other a long and meaningful hug. Sara, usually the one without words, said, "Jason, this is so hard. I have been in school nonstop since I was five. That is twenty-two years of nothing but school. I realize it has affected me in ways I can't explain, and I know that drives you crazy. Please be patient and let me finish this and we'll figure something out. Maybe I can learn not to be robot girl?"

Jason looked down and said softly, "I like robot girl," and gave her a hug.

14

Crawley, West Sussex, England

It was common knowledge within the senior management of the MDE businesses that Bridget had been running the MDE Enterprises for some time. Maximillian had been highly admired, but with so many interests outside of the core businesses themselves, Bridget was the easier of the two to talk things out with. Now that she was the CEO however, there were still many things she didn't know at a corporate level, which she perceived as a weakness.

To avoid people knowing this, she leaned on the Managing Director for MDE Defense, Alexandre Arnaud as her sounding board and advisor. She had just walked down to his office from hers, entered, and closed the door as he looked up. "Ah, Bridget. So, you met with Remy Cadieux and his father, Gustave."

"Yes. It was a long trip for an hour, but a productive one. The father is eighty-six and, while perhaps old-fashioned to a fault, he is quite intuitive. The son, not so much."

"Well, to me, the company within a company is a non-starter. Far too complicated for such a small investment. I would just purchase Cadieux shares and move on. What are your intentions?"

"My first thought was just to help your defense business, but I rather like the entire company."

"Wasn't this around ten to twenty million? Are you thinking something grander?"

"Yes. I'll buy in but want control, meaning I have to get at least thirty percent of the shares to get three of us on their board. I can manage Remy but the father, Gustave, it quite sharp and I actually like him, but if he becomes a problem, I'll need to buy more shares to wrestle control from him. Angus has identified some large shareholders that we'll get to sell their shares to me without paying a premium."

"Why would they sell?"

"It would appear that many early investors had inside information to make their initial purchase. I'm betting they would sell rather than be exposed," as she flashed him a wicked smile.

Angus Adair read the words on his screen for a second time and asked one of his techs to verify the information. Thirty minutes later, he had confirmation and immediately sent a text to Bridget telling he had some interesting news.

Bridget called an hour later and said, "What do you have, Angus?"

"Ms. Drummond, I was looking into Versilant and there is a lot of news over this past month." Angus told her that in the absence of a deal with Cadieux MT, they had gone alone, raising cash, getting the provisional patents, and they were interviewing medical companies who could take them to trials.

"Well, well, well. It looks like Remy Cadieux has let this one get away. Versilant owns the critical aspect of the technology. Anything else?"

Angus paused for a moment, not sure if this was controversial or not, before replying, "Well, one thing. It would appear that a person from our past, Jason Sykes, has resigned from DARPA and is now living in Seattle and working for Versilant."

"Interesting, but it makes sense. As I recall, he and the owner went to college together."

"Yes, true. I also learned he brought in Sara Ricci, the young physicist. She is the mastermind behind the motion control on these nanobots and worked there for about six weeks, although she is back in Italy now."

Bridget gripped the phone now, almost in a trance. She did not say a word and Angus, unsure if they still had a connection, asked, "Ms. Drummond, are you still there?"

Startled, Bridget came back and thought of how to reply. Being less than direct or honest, she said, "Yes. I am here. I have not heard that name in a while and needed to process it. Something about her infatuated Maximillian and his inability to let it go was instrumental in his death. For that reason alone, I hate her very much, but as fate would have it, here she is in my life again."

"I'll send you a detailed version of our notes."

"No bother Angus, I have what I need. Thank you and the team. This will leverage my position. How are things on the other item we discussed?"

"I have nine sources and if we had them all, that would control the board with your planned purchase."

"Have you already contacted them?"

"Only the three we discussed."

"Excellent. I'll let you know when the real fun starts," as she hung up.

Angus sat back, smiling. He and the team were back, just like old times.

Remy Cadieux touched down after the quick hop from Montreal to Halifax, Nova Scotia. Bridget apparently owned a posh condo in a high-rise building downtown on Granville Street with views of Halifax Harbor and had been redecorating it. He climbed out of the helicopter and onto the tarmac, lowering his face in the cold, and headed straight for the car she had sent for him. When Bridget called and asked that they meet, she was vague and stated no reason to do so, but Remy assumed she had information, or perhaps this was like a date. They were going to meet at a restaurant near her condo, which gave him hope.

When he arrived, Bridget was already there, and Remy noticed her bodyguard sitting at the bar. He removed his long coat at the door, handed it to the coat-check and walked over and extended a hand.

"Ms. Drummond, I was so pleased to receive your call. I wasn't exactly sure where we left off."

"Remy, so pretty, but not very observant," was her reply.

"I beg your pardon?"

"Remy, the ball has been in your court. I'm waiting for you, but since I was in town, I thought you could bring me up to speed on your status to secure Versilant over a lovely meal. The chef here stays out of the limelight, but is actually very well known."

He nodded and waved for the server to order a drink and a second for Bridget before saying, "I was in talks with them, but they went nowhere. The owner requires cash and I only have stock, so my brother Henri went with me on several trips to Versilant and they gave us enough information to proceed without them."

"Oh. So, you don't need them? Marvelous. I thought differently?"

"It certainly would have been easier, but within six months, we will have the designs complete, if not sooner."

Bridget took a sip of her Pascal Jolivet, Sancerre 2014 Sauvignon Blanc and asked, "So, how will you get around their provisional patents?"

"Ah, this is no problem. They are not so far in the designs, just design specifications. Henri and I have seen them."

"Well, they have five of the seven designs in proof-of-concept prototypes and have filed provisional patents on them. The remaining two are not far behind."

Bridget was looking right at him to see his reaction, and it was worth the glance as he lost his temper and shouted, "That is not possible; they don't even have equipment to complete them?" as he went from shock to anger in less than a second. Several in the restaurant glanced over to them, and Bridget gave them a smile and look to suggest all was fine.

She then added, "They have raised close to eight million, presumably for such equipment, and are shopping for a new medical partner. My company has worked informally with Versilant before. They are quite capable. I fear the bickering with your father has cost you an opportunity, Remy."

Remy couldn't speak. He was furious that De Vires had been so bold as to go alone, but even worse was once again, this amazing woman that excited him, and scared him, had such information. He took a sip of his exquisitely prepared old-fashioned and calmed. "I don't know how you do it, but your insight is, as always, amazing. I am in awe of your skills and thank you for the update."

"We'll think of something. Let's order, I'm starved. It's my treat and if you're a good boy, you might even get dessert."

15

Rome, Italy

Sara sat in her small campus office with Hernan de Costa, the researcher she had hired to complete her citations eight weeks earlier.

Hernan explained all he had completed, which was excellent, and then discussed those he still had to complete or, better said, those he had found problems with. Although Sara took copious notes over this several year journey, some of these links to the paper or researcher were no longer valid. It could be an error or change in the original IP address, or perhaps the paper had been pulled from that site. After an hour, they had solved three, but failed to find two and would have to research these further. They were running out of comfortable time as she only had two weeks left before the copy had to be in the hands of the print-on-demand book service in Milan.

As suggested, Sara had also sent a copy of her dissertation to Dr. Zimbrean that morning, even though she still had a few edits. She felt a little guilty sending the document to her former chair at MIT and not her current chair, but there was a rationale in this. First, Dr. Ferrera was on her approval committee and therefore could not give her direct feedback. Second, Dr. Zimbrean at MIT was with her the day she made the discovery of Gilberti Ricci's works and had given her the advice on how to make this her thesis. She only hoped Dr. Zimbrean realized her tight timeframe. She didn't miss the cold weather in Boston, but she really missed him.

The following day, the long hallway was busy with students and several dialects were talking at the same time as Sara walked down the hall towards Dr. Ferrera's office. She walked in and his student assistant immediately took her in. Dr. Ferrera rose and motioned for Sara to sit but did not formally great her.

"Sara, How is it going? You look relaxed, so this is a good sign, yes?"

"Yes, Dr. Ferrera. I had actually started on this back in America, so I was several days into it by the time I arrived. Citations are complete. Editing is nearly complete, and I have formatted the text for the book printer. I'm only waiting for a proofreader to give me feedback."

"Ah yes, Dr. Zimbrean."

Sara wasn't sure what to say but managed, "Dr. Ferrera, I hope you understand. I assumed you could not give me direct feedback."

"You are correct and please, had you not considered this, I would have suggested you do so. I must confess, Sara, I have known Adrian Zimbrean for close to thirty years and having you as my student became a bond for he and I to reconnect. We speak often."

Stunned, Sara said, "About me?"

"Well, not usually... but sometimes, yes. Your journey is one so impossible to consider it is noteworthy. But please, we don't talk out of line and all that we discuss is between us. We are both rooting for you and only want to help."

"Thank you for your support and for being so understanding. Did he mention perhaps what he thought? About my dissertation, I mean." Sara asked.

"That is only for him to tell. Be patient Sara. You're almost there."

16

His cell phone rang, and Harley's first reaction was not to answer. He hated the paranoia this situation had caused but clicked the answer key, hoping for the best, prepared for the worse. "Sykes," he said tersely.

As the voice replied, his shoulders dropped. "To avoid the embarrassment of prison for insider trading, you will bring twenty-five thousand in cash to the underpass of I-84 at Centennial Ave. Park at the trailhead on Boise Ave. We'll be watching you. The money should be in a white nylon bag. Deposit it there between 3:00 and 4:00 p.m., this Wednesday."

"I'll need more time to get that much money." Harley said, trying to stall.

"We know everything you have. No excuses. Between 3:00 and 4:00 p.m., this Wednesday. Is there anything about this message you do not understand?"

"No." And the call ended. The game had begun.

Over the next three days, Harley got the money, and purchased a few extra white nylon bags. He expected this would not be the only request.

The day before, he had done reconnaissance on the drop area and drove to I-84 and exited on Centennial Ave. Heading east, he turned left to the Boise Ave. and followed it down to the trailhead parking area. He got out and walked to the approximate place he would have to hike down to get to the drop point. Once there, he looked across the Boise River and found a place to observe this very spot. Hiking back to his truck, he got back on I-84 only to get off the freeway once he passed over the river, exiting onto Old Highway 30 before parking on Towne Circle. Walking down the bike lane toward the river, he hiked until he could see the underside of the highway on the opposite side of the shallow ravine. With the Boise river between them, he took a GPS reading of the location and placed a camouflage canvas bag there under some wildflowers. Without pause, he headed back to his truck, and noted with worry, a hiking trail and a mountain bike trail in the ravine's bottom.

When Wednesday came, he used a small backpack to conceal the white money bag and parked at the trailhead. He then walked to the underpass and hiked down underneath the highway and thankfully, nobody was about. Glancing at the trail across the ravine, his gaze followed it to the bike trail. Nothing. Pulling the white bag out of his pack, he dropped it and turned to head back to his truck.

Retracing his steps, he drove to the spot on the other side of the river and pulled over. Quickly, he pulled a camo jumpsuit over his clothes and headed to his spot. As soon as he was there, he grabbed the camo bag out of the wildflowers and removed a box from within. Quickly, he assembled the rifle, a task he could do with his eyes closed as he added the scope and entered a full clip. After some adjustments, he screwed on a silencer and trained the sight onto the white bag, and waited. He couldn't use the silencer for a long shot, but this was less than three-hundred feet, and an unmuted gunshot here would reverberate all the way up this ravine.

Several hours passed before someone in black pants with a dark gray hoodie came down the embankment. Harley glanced at the two trails, and both were quiet. The figure paused and walked up to the white bag. Looking around, the person bent down, grabbed the bag and, as the figure turned, Harley fired.

Bridget stood on the terrace of the company's London flat looking out to St. James, Piccadilly Circus, and partial views of River Thames. The former headquarters of the White Star Line, of Titanic fame, the once ticketing office was now several large and well-appointed apartments. A forty minute commute to her West Sussex office, the purpose of the flat was originally to house executive clients, and for this; it was excellent. But with no home of her own as yet, she simply had taken it over for the last year.

Still standing, she was listening to her contractor in Scotland explain the situation regarding the residence on the Isle of Skye. A beautiful structure, she and her brother had built this residence for themselves. Under the main house was his private company, all of which sat on a plot of family-owned land her father purchased originally to build a summer home but never did. Both parents died in 1982 following a plane crash and Maximillian commissioned the construction of the residence in 2014, after two years of planning.

The private company was on the lower floor, built into the bedrock and tundra. Atop that was the substantial residence. From the main highway looking toward the ocean, only the large single-story residence was visible, and it was only from the water itself that one could see the glass offices of the private company below.

After the raid by Police Scotland a year before, it had taken six months for the property, a crime scene, to receive clearance for repairs. Until now, it had taken another six months to repair the hundreds upon hundreds of bullet holes and replace the glass windows and doors, so much of it destroyed. At a cost of over one million euros, it was now ready, and as she held this thought, she recalled how close she had been to death.

An unknown officer of Police Scotland had shot her just centimeters from her heart, and it had taken months to recover. The scar itself was a visual reminder, but she also wore a small platinum vial around her neck. Inside were shards of the bullet as an additional reminder—or perhaps an omen.

Bridget listened as the contractor finished and hung up. Her first thought was how powerful it would be to return to the residence. It had been inspirational for Maximilian, and she hoped it would be the same for her. She put that out of her mind and thought to make a call to prepare to move from London to the residence in Scotland, but first; she placed a call to Angus Adair. It was time to own a significant piece of Cadieux MT and seal the deal with Versilant. Sara Ricci would be the prize after a wise investment.

Two days later, a solicitor for MDE Enterprises made a bold purchase. He and a Toronto based broker waited five hours for the stock price to lower in the late afternoon and then executed an order on behalf of a Cayman Islands company. They purchased most all of the available outstanding shares. The transaction was close to one-hundred million dollars, and they had five days to disclose their intentions and file the paperwork with the Canadian Securities Administration and then, the company. This was required anytime a person or entity purchased ten percent or more of any public company. Bridget had chosen not to disclose in advance, but they would do so later.

Bridget had now executed the first part of her initial four-part plan. When Angus was ready, she would gain the shares of Harley Sykes, Liam Boylan, and Jessica Estrada, giving her thirty percent of the company. That guaranteed three board seats of the nine available. With Remy in her pocket, that was four, and she thought enough to control Gustave even though she did not have a majority. If not, Angus had identified six other shareholders she could blackmail into selling and with that, she would have five of the nine board seats. The company would be all but hers.

At the Cadieux MT headquarters, the Vice President for Investor Relations ran down the hall, red-faced and winded, as he stormed into Jenesse Tremblay's office. "Jenesse, something is up. A ghost entity just purchased almost all of our outstanding shares on the open market. We're trying to run it down."

"Have we have received any notification or disclosures?"

"No, nothing."

Jenesse rose on those words. "Let's tell Remy. Such an event is rarely good news." They walked to his office and his assistant didn't hesitate to let them in. Remy was on the phone but quickly ended the call when he saw the seriousness of their faces, and asked, "Did you see the share price? Up almost sixteen percent." He gave a thumbs up and a big smile, but when neither smiled back, he asked, "What happened?" Jenesse explained the purchase and that the buyer was a private entity out of the Cayman Islands.

"Is this an activist shareholder group?" Remy asked concerned.

"It's possible, although to aid their cause, activists are usually very public about who they are and what their intentions are." Just as he finished, Gustave walked in. Remy looked at his father who said, "I assume you have seen the purchase."

Remy explained what they had just discussed and added that they would wait to get the disclosures before they reacted. When he finished, Gustave chuckled and looked at the three of them. "Remy, you remember what I said about Bridget Drummond? And yet, here we are. She now owns twenty-seven percent of the company, which is a likely precursor to three seats on the board. If we don't act quickly, my bet is she's not finished. Jenesse, what are our options?"

A bit in shock, she walked over and closed the door. "Provided you're right, we can await her filing and negotiate a buyout if she would accept it. Otherwise, we would have to allow her purchase and then have an emergency meeting to increase our shares outstanding and immediately purchase them to dilute her holdings. That would wipe out our cash and tank the share price. Remy, have you contacted her?"

"We don't even know it's her?" he yelled.

"So, you don't think it's her?" Tremblay replied with hope.

With all eyes on him, he sat down and shook his head. "No… Dad's right. This has to be her." He paused for a few minutes and said, "I'll call her. Let's reconvene after so we can strategize."

18

Isle of Skye, Scotland

Bridget stood inside the residence holding a glass of Rombauer Chardonnay, looking over the ocean. Execution of the remodel had gone well and if you just glanced; all was as it always had been. She, of course, had made a few changes, some because of what happened and others to ensure that what happened could never happen again.

As she looked back to the ocean, although not superstitious, she felt the power of the residence. The house and offices below were almost empty except for Rex Williams, her head of security, and a few of his men, but they were downstairs in his office. At some point, the entire downstairs would be full of employees as she rebuilt that part of her world. The sound of her cell phone brought her back to reality, even though she was almost in a daze. She glanced down and noticed it was Remy Cadieux. She smiled, knowing the call would come, and sat down as she answered, "Remy, this is unexpected."

"So, you are saying you are not behind the purchase?"

"I said no such thing. I only said your call was unexpected."

"Unexpected? Did you actually think you could purchase a quarter of my company and not get this call?" he practically shouted.

"Well, that was rude and unnecessary. But a few clarifications are in order dear Remy, please. It's not your company, you merely run it for the good of your shareholders. Shareholders like me, so be careful. I take it by your reaction you don't consider your own company an excellent investment?"

"For fuck's sake, Bridget, you know exactly what I mean."

"From where I'm sitting, once your board approves the transaction, I'll have made millions on the increase in market price, and likely much more to come. And you, my dear will have received all the cash you need to maneuver around dear old dad. This is a true win-win scenario."

"Bridget, help me understand your intentions?"

"Intentions? Remy, my intentions are obvious. Cadieux MT is an excellent company but can't act like one because of the tension between you and your father and a pacified board, too lame to put a stop to it. To maximize my investment, that will stop now. The company now has cash, and you have a willing partner to bridge this power gap provided, of course, that you have the balls to take on your father. Alexandre Arnaud, myself, and a person of my choosing will immediately replace three current members of your board, and we'll form an alliance to help you. Last, your solicitors will approach Versilant Nanotechnologies next week and offer them whatever the hell they want for forty-nine percent equity in the new product family. I promise you they'll accept."

Again, amazed at her knowledge and insight of his family, he said softly, "Bridget, I am not alone here. What if the family fights this? We have run this company for over one-hundred years."

"Remy, that is touching, but it's your family, not mine. Convince them to accept my purchase and join me for the betterment of the company. Otherwise, this will end badly for you... and them." Bridget disconnected the call primarily for effect, but also to refill her glass, which was almost empty.

In the boardroom, Gustave, Jenesse, brother Henri, and Remy's sister, Adrienne, sat with several of their solicitors, including Cinead Vass, their longtime family attorney and the heavy hand in the room. Remy eventually made his way there and went straight to the sidebar and made a Manhattan with his own supply of Angels Envy Rye Whiskey. None of the family moved to join him, which was fine. As he sat, Gustave, in his patriarchal manner, asked, "So, Remy, would you be so kind as to tell the family how you gave away almost thirty percent of our company?"

"Watch yourself Dad. Just two years ago, our stock price was forty percent more than it is today. You returned and without my consent, forcefully stopped all grow, fired a senior officer and two board members. You did that as a knee-jerk criticism of me without considering the reaction to our stock price and debt covenants. Even after myself and the former CEO told you exactly what would happen. That and the death march you have imposed since has put this company in neutral, not what just happened."

"Well, well, your new girlfriend has given you some balls?" Gustave replied as the entire room quieted, a few smiling.

Ignoring him, Remy explained the situation. "As you all know, the siblings and their families own twenty-two percent of the outstanding shares and dad owns nine percent. Institutional and common shareholders own forty-two percent. Our new investor, presumably a company controlled by Ms. Drummond, would own just over twenty-seven percent if we approve her filing. She wishes to replace three existing members of our board with herself, the Managing Director of her defense company and an unnamed candidate. She further demands that we partner with Versilant Nanotechnologies in an all-cash deal. These disclosures will arrive tomorrow. I don't have to tell you how much this one-hundred-fifty million in-flow helps our current situation."

Nobody spoke, but Cinead Vass, their solicitor, said what everyone was thinking. "And if we do not approve her purchase?"

"She wouldn't say directly, but would likely approach existing shareholders with a premium sufficient to give her control of the board. We only really control thirty percent." Looking at his dad, he added. "To be honest, we and the board have all been remiss and left ourselves open thanks to our stock restrictions and lack of contingency planning for just such an event. She did this, but we allowed it to happen."

The room went silent. Gustave stood, and although he seemed calm, his face suggested otherwise, "Remy, a word in private." His voice was stern and cold.

One could cut the tension with a knife as the two went to an anteroom. As soon as the door closed, Gustave asked, "Remy, this all seems so perfect, so calculated and I have to ask myself, did you orchestrate all this just to oust me?"

With a look of disgust, he shook his head, dumbfounded. "Dad, I don't agree with you on many things, but no, I did not orchestrate this and as far as ousting you, you're doing that all by yourself," as he turned to walk back.

"Or you don't have the guts to tell me to my face?" Gustave shouted to his back.

"No Dad. That was my knee-jerk response to you thinking I would just give away our namesake."

"Remy, son, you have skill, but I have always been hard on you because you're reckless. But I have always done so to your face. Not behind your back. I'm only asking for the same consideration."

"You must be joking. Do you think I'm not aware of your little club? Do you think I don't know that I'm only CEO because of a fucking PR campaign said you were too old to be the face of a new public company? That is why I took advantage when you got sick; to show what I was capable of. It was the only time in my entire life that you weren't behind the scenes pulled the cords to help me or hurt me. Your actions of the last two years have hurt this company to its core. If you would have just backed me, just once, we would be twice the size with no concerns over cash or debt. I didn't orchestrate this, Dad, but I think it might be the best thing to happen considering our frozen circumstance and passive board."

Gustave was stoic as he smiled and turned towards the door, "Very well, why don't we return to the others?" and walked back into the boardroom. Remy followed in silence. As they sat back down Gustave asked, "Jenesse, can we stop this without bankrupting the company?"

"Technically, yes, but there is substantial short-term risk. Without supporting one view or another, Remy is right in one sense. If our actions favor the stock price, it is unlikely we'll not see any retaliatory reaction if everyone is making money. If we block her, institutional shareholders, and Ms. Drummond herself, will come after us. We lack the ability to respond without significant financial harm."

"So, the board can't allow additional shares outstanding that the company, or family, could purchase to dilute her position?"

"Sir, the board can change the restrictions on family ownership and release more shares, but the company nor the family have one-hundred-fifty million in cash, so we would have to negotiate with our banks. That debt added to our current debt, besides the high dilution factor, would cause class action consequences unless we simultaneously created a reverse stock split to compensate them."

Cinead Vass, their solicitor, chimed in, "Gustave, in my professional opinion, we could only survive such a legal action if Ms. Drummond tries to harm the company through an abuse of her power. As she has not done that, we do not have a legal case against her. She simply purchased shares we made available subject to our approval."

Gustave heard him but did not react, turning back to the CFO, "Jenesse, tell me honestly, have my actions allow this to happen?"

She hesitated. This was a horrible position to be in, but she found her nerve, "Sir, out of respect, I will not answer that directly. I will say…" She paused, "I will say that is likely how shareholders will respond."

Before all hell could break loose, Henri looked at Jenesse and then at his father before settling his eyes on Remy. "I vote we accept this and get the stock up to a hundred dollars a share. We have always been an excellent company. With this financial windfall, we can become a great company." Around the room, it went until the last person was Gustave. His eyes were glassy, and he was clearly emotional as he said nothing but nodded approval. Once Gustave and Remy took this to an emergency board meeting the following day, Bridget Drummond would now own twenty-seven percent of Cadieux MT. She had won the first round.

19

Sara was in the lab when her cell phone rang, and she noticed it was Dr. Zimbrean. She immediately answered and said hello.

"Sara, are you free for a few minutes?"

"Yes, Dr. Zimbrean. Have you read through my dissertation?"

"I have Sara. There are a few holes in your final conclusions and additional research section. But I agree with you, this is difficult to prove in a lab and is best left for industry to solve in a real-world situation. But you need to speak to this directly, so it is very clear to the reader. As it is written now, they might think you missed something. The only other comment is the coating from Cerium Scientific Compounds (CSC). I realize they own this secret and will not disclose it to you, but this is an important element to your invention, the Ricci Gamma Ray Conversion Dish. In your narrative, you only explain it in vague terms. I would strengthen this section with all that you know and add footnotes to frame any missing information within the NDA with CSC. Last, I have emailed you the document with some minor suggestions. That is all."

"Might I ask if I presented this to you? Would you approve it?"

"Sara, it would be unfair of me to answer that, as I am unfamiliar with Sapienza University's criterion for acceptance. Let me say this. The document is well done, and you have successfully proven your thesis. I'm not sure what more one could ask for."

"Thank you so much for everything, Dr. Zimbrean. I'll check those two areas and see what I can do. I have just one day left to get it to the publisher."

"Best of luck Sara. MIT misses you."

"Thanks Dr. Zimbrean, I miss you." Dr. Zimbrean noted she did not say MIT.

Sara opened the box that had just arrived and felt her heart jump as she lifted out the book version of her dissertation. Handling it as if it were a two-thousand-year-old relic, she took a selfie holding it in front of her and texted it to her dad and Jason. She then pulled out several copies and assured that five remained, before closing the box and heading over to Dr. Ferrera's office.

He was busy when she first got there, but after fifteen minutes he was free and came out to see her. "Sara, I trust you have something for me?" Smiling.

"Yes, I have them," as she handed him the box, all smiles. Five copies were for him and her committee. Back in her office was one was for her dad and another she intended to frame in a shadow box.

"Excellent. You have provided enough time for a review so we will keep our original date and time for presentation, yes?"

"Yes, I will be ready."

"Of course. And you will have visitors?"

"Oh right. My dad will be there and possible my boyfriend from America if he can get the time. He is working on an enormous project."

Dr. Ferrera just smiled and said, "Very well. We can accommodate this. I will see you this coming Tuesday at 9:00 a.m."

"With bells on." Sara said, although it was obvious Dr. Ferrera did not understand the saying from the Conestoga wagon era of the United States. A little factoid she had gained in Boston.

Hernan de Costa, Sara's researcher, sat with her as they enjoyed a charcuterie board and a glass of wine at a small *enoteca* near the university. In Italy, especially less tourist centric locations, restaurants and bars have distinct classifications, although in modern times, this has diminished. For example, a *Ristorante* is a place for formal dining. They are likely to have a well-known chef and are located on major streets. A *Trattoria* is also a restaurant, but family run and usually on a side street. A *Pizzeria* is a small place where pizza is made and available for takeout. Historically, this was the Italian equivalent of fast food, and this concept remains in traditional locations. An *Enoteca* is a wine bar, and this is where Sara and Hernan were now, celebrating the end of her PhD effort as she knew it.

"So, what are your big plans after acceptance?" Hernan asked eagerly.

"Well, first thanks. You have more confidence than me. As for the future, I don't really know. Dr. Ferrera wants me to teach at Sapienza and I'm not apposed but industry does more fun stuff. Another option is being a freelancer, you know, a PhD for hire."

"I didn't even know they had such a thing." He took a sip of the reserve chianti. It was good, but not great, according to Sara. To him, it was the best wine he ever tasted.

She continued, lost in her own mind as she rambled, "I have so many questions. In this journey, I have met so many good people, but a lot happened, and I don't know who to trust."

Hernan was not up to speed on Sara's life, but he asked, "What do you want to do?"

"That's the problem. I honestly don't know."

"Well, here's to figuring it out," as he raised his glass and they toasted. In less than an hour, Sara was back at her flat, confused. Hernan had asked such a simple question, but she honestly had no answer.

A day later, Sara was reciting her slides when her phone buzzed as she looked down to see who it was and smiled as she clicked answer. "Jason, how are you? How is the team?"

"Excellent. You'll never believe what just happened. Remy Cadieux called Dann and Susan offering ten million cash for a forty-nine percent stake in the new company."

"Jason, that is wonderful news. Did Dann accept?"

"He did because this solves the trials and go-to-market problems."

"Wow fully funded. I'm so happy for the team. Did the equipment arrive for the last two designs?"

"Yes, but it's still being calibrated. There is also a push to add several military designs based on work that Cadieux MT once did with DARPA."

"What is the difference between those and ours?"

"I haven't seen the design specification, but one is a DNA origami like the virus catcher you suggested, one is bacterial, and the last one involves slowing blood loss from battlefield injuries. That was the original design they were working on with DARPA. I guess Dr. Dubois was right, it's back."

"Sounds interesting. So, all is good there. I miss you and the team."

"I miss you too. Are you ready for next week?" He asked, speaking of her dissertation presentation.

"Yes, it is surreal for it to be almost over after having spent so many years to get to this point. Will you be able to make it?"

"I obviously want to, but with the new venture, there is a lot going on. I'll get back to you. If I can't make it, your dad says he'll FaceTime with me. So, can you rejoin the team here after next week?" Jason asked causally.

"I don't know what the future holds. I'll have to see. Maybe Amy and I can help from here."

Jason, expecting the answer, just said, "I figured as much. Let us know." And after a few minutes of unrelated conversation, the call was over. They had gotten so close, now they were back in their corners.

20

University of Washington, Seattle, Washington

It was just a few hours after sunrise when Jason pulled his Toyota 4-Runner into the parking lot near the Oceanography building on the campus of the University of Washington, his alma mater. This morning, he was taking out his wood kayak for only the second time, having restored it himself. The classic Greenland style, strip-design had taken over one-hundred hours to restore in the small workshop that was part of his guest house.

Carefully pulling it off the top of the SUV, he walked with it down to the water before gingerly climbing into the single hole. Pushing off, he paddled away from Lake Washington toward the Salmon Bay Waterway and eventually his turnaround point at Shilshole Bay near Discovery Park.

He had done this a lot in college and now back in Seattle; he was eager to get back into it. Unsteady at first, he got into a rhythm and, staying close to shore, headed out for his sixteen mile journey.

Even though he was pulling hard and sweating now, he smiled, thinking of his recent life changes. For that moment, he didn't think twice that his shoulders ached and his stomach muscles were cramping. His core was clearly out of shape for these movements, but he thought nothing of it. This was a good pain.

As he neared the turnaround, his phone went off again, this time a text or possibly an email. It had beeped three times since he hit the water. The phone itself was in a watertight compartment in front of him, but he was not yet skilled enough to just sit in the water without forward movement. The small rudder was no match for his larger frame, and the kayak would flip over immediately if he lost concentration. Given the water was quite cold this time of year, even though he had on a dry suit, he had no desire to get wet. Turning, he paddled almost nonstop until passing Portage Bay Reach and neared the campus.

Exiting the kayak rather ungracefully, he managed without flipping it over and pulled down his dry suit down to his waist. Bringing everything up to the truck, he finally pulled out his phone and saw two messages from Susan De Vires, Dann's wife and two from his dad. They had only spoken a few times since he graduated high school and while it bothered Jason early on; he was over it after thirteen years. His dad treated everyone like a recruit and only the subservient stayed anywhere near him. That included his mom and sister. He let his call go, but called Susan. She didn't pick up, so he left a message and loaded the truck.

Monday morning came quickly as Jason pulled into the lot at Versilant, collected his backpack, and headed to his lab. He walked into the side entrance and immediately felt a negative vibe. He had taken Friday off for a three-day weekend but didn't recall any issues when he left, but the long faces and quiet were unsettling as he walked in. When he left Thursday, everyone was euphoric over the Cadieux MT deal.

As he headed for his lab, he hoped to get some answers. Susan De Vires rounded the corner with a tall man in a black suit and stopped. Susan was an attractive woman, but at that moment, she honestly looked horrible. She ran to Jason and burst into tears as she reached up and hugged him. Susan was all but five-foot and it was a climb for her to reach Jason's six-foot three frame, but he ducked to accommodate her, not understanding what was going on. Susan looked up and said tearfully, "Jason, I'm so glad you're here. Dann is missing."

"What do you mean, missing? Is that why you called? I left a message, but you didn't call back?"

"He never came home Saturday night, and no one has seen him since. I'm sorry, this is FBI agent Trevor Davies."

Jason looked at the FBI agent and asked, "The FBI? What's going on?"

Davies looked at Jason and the surrounding area and said, "Let's go into the conference room and I'll bring you up to speed."

Jason looked at Susan and then the FBI agent and asked, "I'm not sure I understand. You're briefing me in? Why?"

All business, Davies replied, "Mr. Sykes, please, the conference room," as he motioned to the room down the hall. With that gesture, Susan started for the room, with Jason following and Davies bringing up the rear. They walked in and he locked the door, waving a hand forward as if to say, be seated. Susan sat and Jason followed. Davies sat on the edge of the table and said, "Mr. Sykes, someone has abducted Dann De Vires, and we elevated this past the local police because of his profile and the fact that this might be related to Cadieux Medical Technologies."

Jason looked at him skeptically and replied, "Cadieux? Agent Davies, we literally just partnered with them. There is no incentive for them to want to harm Dann."

"When was the last time you spoke to your father?" Davies asked.

"What's he got to do with anything?"

"Are you saying you won't answer the question?"

"No, it's just I haven't talked to him in like five years and can't imagine what he has to do with anything."

"So, you don't care for your dad."

"It's more a case that he doesn't care for me. We're not close and haven't been since I disobeyed his direct order to enlist in the Army as an infantryman. To say that Sergeant Major Harley Sykes is unforgiving is not a stretch." Jason replied without emotion.

"So, no contact at all?"

"Well, oddly, he called me twice yesterday but didn't leave a message and I didn't return his call. I'm honestly done trying. He might be the greatest soldier ever in the eyes of the army, but as a dad, he sucks."

"Well, he is a large shareholder of Cadieux MT. Do you have anything else you would like to say about your dad?" he said, eyeing Jason coolly. Even Susan was waiting for his answer.

"I don't know what you're saying. My dad is a soldier, not a businessperson. He's career army, just retired, and lacks the funds to be any company's major shareholder and especially not a company in biotech. I'm not kidding when I say he is just a soldier. Sir, you have your facts all wrong."

"And you would know this because you and he are close and talk with each other often?"

"I'll rephrase the statement. It sounds nothing like him, and I assure you, he is not a wealthy man."

"Mr. Sykes, your father has three million dollars of Cadieux stock, and along with a property in Caldwell, Idaho, worth one million. That sounds pretty wealthy to me."

Jason sat there trying to contemplate all that was being said, but just couldn't bring it together. Both were eyeing him intently now, and he simply asked, "Listen, you're right, I really don't know him, but even if this is true, what does any of that have to do with Dann? Shouldn't you focus your investigation on him?"

"I am Mr. Sykes," as he went to the computer at the end of the table and brought up a camera video from what looked like the Versilant parking lot. He played the recording and Jason could see Dann exit the side door, lock it, and head to his car. A moment later, a man walks into the video from the left and although Jason had not seen his father in almost a decade, the walk and man's build were unmistakable. There was no audio, but the two were talking calmly for about five minutes, when Harley Sykes puts out his hand, shook Dann's. He then turns and walks out of the camera view from the direction he came. Dann then proceeds toward his car, but a large tree blocks the view. Headlights appear from the right and stay there for several minutes, but you still can't see Dann or his car because of the tree. The headlights grow less bright, as if the car is backing away until it is dark again and the video ends. "So that's it, no word in two days and your dad, who can't be located, was his last contact."

Jason was speechless. As his eyes met Susan's, he said, "Susan, I can't explain any of this. I don't know what is going on, but I'll help in any way I can. What can I do?"

21

Cougar Mountain, Issaquah, Washington

Two Days missing. The first thing Dann De Vires noticed was the darkness. Not just dark, but absolute blackness. There was no hint of light at all. It popped into his head that perhaps his other senses might strengthen and try to overcompensate for his inability to see. Groggy but awake, he assumed someone had drugged him; it was the only thing he could think of to explain his headache and uncharacteristic tiredness. He was lying flat on an uncomfortable mattress. This was far from his pillow top mattress at home, likely the type of mattress found on a low-quality pull-out style sofa bed. By the smell of dampness, he assumed the mattress was directly on the floor, a floor of porous concrete or perhaps it was earthen.

His thirty-five-year-old joints, normally pain-free, were now uncomfortable, and he listened with intent for any clue to suggest where he was. The only sound was a slight hum in the distance, and he thought it might be a refrigerator or generator. Based on the dampness and smell, he felt he was still in Seattle or near there. Trying to move for the first time, he placed his hands behind him and sat up, thinking, *why is someone doing this to me?*

Dann De Vires wasn't sure if it was hours or days since leaving his office. He couldn't recall what happened, but thought he remembered talking to someone in the parking lot. Someone that surprised him, but that was all he could recall at this moment. Slowly, he got to his knees and then stood up. He was dizzy and felt awkward, but he got his balance and as he reached out, he touched a wall he couldn't see. He rotated ninety degrees and tried again. Again, the wall was right in front of him when he fully extended his arm. It took just a few minutes to realize he was in a box about six-or seven-feet square. The walls were made of cinder blocks, and the roof, which he could easily touch, appeared to be steel. All surfaces were cold and hard. This wasn't accidental. Someone had built this structure to hold him, *perhaps others before him,* he thought nervously.

He laid down again, letting the dizziness fade, and eventually fell back to sleep. Waking several times, he soon lost track of time, but there was no change to his surroundings. No water, no food, no light, and no reason to explain why he was here. He was weakening and could feel it. Thinking of his wife and girls, suddenly, he heard a snap switch, and a very faint light outlined a small door in his box. He yelled. "Hello. Is someone there? What is going on? Please help me." There was no sound. "I have money. We can work something out. Please." The only reply was silence, although he could feel someone's presence and soon heard small feet moving towards him.

All at once, he smelled food. It was unbelievable how his body reacted, and he realized; he couldn't recall when he ate or drank last. A small door, maybe three inches tall and twelve inches wide, opened at the bottom of the larger door and someone pushed through some paper wrapped items. Three waters followed, and the small door snapped shut and locked. The door was metal by the sound of it. The small feet walked away, and the sound of the light switch snapped as the light outline disappeared. In the darkness, he moved towards the smell and felt with his hands. It was fast food wrapped in paper. There were two burgers and two boxes of fries. He felt for a water and opened it, sipping it slowly and elected to eat half now and save the rest for later, not knowing if they would feed him again.

Dann focused on eating and trying to determine a system for time when he realized he still had on his watch. He felt for the top left button and pressed it. The face illuminated, and it was 11:30 p.m., Monday night. Only forty-eight hours had passed since he left work, but it felt like days. He wound the watch, thankful it was a manual one, although he wished it had GPS.

22

Lake Lowell, Caldwell, Idaho

Harley was in his garage, working on the truck, when his cell rang. He assumed who this was. He answered and the same computer created voice said, "You think yourself clever."

"Not particularly, but I'm not somebody you want to fuck with." Harley replied.

"Perhaps, but this is a game in which your skills are not of much use. It was a mistake to test us. The intermediary we hired to get the money; a young student who was just twenty-three years old is now dead. We took care of the body, but the stakes have just gone up. Considerably."

"I didn't kill anyone, but I promise you this. Someday I'm going to kill you."

There was a pause before the voice said, "I think not. What you will do is sell all of your shares in Cadieux MT within the next twelve hours. We'll remove one million of the proceeds for our price of silence in all matters. We'll be watching the exchange. If the shares do not appear, the world as you know it is over." The phone disconnected abruptly.

Harley knew he was too good a shot to kill anyone unless he wanted to. He had fired a warning shot, assuming the person getting the money

124

was not the blackmailer. No, he didn't kill anyone, but these crazy bastards just might have actually murdered that poor kid just to set him up. They seemed to be a step ahead. He didn't want the publicity of the insider trading, but being tied to a murder, even one he didn't commit, would devastate Annabel and his reputation. This had just gone from bad to worse.

With just twelve hours to save himself, he knew then this had gone too far. He had to come clean and take his medicine. But first, he went into his study, closed the door, and turned on his computer. When it booted up, he went to his trading account and placed a sell order for his entire lot of Cadieux MT shares at market price. The Toronto Stock Exchange (TSX) was closed now, but the order would hit the following morning.

Later the next morning, Angus and his team were monitoring the Toronto Stock Exchange as instructed and waited for the sell execution order to appear for the Cadieux MT stock from Harley Sykes. The minute it appeared; a Toronto based broker executed an order on behalf of a Cayman Islands company for the entire lot through a holding company in the Grand Caymans for roughly three million dollars. No sooner than the sale was confirmed, Angus transferred one million out of Sykes' brokerage account to himself.

23

Rainier Beach, Washington

Susan went about her normal routine as Jason looked on, assuming she was being strong for the twin girls, Amanda, and Breanna. They were five and Susan had just made them peanut butter and jelly sandwiches with juice and some apple slices. Jason couldn't tell them apart and watched them intently, wondering if they had any idea what was happening. He had come over earlier and they spent several hours calling friends, looking for anyone that might have seen Dann, but there were no leads here on the fourth day since he was last seen. Davies had been over earlier and although he didn't say it, concern was etched into his normally emotionless face. Susan stood off to one side, out of earshot of the girls, and asked, "Jason, why does agent Davies look so worried?"

Jason responded honestly, "I think in these situations, they get demands fairly quickly. It has been almost four days and they have nothing."

"So, he's dead."

"Susan, you have to be positive. I don't think so and can only say that actual events are not following normal patterns."

"I'm sorry, but a direct explanation is that he's dead," as she cried, bringing a tissue up to her eyes, thinking about the girls, the business, and the misery of life without him.

"Or, he is being held against his will, for reasons we just don't yet know. We have to help agent Davies figure that out."

Susan said nothing and Jason felt maybe this was her defense mechanism. Assume the worst now so she could deal with it later. Susan patted her eyes and asked, "Do you think his disappearance is related to Cadieux MT?"

"The timing is odd I'll give you that, but I just can't imagine a company giving up all that cash after months of saying they couldn't, then disrupting the key executive of that very business?"

Jason left Susan and the kids and had just pulled into the Versilant lot when his cell rang. The number was not familiar, but a local area code. His truck was too old to have hands free calling and as he went to connect manually, it stopped ringing. As he walked inside, it pinged with a voicemail message. He clicked it.

"Boy, pay attention to this number. When it calls again, answer." The voice was that of his dad. What the hell was going on? He saved the number as contact "Dad" so the phone would remember it and immediately went to his office and called Davies. When he picked up, he asked, "Agent Davies, it's Jason Sykes. Are you by chance in the office?"

"I am, what's up?"

"I need a favor. If I give you a number, can you tell me where it is?"

"Is this about your dad?"

"Yes, it's just a voicemail that says if this number calls, pick it up, but it's his voice."

"Give me the number." He did, and Davies came back a few minutes later. "Can't help. It's a burner phone, untraceable."

"Why in the hell would he have a burner phone?"

"Same reason he is on the run. If he calls, let me know. We might be able to locate nearby cell towers if we have a few more incoming calls."

"Got it and thanks." Jason went to his contacts and found his mom's cell number and pressed send. Jason had been very close to his mom because his dad was rarely home. But when all hell broke loose after high school, she defended his dad, leaving him with no allies, not even his sister. His mom answered on the fifth ring.

"Jason? Jason, is that you?"

"Yes mom. I suspect the FBI is monitoring your calls, but what's going on?"

"Jason, I don't know. Everything your father does is like a clockwork, calculated and easy to figure out, but this? This I don't understand. Believe me, something is wrong. This is not at all like him."

"I know, Mom, but it doesn't look good." Jason explained Dann's disappearance, and Harley's meeting Dann at Versilant and the FBI. He did not explain the Cadieux MT stock.

She pleaded, "Jason, you must help him."

"Mom, that's asking a lot, given what you've both done to me. I don't owe either of you a damn thing."

Almost crying, she said, "He is still your father, Jason. He is a bear; I know that more than anyone, including you. Can you imagine my life? Can you? Please help him. He is a good man, and something is very wrong."

"OK mom, I'm trying. I'll find a way to communicate with you, okay?"

"Thank you Jason. I'm so sorry," she said as he hung up. Within two days, Jason purchased two burner phones of his own and got one of them to his mom.

Davies walked into Jason's small office and lab, closed the door, and sat down. "Have you heard anything from your dad?"

Jason looked up and replied, "Nothing but the message I mentioned."

"You and your dad really don't get along do you?"

"No." Jason told him the whole story.

"Tough break. Tell me about Remy Cadieux."

Jason went on about the entire sequence, from how Dann wanted to do a joint venture with them and wanted Jason to head up the project. He told him about Sara and the Dann's decision to go alone and then, miraculously, Cadieux MT agrees to do all they said they wouldn't or perhaps couldn't. He concluded with, "It just makes little sense that they would do all that and then sabotage it."

"Back to your dad. He has three million in their stock and was the last person to see De Vires. Now this highly trained former army ranger is on the run?"

"Sounds to me like someone is setting him up." Jason replied.

Davies smiled, "That is our thinking as well. If you talk to your dad, tell him to come in. We can protect him."

"I will if he calls but, Davies, you don't know my dad. He is not running from them or you. I think he's going after them, whoever they are."

"Interesting spin. Thanks."

24

South Beacon Hill, Washington

Jason had called Sara in Rome from his office to talk about the activity surrounding Dann and his disappearance. She and Dann had started off a little rocky, but by the time she left to return to Italy, they had a mutual respect for one another. Jason had hesitated to even tell her so close to her dissertation presentation, but knew it would be worse for her if he didn't. Sara was shocked and saddened and immediately offered to fly back and help. Although part of him wished she could, this was her time, and he promptly said no. He then told her about his dad and the Cadieux MT shares. "I told the FBI agent it sure sounded like my dad was being set up."

"For what purpose?"

"No idea. If I could just talk to him, I would at least have some answers."

"You mentioned after Cadieux MT came through with the money, they were pushing some designs from the past that involved DARPA. Can you call your old boss at DARPA, Ralf Müller, and ask him to check on what that project was?"

"I'm way ahead of you. I called a few days ago, but Ralf didn't know. He gave me the name and number of the director who was heading up the Biological Technologies Office back then. Her name is Dr. Caroline Dubois, but I haven't called her."

"I would, it might offer some insight."

"She might not talk to either of us. Tell you what, let's make a conference call and see if she will. She retired from DARPA last year. Hold on." It took a few minutes, but Jason connected and explained who he was and why he was calling. Dr. Dubois knew Jason might call since Ralf Müller had given her a heads up and there was nothing classified about the former project, so she agreed to talk to them. Jason brought Sara back to the call and took the lead. "So, Dr. Dubois, do you recall Cadieux MT?"

"I do. It is rare for us to work with companies off American soil, so when we did, they stand out. An army doctor, something McMillan, had theorized on a way to make a nanobot that could restrict blood loss of soldiers in the field when advanced help was hours away. The concept was this. If you got hit, you would ingest a pill. If you couldn't, someone would inject you. The nanobots were held inside a saline solution would race to the vascular area in distress, band together and effectively create a clot. DARPA went from wanting this to wanting something faster and it was abandoned. As I understand it, the army doctor then took the concept to Cadieux MT, and I stayed involved at arm's length because it was fascinating and someday, I thought DARPA might want to revisit it."

"Do you recall when this was?"

"I believe it was winter, about five years ago."

"Back then, who ran Cadieux MT?"

"I recall an older gentleman, very sharp. I think his name was Gustave, Gustave Cadieux, son of the founder, and not long after, his own son took over, but I don't recall his name."

"Remy Cadieux?" Jason mentioned.

"Yes, that's it. There was a lot of excitement around that time because they were going to take the company public."

"Did the offering go well?" Sara asked.

"Tremendously. This McMillan fellow had been actively telling people to invest, and they would soon be millionaires. Many did."

"Do you recall an Army Sergeant Major, first name Harley, on the team?"

"I don't recall that name, but I do recall a comment from McMillan that having some high-level brass on the team could help our chances at DARPA. Perhaps this Sergeant Major you mentioned assumed that role?"

"Perhaps. Did you invest in Cadieux MT?"

"That is a very direct question, but heavens no. I worked for DARPA, and this was, to me, insider information. Although, given my current retirement, perhaps I should have. The stock is something like ten or eleven times today what it was then."

"Dr. Dubois, you have been very helpful. Thanks for your time."

"It's nice to be needed. If you have any issues with your products, let me know. I can likely offer sound advice and know everyone in the business."

"I might take you up on that, thanks again," and Jason disconnected her, leaving Sara on the line.

"Your thoughts."

"We have to find this Dr. McMillan. I suspect my dad was the brass, and that he invested before they went public. A three-million dollar stake today would have been around two-hundred-fifty thousand back then and while a lot for him, he could have pulled that off."

"Meaning what?" Sara asked.

"Someone is blackmailing him for insider trading."

"Whoa…"

"Yeah. I have to talk with Davies. Hey, good luck on Tuesday. And I'm very proud of you. You'll do great and I'm sorry I won't be there, but I think you understand. We'll watch it on FaceTime."

"Of course, I do. Thanks for telling me. It all makes sense."

The following morning, as soon as Jason saw Davies with Susan, he asked if he could speak with them. It was then he told them the story of DARPA, Cadieux MT, and the timing of his father's involvement and the possibility of insider trading. He included the suspicion of blackmail.

Davies paused for a bit and then said, "Not an impossible theory. Harley meets with Dann to find out about the Cadieux MT joint venture. Likely because he knew you worked here and might figure it out. The question is, how is this related to Dann's disappearance?"

"How could it be?" Jason asked.

"What if your dad is one of many?" Susan asked.

"Even if that were true, what does Dann have to do with that?"

Davies said, "He could be an insurance policy. If I'm right, he is very much alive, and this explains the lack of communication or ransom."

Jason asked, "In what way?"

"The blackmailer is trying to extort money from people that are likely powerful and connected. If they don't agree to his or her terms, he uses the potential death of Dann to motivate them. It also could mean those being blackmailed know Dann personally." Davies replied.

For the first time in a week, Susan smiled, feeling a smidgen of hope.

25

Sawtooth National Forest, Idaho

Harley Sykes was almost to the top of the 5,300-foot peak and between one of the few cell towers near Lake Cascade. He had risen above tree line about thirty minutes before and was aiming towards high ground, which had unparalleled views of the surrounding Boise National Forest. He had told Annabel five days earlier he was going on a backpacking trip to the Bogus Basin outside of Boise, Idaho, but was actually sixty miles north. When he got to the top, he took out his burner phone to make sure he had a signal. This would be the only time he would use this phone. He hesitated for a moment, then rang Jason.

Jason saw the number, answered immediately, "Dad?"

"That's sir to you. Whatever you hear, do not look for me. I'm not important. Your job is to help your mother and keep her safe. I'm being blackmailed."

"I know all about McMillan, the Cadieux stock, and that someone is setting you up. Come in and let the FBI handle it. You're cleared."

"FBI? Cleared? Cleared of what?"

"Dann De Vires kidnapping?"

"What the hell are you talking about? I talked to De Vires last week about this whole mess?"

"I know that's why the FBI are looking for you and monitoring Mom. It has nothing to do with possible insider trading. The FBI doesn't even handle such cases. You are the last person to see Dann before he went missing, and they have it on video. They realize now these are separate events, but if someone is blackmailing you, there could be others. The thought is Dann's disappearance is an insurance policy to the blackmailer if one of you doesn't act."

"Well, that makes sense. In my case, I already sold everything. Bastards took a million dollars of my money to not go public, but I'll get it back. Thanks for the intel. I have some thinking to do." And click. The call ended.

Jason had never heard his dad say thanks, so he had that going for him as he went down the hall and talked with Davies. He explained the call and Davies used FBI resources to trace it, but got nothing. All indications were that he was using a pre-paid phone and a virtual phone number operator's app, so he would have to call again from the same location to get a cell tower location. Harley knew that and wouldn't call again from that phone.

As Jason left Davies, he stopped to talk to Susan. The kids were in school, and she was there to keep busy. He told her about his dad.

"Jason, do you honestly think someone is keeping him just to have leverage?"

"It makes sense, so yes?"

26

Five-Days missing. Dann awoke, and immediately looked at his watch, pleased it was still working. A small thing like keeping track of time was keeping him sane. It was 10:30 p.m. several days later, and he was getting fed once a day, on or about the same time. No sooner had he checked the time, he heard the snap of a light switch and again a very faint light outlining a small door in the box he was in. He again heard the small feet moving towards him.

"Hello. I know someone is there? Thank you for the food, but can you help me understand what is going on? Please. I have money, I can help you. Just you." As before, the only reply was silence, although he could feel the captor's presence.

The small door opened, and the same meal pushed through. Three more waters followed, and the small door snapped shut and locked. The small feet walked away, and the sound of the light switch snapped as the light outline disappeared.

He felt for the food and thought back on the strange events, as his memory had become clearer. First, he meets Harley Sykes, Jason's dad, in the parking lot after work who says he is being blackmailed over an insider trading issue with Cadieux MT shares. Then he was abducted. Is this related to Cadieux MT? Is Remy Cadieux involved?

27

Rome, Italy

Hernan De Costa walked briskly toward Sara's small office in the physics lab, hoping he wouldn't be late. Today, he and Sara were going to roleplay defense questions from her acceptance committee. Although she did not have to defend her written dissertation, she still had to answer their questions. After talking with former Sapienza PhDs, they insinuated that how she held herself, and how she answered, were also factors in her approval. She had sent Hernan a list of questions she expected, and he was going to ask her to see how she responded. They were taping this, so Sara could play it back.

Hernan walked into her office just as Sara was setting up the microphone to her computer. "Ciao Hernan, right on time. Are you ready?"

"Not that I must be ready. Are you ready?"

"Let's find out," as she laughed nervously.

Sara sat in front of the microphone, and Hernan sat in front of her desk. When Sara gave a thumbs up sign, he began.

"Ms. Ricci, in your final experiments, you used four incoming power levels. You relate these values to distinct groupings of data in a paper you authored regarding sensor and satellite data from actual Terrestrial Gamma-Ray Burst events. If we understand this correctly, your sensors had a limitation of six-hundred million electronvolts. How did you establish the higher values if your discrete data did not support this?"

"Thank you for the question. You are correct that the application specific integrated circuit in my sensor had this limit. Data table 27 shows that sixty-one percent of the sensors offered discrete data ranging from eight thousand to five-hundred-ninety thousand electronvolts. The other thirty-nine percent were higher, meaning they exceeded the sensor limit. However, this data also had altitude, longitude, and latitude records and allowed us to create the exact location of the power readings within the thundercloud. We then took known satellite data from proven TGF detectors, data that had no limits, to correlate those points to our points relative to their location within the thundercloud. We then extrapolated the incoming power from the satellite data and applied it to the sensor data with allocation accuracy of approximately a hundred feet in all directions."

Hernan looked at question sheet and said, "But that is just a guess Ms. Ricci. There is no basis of fact that the satellite data is the same as your sensor data."

Sara responded. "That is partially correct and explained in the footnotes and the 'Additional Study' section. There you'll note that of the three satellite datasets, there was a seventy-seven percent correlation between them when you compare them in the same manner. This means from one, you can predict the power of the other two based on altitude, longitude, and latitude. Given that, the error rate is fourteen percent, and the Data Table 27 suggests a fourteen percent error rate."

Hernan gave Sara a quick clap and went on to the next question. It was over four hours later when they finally stopped. Sara asked Hernan, "So, how would you grade me?"

"Your recall is amazing, so to your answers and its relationship to fact, I don't see how you could improve this. Where I would caution you is that although you have premeditated these questions, you have also shown some bias."

"I don't understand, bias towards what?"

"On a few, your answer might be accurate, but your tone is condescending and a tad bitchy, just saying."

"Okay, I know me, that's fair. I'll just have to mind my manners. How about a beer as a reward?"

"Let's go, I thought you'd never ask?"

Susan De Vires glanced at her phone and thought to call Lillian Boylan again. They were not great friends, but with Dann's involvement in their business, CSC, and Liam's involvement in Versilant, it gave them a natural reason to talk.

Lillian was a scientist herself and sometimes it was hard to get immediate hold of her, but that could be measured in hours, not days. Susan had been trying to call her for six days straight and nothing. That was very odd. She had even tried to get hold of Liam, but he didn't call back either, although she expected that. He was crazy smart, but a really weird guy.

Susan pressed send to call again. The phone rang and went to voicemail, and Susan left a message. "Hey Lillian, it's Susan again. Not like you to not answer or call back. Please call when you can, I'm getting worried." And she hung up. If she didn't hear from her soon, she'd let agent Davies know about this. Something was not right.

28

Nine-Days missing. Dann had been awake for some time and was doing modest stretching and exercise to keep his body moving. At some point, an opportunity to escape would present itself, and he needed to be ready and able.

When he heard the snap of the light switch, he stopped and looked at the door. His watch said it was 10:37 p.m., right on time. He also heard the small feet moving towards him. In a change or habit, he decided not to talk. He hoped it might scare the person into opening the door to check on him, as if he had fallen ill.

The person was there at the door, and he could smell the food. De Vires had always had a strong sense of smell. Whether it was wine, food, anything, he could separate smells and his brain identified them. At that moment, he could smell the food, but something else. It was a fragrance. A woman's fragrance, although he had not noticed it before.

As the small lower door opened, the paper food tray came in, followed by three waters. The door closed quickly, latched, and the scent attached to the small feet went away.

Although his tactic of silence had failed to rouse suspicion, the scent was a clue. The problem was that scent belonged to Lillian Boylan, his friend and wife of his business partner. That just couldn't be.

29

Montreal, Canada

A light snow had fallen within the hour as Remy Cadieux looked out of his window, heading towards his desk. His entire office was glass walls, floor to ceiling, and despite the lack of better insulation, the room was warm and comfortable. He picked up the phone and had his assistant connect him to Jason Sykes at Versilant.

When Jason answered, he said, "Jason, it is Remy Cadieux. Do you have a moment?"

Jason, shocked by the call, replied, "Yes sir, what can I do for you?"

"Jason, in Dann's absence, I thought I would call you directly. There is a symposium in New York, for two days. I knew of it but didn't think it had much relevance to our needs, but have since learned that there are two speakers that might allow significant future guidance. Many companies operating in our space will present product portfolios at a small convention attached to the event. I'm sending two from our team and thought if you and Ms. Ricci were there, it would help the team bond and also help generate ideas for the next phase of the product family."

"Thank you, Mr. Cadieux, but our situation here is unchanged and I cannot allow funding for such a trip under the circumstance."

"I realize Dann's disappearance is a horrible distraction, and we here at Cadieux MT, we hope for the best, but business goes on, Jason. Perhaps a break for a few days is exactly what you need. This has to be tough on you. Please, Cadieux MT will pay for everything. Can I count you in?"

"Sir, I'll have to consult with Sara. She is in Rome and less than a week from her dissertation presentation and seriously doubt I can persuade her, but I'll ask. I can be there, I guess."

"Excellent. Use your charm on Ms. Ricci. You would only be in town for twenty-four hours. Here is a number to call to arrange your travel, and we look forward to seeing you both." Remy gave the number, which Jason wrote and down as Remy hung up.

Jason glanced at the time and realized Sara would still be up, so he called and explained the trip and the benefits despite the not so ideal timing. Sara replied as expected, "Jason, normally that would be great, but I just can't risk leaving now."

"It's all paid for and first class even. Are you sure? You could be in and out in a day and a half and perhaps, like me, a day away from the current state might make everything seem better."

Sara was thinking quickly and figured, what the hell? He might just be right, as she could relax and switch gears. "Okay, text me your arrival times and I'll book my flights and please understand, I only have the forty-eight hours, no more."

"Cadieux has a travel agent that will do this for us. I'll text the name and number. You won't regret this, and I can't wait to see you," he said with a smile.

The Delta flight from Seattle landed early at John F. Kennedy Airport and taxied into terminal two. Jason arrived a few hours before Sara and, after several minutes, he deplaned and, with his small carry-on and made his way to the AirTrain, which took him to Terminal four. This is where he would meet Sara, and he stopped at the Tigin Irish Pub and had a beer to kill some time as he waited. While he couldn't get to her gate, he would be right outside customs and texted to let her know.

Forty minutes after her Alitalia flight touched down, Sara emerged from the baggage claim as Jason waved. They had a hug and a long kiss before heading to a taxi that would take them into lower Manhattan. Their hotel and the convention were at the Millenium Hilton, New York Downtown on Church Street, in the financial district. After a nice but expensive meal, they went to their suite for a good rest before meeting the Cadieux MT team in the morning. This would be the first time they and the two leaders had met face-to-face.

The next day was a blur as they met the two bioengineer leaders from Cadieux MT. They all attended two seminars that discussed the future of nanotechnology and upcoming trends, the focus being viruses and dentistry. After that, they had a quick lunch and, after a third seminar, headed for the small convention. As they walked through, they noted their competition and what they were saying to differentiate themselves. Most of which was future speech. It was like a politician that says all the things they're going to do, all the things you wanted to hear, but in reality, none of it will ever happen. But that kind of talk resonates with the human spirit and brings in votes. Here, it brought in product hype. Product hype brought in investment dollars.

It was soon evening, and after changing into dinner attire, they went into a large ballroom to the left of the convention for a hosted cocktail session. Jason and Sara hung with the Cadieux MT engineers most of the time, but they also mingled a bit with others.

On the second floor, Bridget Drummond was near the rail to the floor below, talking to another CEO as she glanced down at the crowd. Her eyes wandered aimlessly but stopped when she noticed an attractive man, perhaps private security and a stunning woman that looked familiar, but she couldn't place her. She motioned for her security head, Rex Williams, to come over and asked as she pulled him aside, "Who are those four there? One is wearing a Cadieux MT shirt."

Rex pulled out a mic and asked a question. Moments later, he said to Bridget, "The two young guys are bioengineers with Cadieux MT and are leading the new nanobot effort from the Canadian side, while the others are from Versilant Nanotechnologies. The tall guy is Jason Sykes, formerly with DARPA. The woman is Sara Ricci."

Bridget stood rigid as stone. She regained her composure and explained the situation to Rex. His face turned very serious, and he backed away and spoke again into his mic as Bridget stared at Sara. Her haunting eyes now gazing down on her like a death ray.

Below, Sara was laughing at a lame physics joke and as she turned, she glanced across the room and up. As she continued glancing to the right, she snapped back to the left where a tall, exotic looking woman, standing at the rail, was staring at her with the evilest eyes. Sara looked away and then instinctively glanced back. The woman was still there and still staring at her. Feeling uncomfortable, Sara wondered what the hell the women was staring at, although it appeared to be her.

Sara looked at the older of the two bioengineers and asked, "Without being too obvious, behind me is a woman on the second floor. She seems really pissed and I think she's staring at me. Do you know her?"

He looked up casually, and the bioengineer said, "Yeah, that's Ms. Drummond. As of a month ago, she is the largest single shareholder in Cadieux MT. It is the reason I'm told we finally got a deal with you guys at Versilant." Sara almost screamed and turned a shade of pale as the engineer asked if she was alright. Jason immediately looked around the room. His training allowed him to see security in each corner of the room. Each was cupping their non-shooting hand around their ear to receive a message in their earpiece and moments after, promptly looked in their direction. With no other thought, he grabbed Sara's hand and said firmly, "We have to go. Now."

He literally pulled her away from the stunned bioengineers and started through the crowd and headed to the exit directly in front of them. A security guy was there and as soon as his head came around in their direction, Jason hit him hard, with no warning. As the man went down, a few people saw the exchange and gasped. Paying no mind, he grabbed Sara, and they ran out of the crowded room as that area erupted in shouts and screams. With no chance to get back to their rooms, they ran out of the hotel onto Church and headed for Dey street, towards the Westfield World Trade Center. At least two guys were following, likely more. As soon as they crossed the street, Sara stopped and pulled off her high heels before sprinting off. The faster of the two, she was slightly ahead when Jason told her to get a cab and head to the Roxy Hotel in Tribeca on Sixth Ave. He would meet her there. She gave a thumbs up as he turned right and ran as fast as he could. Breaking them up would make it harder to follow.

Jason ran across the stalled traffic in Greenwich, ignoring the honks but still not looking back as the noise all but told them where he was if they were well trained. He went left to Liberty Street and took off his jacket, casually walking towards the corner. If the security guys were there, it wasn't obvious as he jumped into a cab, a little out of breath, and told the driver to go to the Roxy Hotel in Tribeca.

The driver glanced in his rearview mirror, nodded, and drove off. A few minutes later, they pulled in front of the Roxy Hotel and Jason climbed out, looked both ways, and paid the driver. He then walked inside and glanced around. Sara was in a dark corner of the bar when he first saw her. He walked over and gave her a hug. "That was close."

She held him with everything she had and asked, "What the hell just happened?"

"Drummond must have found out who you were and sent her security team to us. Those guys weren't associated with the hotel. The convention security all wore black suits. These guys wore MDE colors, dark blue with a MDE crest on their lapel."

"But why?"

"Perhaps she found out what really happened on Heard Island."

"Dr. Berniece told her?"

"That's my guess. He was under a gag order, but knowing her, they likely threatened him with his life."

"Really, I have to go through this shit all over again?"

"It's only seven. Let's head to the airport and get you out of here. But first, hang out at the bar for a bit. I'm going to get a NYPD friend from my army days to go with me into the hotel to get our stuff. I'll be back in an hour. You okay?"

"Are you kidding me? Of course, I'm not okay. Why can't I come with you?"

"Sara, it's you they want. With the police escort I'll be fine, but if you're there too, it's just asking the MDE security team to play their hand and I don't think they'll back off for one police officer."

"Okay, fine. God knows I need a drink. Please be safe, I need you to keep saving me." She said as she winked at him.

"That's all part of my master plan." As he smiled and called a number. He waited for the NYPD cruiser to pull up and met his friend, now a ten-year veteran of the force. He explained the situation, and they drove to the Millennium Hilton. They parked right out-front, lights flashing. Waving off the doorman, they walked cautiously into the hotel and went to the front desk. There, the officer told a bewildered manager to send security to Jason and Sara's suite, pack, and bring down their two small bags. The entire time, Jason kept lookout and his friend stood rigid, facing out, with his hand on his holstered but unclipped Glock 19 service weapon.

As Jason looked at the vast reception area, he counted three security all looking at him, but none made any effort to move toward him. One spoke into his comm, but nothing happened. Although he might have been a bonus, it appeared they didn't want him as he expected. Once he had their stuff, they drove back to the Roxy and Jason thanked his friend for his support.

Less than an hour later, Sara and Jason were back at JFK International and would spend the night there. They had dinner and Jason used cash to avoid any trail back to Cadieux MT on the chance this was a setup.

As the server removed their plates, Sara asked, "I can't believe this. Remy Cadieux and Bridget Drummond are a team?"

"I need to find that out, but it seems that way. He insisted we both be here and must have known she was here, but of what I know of her, she calls the shots. If she is using him, he might not have a clue."

"How can you find out?"

"He'll be in Versilant in three days, I'll just ask him." They finished up and found a set of empty seats in a crowded part of the terminal to rest for the night. It was a risk, but Jason slept with one eye open. Sara spread out, leaning on his chest, and slept.

Early that morning, Jason kissed a nervous Sara, who headed down the jetway for Rome while he headed back for Terminal 2 for his own flight. He had to figure out the connections between Cadieux MT, Drummond, Boylan, De Vires, and his dad.

30

Ciutadella, Menorca, Spain

Somewhere in the mountaintop home, a phone was ringing. Jessica Estrada knew it was her cell, but had no idea where it was. Seeing it now on the couch, she grabbed it and answered, but immediately wished she hadn't.

The computer's voice was blunt. "You have chosen to test us. There will be no negotiation, but there are new terms. We know about your husband. Perhaps you recall killing him. The stakes have risen considerably."

Taken aback and flustered, she held herself and, playing dumb, responded, "I… did no such thing. How dare you?"

"You are a resourceful woman, but you are no match for our knowledge. Tomorrow morning you will sell your entire stake in Cadieux MT. The cost of our silence is five million dollars. If you do not sell the shares within one hour of the TSX opening, we'll reveal you and his murder to the world." The call ended.

Jessica was used to dealing, not running, but if they really had proof of what she had done, she was in big trouble. How in the hell could they have possibly known? If all they wanted was money, five million was a pittance compared to her empire. She would do this, but then get some competent thugs to find and kill this bastard.

Angus and his team, now back at the residence on the Isle of Skye, sat in their old offices watching the TSX market the next morning. Sure enough, the shares from Jessica Estrada were up for sale. Adair, using the same Toronto based trading house, immediately purchased them using the same Cayman Islands company and transferred five million from her brokerage to his own account.

The Cadieux Jet landed at Renton Municipal Airport and Remy Cadieux, traveling alone, waited for the plane to stop. He spoke with the co-pilot briefly and once the door opened, headed to the hired car in a light rain. They were at Versilant within fifteen minutes and Susan and Jason met him at the door, and they went into Dann's office. Remy spoke first. "Mademoiselle, the recent events saddened the entire Cadieux community and me. We hope and pray for a successful outcome."

"Thank you Mr. Cadieux, it is all still a shock, and we still know nothing."

"Nothing at all?"

Jason responded as Susan had become distressed, "Mr. Cadieux, neither we nor the authorities have received any demands or communication."

"I am just a business executive, but I understand how this silence must make a tense situation even worse." Susan had tried to hold it together as long as she could, but quickly excused herself.

"Perhaps this visit was ill advised. I should go." Cadieux said as he turned to go.

"Sir, you're here. Let me get the team together so we can update you." Jason replied. He was halfway to the door when he turned and asked, "Mr. Cadieux, how well do you know Bridget Drummond?"

Remy tilted his head and, not sure where this came from and replied, "And how do you know of her?"

"When I worked for DARPA, I was on a joint raid to apprehend her brother and his security officer for crimes. Maximillian, her brother had kidnapped Sara."

"Ah, that is why her name is familiar." Cadieux said, already knowing the story but playing dumb.

"What do you mean?"

"When I first met Ms. Ricci, the name sounded familiar, but I couldn't place it. Now I recall her story."

"All that happened last year and while it was going down, Bridget Drummond was near death and recuperating in Scotland. Police had shot her during a raid on her home on the Isle of Skye."

"I was not aware of that. Tell me, Jason. Is there a purpose to this conversation?"

"Mr. Cadieux, Sara, and I left the convention in haste when eight men, all part of her private security force, tried to kill us. I want to know why."

Cadieux was hardly a physical man, but Sykes was, so he calmed himself and smiled, "You are worried for Ms. Ricci, yes."

Jason looked down and replied, "Yes. She has been through a lot and this attempt has brought back many old memories. Memories she doesn't need. Please answer the question."

"Jason, I understand your concern, but I do not answer to you, so please note to whom you are speaking. That said, I actually know little of Ms. Drummond. She is clearly a smart and beautiful woman but plays by her own rules. I do not know why she would want to harm Ms. Ricci or yourself, but I am also smart enough to not ask or involve myself. My interest in MDE is a financial transaction, nothing more. Cadieux MT has no agenda other than a new product family of nanobots."

"You don't find it odd that in your quest to get funding, a woman with a grudge steps forward and then forces you to invest in Versilant?"

"Jason please. You are no doubt an experienced solider and a fine project manager, but I am not aware of your right to question my business judgment."

"When people try to kill me and my girlfriend, I get very involved. Watch yourself Mr. Cadieux. You insisted we be there, and you were especially interested in making sure that Sara was there. God help you if I find out you were setting us up?"

Remy Cadieux said nothing. He simply tilted his head and headed for the door. Jason had obviously offended him and as he left, Jason went down to tell the team the presentation would not happen. He also needed to talk to Susan. He had no problem with what he had said but hadn't really considered any blowback on Versilant.

31

Sapienza University, Rome, Italy

Sara had barely slept since returning from New York. Her mind was running wild at the possibility of yet another attempt on her life and sadly, her dissertation presentation was almost the last thing on her mind. When she returned to Rome, there were emails, texts and calls demanding to know where she was; she had told no one about heading to New York. She simply told all that asked that she had sequestered herself to prep for the presentation. Nobody thought different. Except Sara, who now regretted the decision to go, although she was having tremendous fun until her eyes locked with Bridget Drummond. She would never forget that face.

Her dad had come to town the night before and was staying with her; the last thing she really needed at that moment, but this was her fault, not his. He was in the other room getting dressed, and Sara was trying to do the same as *Fantasy in F#*, by American pianist Richard Kastle, played softly in the living room. Sara wore a black pants suit rather than a dress, trying to be conservative. Less than twenty minutes later, with her proud dad beaming from ear to ear, they walked together over to the conference area. He mistook her apprehension for nervousness and told her she would do great.

As they entered the room, both felt it. This room, in particular, was hundreds of years old. The rich wood construction resonated its 800-year-old long history, and you could feel the spirit of those who had gone before her. Sara wondered how many had stood exactly where she was now.

Now inside, her dad sat in awe, admiring the woodwork while she attached her computer to the projector. She turned it on and made sure it worked. She would have fifteen to twenty minutes to present a synopsis of the dissertation she had already submitted. As she turned to sit with her dad, the door opened, and she immediately burst into tears and ran to the door.

Dr. Zimbrean, her former thesis chair from MIT, walked in and offered her his hand, which she took immediately and looked over at her dad. "Dad, did you do this?"

He brushed her off, saying casually, "Sara, we have spoken from time to time, and he wanted to be here, so he is here. It is as simple as that."

Sara knew it wasn't, but this was just the pick-me-up she needed. She turned to her mentor and said, "Dr. Zimbrean, I cannot tell you how much this means to me."

"My dear Sara, our relationship requires no words. I am honored to be here, and it will be fun to watch this as a spectator. This is a rarity for me." With that, they all sat down and waited. It was just minutes before a side door opened and her committee, led by Dr. Ferrera, walked in. They all sat, but Dr. Ferrera came over and met her dad, Giovanni, and he and Dr. Zimbrean shook hands fondly, given their years of mutual respect. Dr. Ferrera returned to the table. The five of them were now facing Sara, who sat alone, and behind her were her two guests. Giovanni had his iPhone on to FaceTime with Jason who had it hooked up to a projector in the crowded conference room in Versilant. The whole team was there.

Dr. Ferrera brought the room to order. "Welcome Ms. Ricci. This is a big day for you. I trust you are adequately prepared." Everyone chuckled, but Sara, who had barely taken a breath. He then went on to the opening prayer and formal introduction of the committee and candidate. He then motioned to Sara and said, "Please begin, Ms. Ricci."

Sara had practiced this many times and never looked at the slides. Reading from script was not acceptable as she went through the twenty slides in sixteen minutes and on the last slide; it asked the committee for questions.

Expecting the worst, she assumed there would be no questions regarding the Introduction or Abstract, but Validation and Proof of theorem. They surprised her with the first question regarding the Conclusions chapter.

"Ms. Ricci, after proving your theorem, you offer the ability to promote your discovery to industry. You, however, chose not to quantify this during your own research. Can you explain this?"

"Thank you for the question. My thesis was only to quantify the energy available from a TGF and determine the potential power such energy might produce. My early funding allowed me to go one step further, and I created the Ricci Gamma Ray Conversion Dish to determine this. That I converted an average of forty-six percent of the incoming gammas is already a breakthrough to our understanding of its commercial value. That said, I can answer your question directly. All of my experiments used an x-ray machine set to one of four incoming power levels to mimic a gamma ray. These incoming power levels were not exhaustive, simply the sub-groupings from the actual sensor data. It is not possible to extend the x-ray power much beyond the maximum used, which was five million electronvolts. As outlined in Appendix 37, I describe a series of estimates on what it would take to achieve all power levels received from the actual satellite data, the only absolute facts. The estimated cost is one-hundred-million dollars and would take ten years to complete. Such power requires colliders, such as CERN. It is with that understanding that I conclude in the Future work section, that if industry simply produced my invention and sent it to Low Earth Orbit on a satellite for one year or less, they would have the actual potential at far less cost and time. Thank you."

"Thank you, Ms. Ricci."

The next question was related and expected. "Ms. Ricci, you are correct that your invention changes our understanding of gamma ray capture and conversion. If I recall a footnote correctly, this is not your invention but a company in America, Cerium Scientific Compounds. Is this correct?"

"Thank you for the question. That is not correct. There are two design cruxes for my invention. The irregular parabolic shape which traps the interactions, and the coating you have mentioned. My research created the parabolic design, and I determined the material make-up of the coating, and even purchased the materials themselves. Knowing the exact process used to bind the coating to the dish would have been nice, but CSC, as a business, owns that proprietary right and their NDA to me, supports that decision. That said, CSC will gladly coat any surface with my invention for a price. So other than being a sole source, there is no detriment to anyone being able to replicate my invention with my approval. Thank you." Sara glanced behind her as Dr. Zimbrean motioned for her to relax. It did no good to fight with them.

The various exchanges went back and forth for another thirty minutes when a question arose that Sara had dreaded and hoped would not arise, but here it was. From none other than Dr. Ferrera.

"Ms. Ricci, this committee understands your relationship to the distinguished Dr. Gilberti Ricci. I believe he is your great-great-grandfather. Can you explain to the committee how he influenced your work?"

Sara stumbled for a moment and glanced backwards at her dad and Dr. Zimbrean. Both looked at each other and then back to her, and Dr. Zimbrean shrugged his shoulders as if to say, go ahead, tell them.

Sara turned back to the committee and spoke. "When my original thesis was disproven and my mother passed, I gave serious consideration to ending this journey. I was overwhelmed. I knew who Gilberti Ricci was to me, but in my darkest hour, I also learned of his depth, his passion, and his ultimate sacrifice. One that he did to assure his family, students, and his university would not suffer under Nazi oppression. That he took his own life for them strengthened me." The committee gasped.

Sara continued, "That knowledge made me want more. As outlandish as his theories might have appeared on paper, I elected to consider if it was possible to prove them. I can honestly tell you this became more about making his life choice worthy than earning my PhD. He did all the work, I merely proved him right. With the generosity of my mother and father, this became a journey for the entire Ricci family, and I am honored to be part of it. Someday soon, I will honor Gilberti Ricci and publish the work from his amazing mind for all to see. Thank you." Sara dabbed her eyes, trying not to cry, not unlike several on the committee.

Dr. Ferrera rose, composed himself and thanked Sara, and then politely asked her to leave them. She met her dad and Dr. Zimbrean, and they walked out together. This was it. The committee was now in deliberations. In most institutions, a disapproval is not final. They will generally give the applicant one more attempt before they ask you to leave the program.

Sara was hopeful, but at the same time, unsure. If anyone had asked, she would not recall what they discussed while they waited. She was nervous, but only twenty minutes passed before they summoned her to return. Her dad reestablished a connection with Jason, as Dr. Ferrera made a few comments regarding minor suggestions. Sara wrote each down and while it didn't seem like a big deal, she couldn't tell where this was going. At long last, he gave his final remarks as her chair, and said the closing prayer.

When Sara looked up, his face was tight, and he had a look of concern, which caused her to become concerned. The room was silent and even Jason, on the end of the line with the entire Versilant team watching in the conference room said nothing.

"Dr. Ricci,... your committee approves your dissertation without revision." He smiled now and Sara, perhaps expecting the worst at first, did not react. She heard the words, Dr. Ricci, but didn't grasp the significance until she heard her dad behind yell, "That's my special girl" and clapped. Dr. Zimbrean, all smiles, joined in and the committee rose and added to the chorus. Sara mouthed a thank you to Dr. Ferrera and then to her committee. She then turned to her dad, giving him a hug that was decades in the making. She did the same to Dr. Zimbrean and blew a kiss to the phone in her dad's hand. Jason was still on the other end, giving a fist pump as the Versilant team yelled in the background with

Alice Cooper's *Schools Out Forever,* playing in the background. Sara laughed and if she had known how, she might even have danced.

She had finally done it. She was now and forever Dr. Sara Ricci.

32

Thirteen-Days missing. Dann had been doing his exercises for almost two hours and had even worked up a little sweat, although that was not his intention. It was too cold to be in wet clothes. Glancing at his watch, he knew food would soon come and intended to be bold. Feeling strongly that he had correctly isolated the fragrance smell from all others, today he would find the truth.

He had stopped moving now and for ten minutes, just waited until he heard the snap of a light switch and the faint light outline of the door. As the small feet approached the door, he yelled, "Lillian, is that you? What are you doing? How could you do this to me, of all people? Do the right thing, open this door and I promise you, I'll tell no one."

He heard a gasp. A female gasp. Then the sound of his food being dropped on the floor, realizing at that moment, he should have got the food first and then spoke. Thankfully, he had banked several burgers and waters. With no bathroom, he was trying to limit his intake, as the urine and excrement in the room was getting to a powerful level.

The small feet ran out of the room, and he heard a door slam. *Oh shit. It really was her. What the hell is going on?*

33

Lillian Boylan ran out of the house into the mist covered night. The light over the one stall garage was on, and she raced around her 2003 Subaru Outback and into the driver's seat. She started the car and drove slowly down the dirt road, almost hysterical. How in the hell had he figured out it was her? She had been so careful, but he knew. How? What the hell were they going to do now?

She turned in the light rain onto the Renton/Issaquah Road towards her home as she fumed. How could Liam do this to her? Why had she gone along with it? She was an accessory to a crime, a fucking Federal crime with the FBI leading the investigation no less. As she gained speed, the madder she got. She was going to confront Liam and force him to turn himself in. It would ruin their business and everything they had worked for, but this couldn't go on.

Driving recklessly now on the two-lane highway, she considered Dann's words. *Let me out and I'll tell no one.* Could he? Would he? She slowed and pulled over, thinking to herself, *perhaps she should go back and release him. While Dann was never to be harmed, she had the power to end this right now. Fuck Liam.*

Lillian took her foot off the brake and turned around, heading back to the cabin she had inherited from her parents. It was still in their name. She was heading up the grade as the rain became heavy and the roadway veered left.

Billy Meadows had been driving a truck since he was twenty. It was not particularly the job he wanted, but it paid well, and it was easy enough to get into. Meadows had driven most all trucks at some point. He had run hogs, carried beer, heavy freight and for a couple of years, he even did some ice road driving in Canada, but two years ago, he switched to logging. He enjoyed it because it was the type of job where you made as much as you were willing to work. Once, when he needed cash, he had driven this route ten times in one day. Wicked money, but that was an eternal day.

He and a buddy had stopped in Issaquah and had a few beers hours before. That alone partially explained why he was flying down the Renton/Issaquah highway at 11:30 p.m. As he banked wide to take the turn, he suddenly saw headlights and yelled "Oh shit," as he let off the gas. This activated the truck's air brakes, and he tried to swerve to the right, but as he did, the rear slid in the rain. Inertia forced the truck to stay on its original path.

In front of him, Lillian saw bright headlights fill her entire windshield and protectively raise her hands to her face. She had no idea there was a huge logging truck behind the light as it slammed into her car.

Given the huge truck outweighed the Subaru by twenty times and was going thirty miles an hour over the speed limit, the kinetic energy was massive. It crushed the Subaru and then tossed it hundreds of feet, completely off the road and down into a deep ravine.

There was no question. Lillian Masters Boylan was dead.

Washington State Patrol (WSP) was on the scene in fifteen minutes as Meadows had called 911, knowing he had killed the women in the car. Her face of panic and surprise would haunt him his entire life. There were few homes on this stretch of highway within the Cougar Mountain Regional Wildland Park, so nobody came out, but two trucks coming down the hill had stopped behind his now immobile rig. The drivers comforted Meadows. Not long after, a sheriff from Kings county arrived as well as a police officer from Issaquah, just before a fire engine and paramedics pulled up.

One of the Sheriff's and an EMP rappelled down the deep ravine to the car, if you could call it that, using over one-hundred-fifty feet of rope. Once they arrived at the wreckage, it was as they had assumed. There wasn't an intact body. Lillian was simply part of the car now, entombed in steel and plastic. The rear license plate was there, and they would get information regarding the owner and, likely, the occupant. Meadows had told them he was positive that in a split second, he had seen a woman driving.

In time, two heavy duty tow trucks arrived, and one removed the logging truck, which allowed the highway to reopen on the southbound lane while the other brought up the remains of the Subaru. The car was no bigger than four-foot square and the EMT pulled a tissue and blood sample for DNA confirmation. It was close to five in the morning when the accident had been cleared and the State Patrol drove to the house of Liam Boylan in East Renton Highlands to break the sad news.

Liam Boylan awoke on the sofa to a knocking at the door. It startled him, having fallen asleep as he waited for Lillian to return. He got up and looked out the window to the side of the door and saw the WSP cruiser and two patrolmen standing at his door. Panicking, he thought of Dann, but realized WSP would not be here for that. It would be the FBI or police. At that moment, he realized Lillian had never come home and panicked for a different reason. Sleepily he opening the door and the officer asked if they could come in. Putting a hand on his shoulder, the officer paused for a moment and then said he was sorry to tell him about a violent accident on Renton/Issaquah highway. It had claimed the life of his wife, Lillian. Liam burst into tears and the officers at first did nothing, but soon guided him over to a chair. When he sat, the larger officer asked, "Mr. Boylan, do you recall where was your wife going so late at night?"

Thinking fast, he said somberly, "Lillian has a very active mind. When she can't sleep, she takes a drive. I'm so used to it; I don't question her anymore." He lost it again, and after a few additional questions, they left, telling him to call a friend or family to be with him. It was best at a time like this.

In the darkness, the news devastated him. He had done this. To avoid blackmail, he had agreed to grab Dann and hide him. He thought he could avoid it all coming out if he agreed. He had potentially saved some money, but paid a price far greater. Sadly, for Dann De Vires, Boylan was so distraught he hadn't thought of him, unfed and still locked in the cabin.

In his panic and grief, a thought struck him. Why was Lillian going *up the mountain at that hour? She should have been returning.*

34

South Beacon Hill, Washington

Jason closed his door as he looked down at the phone that showed an incoming call from his dad. He answered on the third ring as his dad said tersely, "Any news?"

"No. The FBI wants to talk to you about the blackmailer."

"In time. I'm working on a few things. I'm not running, just thinking without distraction."

"Okay." Jason told him about the incident in New York with him and Sara, explaining Bridget Drummond. While they didn't understand it yet, there was a link between all these separate events.

Harley replied, "This Maximillian Drummond, the guy killed on your mission. That is her brother?"

Surprised his dad knew the story, he said, "Yes. He was a nasty guy, but I suspect his sister might be worse."

"You might be right. Keep your head down, boy, and watch after your mom. I'll call her right after this. Also, tell agent Davies I'll come to him soon."

"Thanks Dad. You're doing the right thing." There was no reply, just silence as the phone call ended. Harley destroyed the phone.

Hours later, Annabel picked up the burner phone Jason had given her and answered, assuming it was Jason. It wasn't it was her husband.

"Hey love, sorry about the scare. I needed to think."

"Dammit, Harley, it's been a week. Where the hell are you?"

"I'll be back in town in a few days."

"Harley, what is going on?" Harley took a few minutes to tell her the entire story and asked for her forgiveness.

"Harley, we've never had secrets, so that is disturbing, but doesn't this mean we're millionaires?"

"Yes, but if this really is insider trading, I could go to jail. The worst part is the money drop. The blackmailer claims I killed the person I was trying to scare off."

"Harley. Listen to yourself. If you wanted to kill someone, you would have done it. This is just extortion. What are you going to do?"

Happy she was on his side, he said, "The boy says he cleared things with the FBI. I'm going to turn myself in and see what happens. He says they'll question and release me. They only want to know about the blackmailer."

"I suspect that is best. I'm glad you talked to him."

"Don't make more out of this than it is, Annabel." They finished the call and Harley walked to a rental car he was using as he tossed the burner phone in the trash and pulled out another.

An hour later, using his new phone connected to the rental car, he called Davies.

"FBI, agent Davies. How can I help you?"

"Davies, it's Harley Sykes. I'm driving to you tonight. Where do you want to meet?"

"Mr. Sykes, we want to talk to you about the blackmailer. There is little need to come to Seattle unless you wish to. I can arrange an agent out of the Boise office to take your statement if that is where you are. The only thing I ask is no more hiding. Just be yourself and use normal communication if we have to get hold of you."

"Fair enough. What is the name to contact in Boise?"

"Special Agent Jayden Thompson. When can he expect you?"

Harley got his bearings and replied, "Little over an hour," and hung up.

Less than fifty minutes later, Harley pulled into a public parking area and went into the FBI field office on West Main and 9th street in downtown Boise. This part of town had been modernized and was a perfect tourist attraction and college party place. He asked for Special Agent Thompson and met him a few minutes later, immediately handing him a locked gun safe bag. Thompson cautiously accepted it and set it down in the corner. Over the next hour, being taped, Harley told Thompson about the entire circumstance that led to the purchase of the shares, the army doctor, and the blackmailer's computer-generated calls, that started six weeks ago. He told him of the money drop and the shooting, reiterating he was an expert marksman and didn't hit anyone. When there were no questions left, Thompson rose and told Harley, "Mr. Sykes, regardless of the blackmailers claim, we are unaware of any suspicious gunshot wounds or missing persons matching the description you have given. That may or may not be a fact, but you'll have to surrender your weapon." Harley motioned to the locked bag in the corner and told him he assumed as much. He gave the agent his contact information and left.

35

Rome, Italy

Sara was smiling from ear to ear and had been for the last several days. Of course, she loved to learn, loved being on campus and being around smart people, but at least for now, she was just so very glad to be done. Sitting in her bedroom, she could finally look to the future and not what had become mind-numbing hours of writing and editing.

Hours before, she had discussed the timeline regarding her adjunct professorship at Sapienza University with Dr. Ferrera. She had agreed to teach for just one year while she sorted out the concept of working for a corporation or, most likely, using her skills for hire. She hadn't ruled out academia entirely, but really believed a freelance assignment better suited her. Despite the scares of the past year, it had made her tougher, less vulnerable, and more willing to extend herself. She felt she needed excitement in her life. Robot girl was still there… but slowly going away.

Her suitcase packed; she rolled it into the corner. She had spoken to her dad and told him she was flying out to Washington to see Jason and help with Dann's disappearance. He had muttered the usual concerns and something to the effect this was hardly the work of a PhD. Sara had become quite adept at brushing it off and told him it would only be for a few weeks before she had to return and start her teaching assignment. As she prepared to hang up, Giovanni asked almost casually, "Sara, do you remember when you answered Dr. Ferrera's question about Gilberti, and mentioned you might tell the world of his genius?"

"Of course, I think it deserves to be told. Don't you?"

"I do. Perhaps at some point, we can discuss how to do this. I would enjoy working on this with you."

"I would like that Dad. I'll think through how to do this."

Sara's plane landed the next afternoon and again Jason was waiting for her. Part of him had actually not wanted her to come, as the pain of her leaving was tough, but this was their thing. Right? He also knew the team could use the help, as Dann's disappearance made it difficult for them to move forward.

Suddenly, none of that mattered when Sara came around the corner, smiled, and he melted. After a quick hug and kiss, they headed straight for Versilant and went right to the team huddle. All were excited to have her back, and it was just minutes before they were at a white board seamlessly discussing problems.

One of the newer military designs was what they called a swimmer. It was a cell-sized robot that was powered and steered by ultrasonic waves. For reference, bacteria and sperm use flagellum, a whiplike motion to move forward, but from a manufacturing process, Versilant couldn't add a battery to start the initial movement. It made the microscopic device too heavy to move. Ultrasound waves were a better choice and were also FDA approved, saving lots of time in the medical approval process. The problem was, the normal process to make such a device was photolithography. Often used in nano-circuits, they apply light to a mask of the circuit. The light passes through and creates an image on a lens that, from the opposite side, reduces the size of the mask and makes a die of that image on a wafer. Their nanobot worked more or less the same but results after several trials were poor. Using funds from Cadieux MT, they purchased a laser lithography system with much better results. It allowed them to create small cavities into the backbone skeleton that created a stream of microscopic air bubbles caused by the ultrasound waves. This propelled the swimmer forward. Amazing stuff.

The team mapped out a plan to proceed, and Sara went to work with another engineer, designing the signal strength they would need. It was tedious work, but promising at the same time.

Susan De Vires had tried to get hold of Lillian once more and was now beyond concerned. She escalated this to Davies, unaware of the accident. Over the phone, she said, "Agent Davies, I have been trying to reach Lillian Boylan, my friend, and the wife of Liam Boylan, but it's been over a week and a half and nothing. It's just not like her to not return my calls."

"Ms. De Vires, I'm so sorry. I thought you knew. Lillian is dead."

"What? When did this happen? How?"

"She was in a horrific car accident on the Renton/Issaquah highway, close to midnight three nights ago. A logging truck hit her, and she was killed instantly."

"Midnight? Why would Lillian be in the mountains at midnight?"

"We're not sure. The husband told WSP that she often could not sleep and liked to drive around to relax."

"What? That's pure bullshit. Lillian could fall asleep in a packed football stadium and hated, I mean hated, two-lane roads. No, something is wrong here." Susan all but yelled.

"Ms. De Vires, you're under a lot of pressure and I know this is a shock. I'll follow-up but I'm pretty sure this was just a terrible accident."

"Agent Davies, please do. This was not a simple accident. She would never be on that road alone unless someone made her."

Back in the FBI field office, Davies had the team dig deeper into Lillian Boylan. To Susan's words, they interviewed two other friends, who both confirmed she had no trouble sleeping, and didn't like to drive at night, especially on two-lane roads.

That left Agent Davies wondering where she was going. At the end of the Renton/Issaquah highway, she would have come into Issaquah, but it did not appear she had any friends or relatives there. But first things first. Liam Boylan had lied to the WSP. Why? Davies grabbed his credentials and he and a partner headed to Cerium Scientific Coating (CSC) to question him.

When they arrived at CSC, the lot was half full. They exited and walked into the lobby, where a receptionist met them. "Hello, how might we help you today?"

"Were looking for Liam Boylan."

The young girl frowned and replied, "I'm sorry he is not in and we're not sure when to expect him?"

Davies flashed his FBI credentials. "This is extremely important. Are you positive you do not know his whereabouts?"

"No, sir, no one here has seen him. He hasn't been himself since Lillian passed. That's his wife." No sooner had she said that when the door to the factory behind her opened and an engineer walked into the lobby. The receptionist mentioned the FBI in front of her and that they were looking for Liam.

Looking over to them, he said, "The Boylan's run this place like a maximum security prison. Everything runs through them and with Ms. Boylan gone and now Mr. Boylan missing, we're barely able to run the factory."

"When did you last see him?"

"Three days ago, he was here in the morning, and nobody has seen him since. He drives a black Ford Explorer, pretty new, and it's gone as well. I went to their house yesterday, and he's not there, nor is the SUV."

"When you saw him last Tuesday, how was he acting?"

"To be honest, he was a zombie. Since the accident, he's been a mess. So not good."

"Did anything abnormal happen that day or in the days since he went missing?"

"No, not that I'm aware of."

"Okay, thanks. We'll likely be back." As they were leaving, the engineer said, "Hey, this might mean nothing, but last night around ten, Mr. Boylan logged into the system from outside the company and downloaded all the CSC recipes."

"Why is that noteworthy?"

"Mr. Boylan is a very paranoid guy. The recipes are the secrets of how each coating is made. Once they are complete, only he and his wife have access to them. The recipes are held offline away from our normal servers, and we can only access them once they download them to the tablets that the teams used to run the factory. Occasionally, they log into that personal server, but they never download, they only add new recipes."

"Thanks." Agent Davies handed them both a card and told them to call him if anything came up, especially if Liam contacted them or came into the office. As they walked back outside, he added to his partner, "This is weird. Let's get out an APB on Liam Boylan and I'll try to get a warrant to dig into that server. Maybe we can get a trace from where he came into the server from."

36

Seventeen-Days missing. Dann was asleep when he heard a door slam above him. It woke him right up, given it was the loudest noise he had heard since being here. Counting backwards, it had been three days since Lillian had been there and fed him. Thankfully, he had stockpiled two hamburgers, two French fries and three waters, which he had been living off since. He was weaker, and his exercises had become more difficult, but he persevered. Hopefully, he would get fed now. The light switch flipped on, but this was clearly not Lillian, as heavy boots stomped in his direction. As he tried to listen, waiting for the small food door to open, the entire door flew open unexpectedly and the bright light blinded him, his eyes sensitive to that much light. He tried to raise himself, now was his chance, but he was too weak.

A large man, all muscle, grabbed him as he tried to fight, but he got a quick slap across the face and felt a pick on his neck. The attacker yelled, "Man, it stinks in here!" With one hand behind his neck and the other holding him down, Dann felt the room spin and knew this was it. He tried once again to fight but had nothing as he thought, *Susan, I love you.*

My beautiful girls, Daddy loves you. Why are you doing this? As the bright lights faded to blackness.

37

Isle of Skye, Scotland

Angus Adair sat quietly in front of his computer, as he prepared to call Liam Boylan. His idea from the beginning, not only did Bridget want his Cadieux shares, but the accidental death of the wife, allowed a perfect opportunity to raise the stakes. He knew Boylan was running, but had no idea where he was going. He also knew he had a secret company credit card and a cell phone, which he was now tracking. According to his computer, Boylan was currently on State Route 2, heading towards Spokane and would soon be in Idaho.

Angus and his team had been behind Maximilian's need for information and, while well paid, they were just a tool in Maximillian's arsenal. Bridget, however, allowed Angus to run the show. When she asked how to get more shares of Cadieux stock, Angus had researched the top holders and found information that allowed Bridget to get the shares without having to pay a premium. These three, Boylan, Sykes, and Estrada, were just the beginning. He had six more, and the best part was that Bridget only cared about the Cadieux shares. He could shake these marks down and keep the money, and he now had millions.

At 6:00 p.m., Mountain Time, Angus called Boylan's company cell. When he answered, Angus spoke into a mic, which the computer turned into a synthesized voice. "Dann De Vires has died. Not feeding him was too much." Boylan screamed as he abruptly slammed on his brakes and pulled onto the shoulder as a semi-truck horn roared behind him and moved into the next lane, barely avoiding him.

"No. No. That is not possible. He was fine." He yelled, not really sure if that was true. With all that was going on, he had forgotten him. *Oh, fuck, what have I done?*

"The last person to see him was your wife four days ago. We are sorry for your loss, but De Vires' death raises the stakes considerably. We have removed the body."

"But it's not possible…"

"Please listen. Before tomorrow morning, you will sell all of your Cadieux shares at the opening bell. You will also transfer all CSC recipes to a dark web address we will soon send you. That will be your cost of silence in both matters."

Liam sat on the road thinking of what to do. The blackmailer was still connected, but Boylan was thinking, *why the fuck should I do this? Lillian is dead, Dann was dead. I'm all but ruined.*

Angus expected this and continued, "We know you are thinking, why bother?"

"No, no… I'm just in shock."

"Boylan, you are on the run with nowhere to go. We can help you, but only if you help us. Sell the shares, transfer the recipes and I'll call back on this same phone to assist you."

Liam wasn't sure if he believed the voice, but whoever this was, they were correct. He had no idea what he was doing. "I don't understand. Why the recipes from CSC? They are useless to anyone but my company."

"Do not test us Boylan. Just do it and we'll help you. You have twenty-four hours." Angus disconnected. That had gone well, he thought.

First thing the next morning, from his computer, Angus and one of his analysts watched the opening movements of the TSX market, and so far, it looked to be a hot start. His computer was tracking volume exceptions when two-hundred-thirty thousand shares of Cadieux MT came up for sale in a single block which triggered an alert; an alert they were waiting for. Angus nodded as the analyst started a buy order of the same amount. In Toronto, a broker executed an order on behalf of a Cayman Islands company. Bridget now owned thirty percent of Cadieux MT and would negotiate her third board seat. Angus told the analyst to be on the lookout for the recipes.

Thousands of miles away back in Washington State, a dark green minivan without windows was parked in a line of other cars and trucks on a Washington State ferry heading from Renton to Whidbey Island. Rex Williams, Bridget's security team leader had grabbed a coffee and was sitting back in the van drinking it. He had stayed in the van on the odd chance that Dann De Vires would wake from under the tarp in the back of the van after Williams had drugged him and brought him here. His orders were to get to the island and wait until Angus had receipt of two items. Being stuck on a ferry and then driving around with him was a high-risk assignment and Williams demanded hazard pay for this one.

Angus soon texted. The first item was complete. He was just waiting for the second. Ten, maybe twelve hours to go before he could head back to Scotland.

Liam Boylan was not much of a drinker, but the day's events had done him in. At a small roadside motel, a dump actually, he was having a beer, thinking about his options. In the trash can next to him were three empties, perhaps the most he had drank in a single setting since his college days. His estate was worth millions, but with no children and no family, he realized it was all for naught.

He and Lillian had concentrated on themselves, with little to no thought of what might happen if they were gone, but he had an idea, one he thought of on the drive here. With the Cadieux stock sale, he had five million cash in the brokerage account and quickly transferred it into a private account. The FBI could follow this, but he might need access to additional funds if they didn't freeze them.

He noted the time and called his attorney. He needed to change the Liam and Lillian Boylan Trust of March 2014. The attorney was adamant that Boylan reconsider, but his mind was very much made up. The attorney also told him he had to come into his office to provide wet signatures, but Liam told him that was not possible and to send him the documents in DocuSign. It was unclear if that would be binding, but besides his words, Boylan had previously sent him a written instruction with his wet signature. He had mailed it the day before.

That done, he took a swig of beer and wondered again if the blackmailer would actually help him. He assumed they wouldn't. As he attached the zip file of the CSC recipes to an encrypted email, it still puzzled him. Why was this file worth more than the five million in cash the blackmailer knew he had?

It was at that moment the ghost of Dann De Vires came into his head as he recalled the fear of the young PhD student, Sara Ricci. He recalled her wild ideas of how the Scottish company, MDE Enterprises, was after his coating for her invention. Now she was working for Dann or had worked for Dann, and he recalled Dann's visit several weeks back, telling him to watch himself. Now Lillian and Dann were dead. Were these both tragic accidents? Or had this group done all this just to get the fucking recipe for Sara Ricci's coating?

His first thought was not to send the email, but at the same time, he needed help. If they could do all this, then they had the skill and resources to help him out of the country. But would that even work? He had caused all this. Was life even worth living? He took another sip of beer and held off, sending the file.

Boylan woke to the sound of a large semi-truck as he tried to focus on where he was and what he had done. He lifted his head from the table and realized he had passed out in the chair at the desk. He glanced at his watch. It was 3:10 a.m. and his head was throbbing as he noted six beer cans on the table and the trash. Who in the hell drove at such an hour? He glanced out the dirty window to watch the enormous truck slowing driving out of the parking lot. He rose, urinated, and grabbed two Advil from his overnight kit, drinking them down with a full bottle of water.

Back at the desk, he clicked to refresh laptop screen, and it came up to his send page. Shit, he had done it. He had sent the recipe file to the blackmailer. Liam knew he wouldn't be able to go back to sleep, and at that same moment, realized he was in too deep. Everything would soon fall apart, and the help promised by the blackmailer was not likely to appear as he wept, knowing the decision he had to make. The consequence he had to accept.

After opening his email, he wrote a message to Susan De Vires. He hesitated for a minute and then hit send before shutting off the computer and disabling his phone. Pulling out the SIM card, he packed everything up and headed out to his SUV. Fifteen minutes later, he was back on I-90 going west towards Seattle.

At the exit for State Route 12, he slowed and left the highway. He paused at the bottom of the off ramp, and with a sigh, turned left, which took him into the Nez Perce Clearwater National Forest.

At Versilant, Susan De Vires had just left the office of their controller and was walking down the hall. As she passed the conference room, she poked her head in and said hello to Jason and Sara, who were noodling something on the board.

"Morning kids." Susan said with a tired voice.

"Morning." Sara and Jason said together. Sara got up and followed her.

"Susan, is there anything I can do for you?"

"No, but thanks for asking. It's just another day. Thank god my mom can watch the girls. Being in the house all day makes my mind go crazy. I really need to be here as much as I can." By now, Susan was in Dann's office and as she sat down at the computer, she looked back at Sara.

"You and Jason should come over for dinner. Mom is making enchiladas tonight. They're fantastic." As she waited for a reply from Sara, she glanced at her company email screen and saw an email from Liam Boylan. She knew the FBI was looking for him and saddened at the thought of Lillian's death, but clicked open the email, forgetting at that moment that Sara was talking. A second later, she screamed. Not a whimper, but a blood-curdling scream. Sara jumped up and came around the desk to her as Jason and most of the company came running down the hall.

Sara grabbed Susan and hugged her. She was now crying hysterically as Sara looked at the screen and saw the email from Boylan. She glanced at the words and stopped when she got to the passage,... *I didn't mean to kill him. It just happened. Please forgive me.*

Sara yelled, "Jason" just as he ran into the room. Sara was on her knees holding Susan as Jason came around and Sara eyed the screen. He looked and like Sara, stopped at the passage and saddened. Trying to hold it together, he grabbed his cell and called Davies and told him what had happened and went into the hall to settle the team.

39

South Beacon Hill, Washington

Davies and two others were in De Vires' office, trying to piece together what had transpired. Sara had driven Susan home after they talked to her and a grief counselor with the FBI was on her way to Susan's house in Rainier Beach. An FBI computer tech at Versilant had tried to match the IP address of the sent file, but it was not using a conventional Wi-Fi. It was using a personal hot spot, which he traced to a cell phone. A warrant to the carrier established what they had not known previously that Boylan had an additional phone under a different name than his own. They traced the signal to the vicinity of Lolo, Montana, and Davies got agents from the Missoula field office involved. It didn't take them long to find the roadside motel where Boylan had stayed. It contained evidence that he had been there, but offered no clues to his whereabouts. He had paid with a credit card under the same name as the phone, so if he used it again, they could trace him. Boylan was on the run, or so they thought.

In Montreal, Remy Cadieux and his father Gustave were in his office with CFO Tremblay as they discussed the events of the past few weeks.

195

Three long-term stockholders had sold entire lots of their stock only for someone, a ghost company out of the Cayman Islands to buy them up.

"And there is no way to determine who is behind this company in the Caymans?" Gustave asked.

"We hired a firm through Cinead Vass to understand the lineage, but and as of last night, they have linked it to fifteen different companies and are still at it. Whoever this is, they know full well how to hide their identity, but I still suspect it is Drummond. As I'm sure you do as well."

Remy said nothing as his father's gaze came around to him. "So, if we assume these companies are under her control, she now owns 30 percent of the company. Remy, had she contacted you?"

"No, I tried to call her, but no answer."

"Well, try again. The Cadieux family has controlled this company we founded for over a hundred years, and I will not allow that ruthless bitch to steal it from us. Jenesse, convene an emergency board meeting. I'm changing the family voting rights and issuing an additional ten million shares outstanding. We can survive a shareholder lawsuit on dilution, but we must call every large block shareholder to offer them a premium on their shares should she approach them."

Remy, knowing his dad was on a roll, asked, "What do you want me to do?"

Without hesitation, Gustave looked at him and said with all present, "I want you to resign."

"What does it matter?" Remy fired back. Gustave gave him a stare.

"Remy, I'm serious. Do it or I'll have the board remove you."

"Dad, given the trajectory of the stock price, I don't think you'll get the votes, but to be honest, I'm so sick of your shit, I just might just take you up on the offer. So go ahead, change the family voting rules. That's all the incentive I need. Maybe I'll even sell my shares to her?" he nervously, trying to muster a smile.

The next day, Remy climbed into the helicopter on top of the Cadieux Headquarters with a small duffle and headed to Nova Scotia, *New Scotland*, to meet with Bridget. He had finally got hold of her and asked if they could meet, and she agreed. He had said nothing of the share purchases or his father's ultimatum.

A hired car took him down Granville, past her condo overlooking Halifax Harbor, to the same restaurant they had gone to a month before. In a similar fashion as he walked, Bridget was already there, and her bodyguard eyed him from the bar. He walked over to her, and she extended her hand.

"Bridget, thank you for seeing me."

"You seem tense. Troubles Remy?"

"Yes. Thanks to you."

"Remy, I more or less told you what I was going to do. Are you shocked that I do as I say?"

"Bridget, that scenario was under the caption, what if the family was to fight you? At my insistence, they approved your purchase. So, it is of interest because you have come after us, anyway."

"Remy, I'm not coming after you. Your father is still driving the bus and my intention is to oust him and not let him oust you. Stay out of the way and all will work out."

"How do you know about that? Do you have fucking spies in the office? And what if I don't want my father ousted?"

Bridget, drink in hand, motioned for the server and replied, "Much too late to be sentimental. Either you're with me or you're out, too. What would you like to drink, Remy? My treat." Remy had known since day one she outmatched him, but he now understood what his dad was trying to tell him.

40

In the Seattle field office, Davies and the team had been digging deeper into Boylan now. He was their prime suspect and in less than two hours; they made the connection to Lillian's parents' cabin. It all fit. That was where she was really going the night she died. He and his partner climbed into his SUV, and they took off for the cabin off Renton/Issaquah highway, just past Tibbets Creek. The King County sheriff would meet them there.

They made good time and Davies slowed as they came to the location of the accident. It was one of just a few sweeping turns on the highway. Her turnoff was just a 1,000 yards from the scene of her death. The turnoff was a dirt road but well-groomed and the sheriff was already there, parked 300 feet from the house. Pine trees were thick and there were only three houses here, two of which looked unused and were boarded up. He got out as they arrived. They conferred for several minutes before they drew their weapons and walked down the drive. The sheriff went around the back, Davies went to the front and his partner stayed on the drive. They slowly moved in place. Davies knocked on the door loudly and shouted, "FBI." Several minutes passed with no sound, no activity. He repeated the command. Nothing. He tried the door, but it was locked. With a swift kick, he broke the lock and pushed the door open with his left elbow. His gun was still out in front of him as he swept it across the room.

The sheriff had done the same seconds later from the opposite end of the house. He was in the kitchen and shouted. He doubted anyone was there, but needed Davies to know where he was. They met in the hallway and then, together, searched the two rooms. Nothing.

As they walked back out, the sheriff noted a heavy door.

"This is to the basement. It's a fire door, but this one is uncommonly robust. He tried the door, and it was also locked. We won't be able to kick it inward. Let's see if there are any keys in the kitchen." It took just a minute before they found a ring of keys. With gloved hands, they tried them one by one, producing a click on the eighth key. The sheriff opened the door. It strongly smelled of urine and feces. He felt for a switch and clicked it on. The snap switch made a loud click. They both walked down the stairs as the smell of excrement increased and soon came to the concrete block cell in the center of the basement. The door was open and inside was a cheap mattress and weeks of excrement and fast-food wrappers in the corner. No one was there. But someone had been.

Davies and the sheriff returned upstairs, and the sheriff called in support. In less than two hours, they had a cadaver dog, a tracker dog, and their handlers on site as they searched the twenty-acre parcel and any unfenced area on either side. Within twenty-four hours, they had found no sign that De Vires had been killed or buried there, but the tracker dog got a scent in the driveway. Davies suspected the body had been removed.

Looking to the sheriff, Davies asked, "So these dogs would only signal on a dead body?"

"The cadaver dog, yes, but the tracker scented off the mattress."

"So, are you saying no dead body was here, but the tracker scented De Vires alive?"

"Could have been when he arrived here, but if the scent is from him leaving, it only confirms they did not kill him here."

"Okay. Once we have the DNA evidence from the cell, we can process it. Thanks for the assist." Davies thought for a moment, *there might be hope.*

Sara and Jason were in the conference room at Versilant, but they weren't talking about nanobots. They were trying to find a common denominator between his dad, the Boylan's, and the De Vires. Versilant was basically a tech company of the scientific sort, meaning they had several *geeked-out* computer guys who could help them, and Jason knew they did a lot of freelance work. Two of them were now in the conference room, and Sara explained what they were looking for. They were pretty sure the link was Cadieux MT stock since they knew of the situation regarding Jason's dad. They needed the programmers to hack into whatever site might let them understand who else might be blackmailed.

Neither Sara nor Jason really understood the process, but it was like pulling one layer of an onion off at a time. The guys were moving quick, going from clue to clue until the taller of the two said, four hours later, "I think I have something." He turned the screen around as Sara and Jason looked on.

"In the last two months, three shareholders have sold their entire positions in Cadieux MT and immediately, those shares were repurchased. The new owner in each case is an untraceable company in the Cayman Islands, but here is the deal. One of those shareholders was Harley Sykes, one was Liam Boylan and the other, Jessica Estrada in Spain."

Jason replied, "So my dad and Liam are linked, but I've never heard of this person, Jessica Estrada."

"She runs a company called Imagen International, it's a PR firm."

"Is there any way to see if she ever worked for Cadieux MT?

"Sure, give me an hour."

Time stood still as both were looking into the request when the tall one, clearly the faster of the two, said, "The answer is yes. Imagen was hired by Cadieux MT about four years ago to prepare the company to go public."

Sara looked at Jason and said the obvious, "So that makes sense right, they went public shortly after that, so likely, this Jessica Estrada is also being blackmailed."

"Okay, that I get, but what's the tie to Dann?"

"Perhaps he was only an insurance policy for Liam and your dad."

"But Liam says he killed him. Why would he do that?"

"He implied it was an accident which could have happened. But it's also possible based on what they told your dad, the blackmailers might want him to think Dann is dead so they can, I don't know, extort more money from him?" Sara added.

Jason looked at the team and said, "We have to tell all this to Davies. It might be important, but we can't say how we found out."

At the Seattle field office, Jason and Sara met with Davies. They were in the lobby when Davies came out to get them. "Morning guys, what's up?" he asked as they walked to his small office.

Jason replied, "We have been looking into a connection between my dad, Boylan and De Vires and think we might have found something." Jason explained the stock and likely blackmail connection.

"And it's plausible that Liam Boylan didn't really kill Dann, they just want him to think he did to get more money or leverage." Sara added.

Davies leaned back and looked at them both. "I don't know how you got this information and won't ask. That said, you're spot on. Our analysts found the same thing. There is a DNA match to De Vires at the cabin cell. We also got a scent from a tracker dog, meaning a live person, was there recently. The cadaver dog did not spot on anything. We have international field offices, so I'll get our Madrid office to work with Interpol and understand more about this Jessica Estrada."

41

South Beacon Hill, Washington

Sara was seated with two Versilant bioengineers in the main conference room discussing the new military bots. They weren't, however, discussing ways to advance the design, rather, they were trying to understand the timing. Sara was convinced that all of this was related. Dann's disappearance, the investment by Bridget Drummond, the deal between Versilant and Cadieux and then a fast-track order of these added nanobots for the military. It was just too much, too soon, and in the back of her mind, of course, was Bridget Drummond. She didn't want to admit it, but maybe it was just that simple.

Sara had drawn these relationships on the whiteboard and was pondering them as Davies walked by. He glanced over and walked past when his brain connected to the timeline she was drawing. He stopped and went back to the room. As he entered, Sara noticed his interest and told him what they were looking into. Davies nodded and asked them to keep him informed if something concrete came up from the exercise. As he left, Jason walked in.

"Hey, are you working on the military bots?"

"Not really, I just think all this is related." Sara replied.

Just then, an engineer walked in as Jason said, "Well, if you have a second, I think we have a problem with one of the Cadieux MT military grade nanobots from variant U-23."

Sara turned to look at Jason when the bioengineer asked, "Like what? Do you mean… with the design?"

"Yes, we have been monitoring the variants and one has, I don't know, mutated."

"Mutated? Mutated how?" the engineer asked.

"The nanobot prototype has gobbled up all the healthy cells. The virus is still there, and the bacteria is there, but the normal healthy cells are gone."

"And this is variant U-23?"

"Yes. This variant is from Cadieux MT and, as designed, was to be a transport vehicle for drugs. It is a spinoff of Sara's idea of the hollow bot made from DNA strands."

"That shouldn't be possible. The DNA hollow bots are targeting viruses which have no metabolism. Mutation is not possible, although I guess someone could have reprogrammed them."

"Well, we can't do that here. We don't even have a DNA programmer." With that, they abandoned the timeline and headed to the lab. Over the next several days, they went back and forth with Cadieux MT. The Cadieux team leaders felt that this must be contamination caused by human error during the building process, but the team at Versilant did not agree and told them someone had reprogrammed them.

In Seattle, an FBI analyst came into Davies' office and said she had something. She explained. "So, with a warrant, we dug into the accounts of Harley Sykes, and two-point-eight million was deposited into his brokerage account and immediately one million was wire transferred out. The entity it went to is best we can tell is a Swiss bank account, but we're not aware of which one. Jessica Estrada shows just over eighteen million went in, but five million came out and went to the same Swiss account. Here's the interesting part: Liam Boylan has five million go in and all five million goes out, but not to the Swiss account. It is a private account under Boylan's name and the money is all there. None is missing."

"And this means?"

"Well, we think it means the others paid a price for silence, but Liam didn't. The implication is he is central to this?"

"When we went to CSC to meet with him, an engineer mentioned that Boylan had downloaded all the secret recipes of the coatings his company had done for others. They have amazing security and military like controls and the engineer thought it was strange that he would copy these files off the server. Do me a favor and check if he sent a large data file from his hotspot in Montana and if so, where did it go?"

The analyst scurried off only to come back forty minutes later. "I'm not sure how you knew this, but yes, his hotspot shows a one-gigabyte file came in when Boylan accessed his own server at CSC. A file the same size was attached to an email and sent back out three hours later. He sent it to a dark web IP address and not a normal email account. The team is looking into it, but it is not likely we can trace it."

"So, to your earlier reasoning. Maybe Liam paid a price, but instead of cash, it was the recipes that make up the intellectual capital of his business."

"That makes little sense. Five million dollars in cash is real. A file full of materials and methods is useless without a factory to use them."

"Possibly, but in this world, there are such factories. Write this all up and add it to the case file, it might become useful." Davies said more confident that earlier.

Several thousand miles away, Interpol agents, an FBI agent from Madrid, and a local Guardia officer from Ciutadella arrived at the home of Jessica Estrada. Given who she was, she had received ample warning and was ready for them. She knew what this was about. Her security team let them in at the gate to the long sweeping drive that went to the mountaintop home where a second security team checked them and brought them in to the house. Her bodyguard was in the room with her when they came into her study.

The Interpol agent asked, "You are Ms. Jessica Estrada?"

"Yes, what is this regarding?"

The FBI agent gave a rundown of the stock, the blackmailer, and that there were others. Jessica used every ounce of energy she had to not reveal any facial reaction, as all eyes were on her for a reason. In her line of work, having a good poker face was mandatory. When he finished, she said with a smile, "That is terrible, but after all, they broke the law."

"And this blackmailer also contacted you, is that correct?"

"No. What made you think that? I have owned these shares for years and the company has been floundering, so I sold on the advice of my broker. That is not a crime."

"Ms. Estrada, this is just an inquiry at this point. It is best that you cooperate."

"And by that, you are suggesting I haven't?"

"Five million dollars was removed from your account almost as fast as the money from the stock sale was received. We believe this was a price for silence. We believe you were also being blackmailed, Ms. Estrada."

"Well, I'm sorry to disappoint you, but that is not the case, and what I do with my money is not your concern." She went to her purse and pulled out a business card. "This is my solicitor. All future questions regarding this matter can go through him, since you have chosen not to believe me. Please send him a copy of the warrant used to access my accounts. If you can't produce one, this will become very difficult for you, agent," as she offered him a wicked smile.

The agent took the card but paid it no attention. He then handed her a sheet of paper with three phone numbers on it. "Ms. Estrada, phone records reveal you received a single call from each of these numbers. Do you recall them?"

"You must be joking. I receive no less than fifty calls every single day, sometimes more, and you think I can recall individual numbers? I have no idea who these numbers belong to. Perhaps you should call them and find out?" She barked, getting annoyed.

The agent held up the solicitor's card and glimpsed at it before he shrugged, and they all turned and walked out. Jessica watched them go, happy that they were looking into this and hopeful they would catch that bastard.

Special Agent Jayden Thompson was driving in his truck in Boise, Idaho when his cell ran. He connected and barked, "Thompson."

"Special Agent Thompson, it's Agent Smalls out of Missoula."

"What can I do for you Smalls?"

"I'm heading up Highway 12 to a trailhead in the Nez Perce Clearwater National Forest. We got a tip from a ranger with the Fish, Wildlife and Parks (FWP) that a Ford Explorer has been there for several days. He normal doesn't bother much with parked cars as backpackers use this area from time to time, but inside the SUV through the window, he saw a computer and other personal stuff. He called in the license plate, and it belongs to Liam Boylan."

"What's the plan?" Thompson asked.

"I'm joining with two FWP, and a sheriff from the Missoula Country to see if we can find him. He's not an outdoorsman, so we're hoping this is quick. We'll have the SUV brought down the hill for the techs to go through."

"Nice work, Smalls, and let me know if you find anything." Thompson clicked off and made a call to Davies in Seattle. It was a start.

42

South Beacon Hill, Washington

Sara was alone in the Versilant conference room that was acting as her office. With an expresso shop infused grande Starbucks drip coffee in front of her, she took a sip and realized that once again; she was frightened. The common denominator in this maze was the stock, but the fact remained that Bridget Drummond was the largest shareholder to Cadieux and the kingpin to the Versilant deal. Based on the events in New York, it seemed obvious she knew Sara had shot and killed her brother, and that once again, she had become a target.

Davies came around the corner and silently watched her. Something was up, and he had learned to trust her instincts. He walked into the room and closed the door. "Ms. Ricci, are you okay? Anything you wish to share?"

"I'm just thinking about some scary connections. It's nothing really."

"Let me hear your thoughts, perhaps it is something."

"Okay. I know you have access to information about me, but last year, Maximillian Drummond abducted me and threatened my life. To save myself, I shot him, and he died. I think his sister, Bridget, knows this and all of this is related to her trying to get to me."

"Ms. Ricci, I am aware of your background, and you have been through a lot. I'll give you that. But Bridget Drummond could have you killed easily if that was her intent. Why the blackmail and multimillion-dollar investment in Cadieux, not to mention the shares of the blackmail victims?"

"I've given this a lot of thought and think when she started this, it was all just a business transaction. At some point, she found out I was with Versilant and switched gears. She is operating just like her brother. She has ten oars in the water, and each is related but separate at the same time."

"Well, I don't have your history, but I understand what you have said and will put this in the case notes. Every day, this turns a different direction, but we agree with you on one front, all of this seems related."

"One last thing. And it might be a big thing. It's about CSC, the company that Liam Boylan runs."

"What about it?"

"My PhD thesis was on a phenomenon called a terrestrial gamma ray flash. Besides locating and quantifying the power of the burst, I invented a method to capture and convert the gamma rays from it into useable power. Enough to power a satellite. The key to my invention is a coating that CSC produces. It is proprietary and although I created the material ingredients, I do not know the exact quantities or process to bind them."

"Okay, so that ties CSC to your research."

"Getting that recipe was one reason Maximillian Drummond abducted me. He wanted to use my invention for commercial gain and at one time offered to pay me a royalty. Perhaps because I refused, he made it a demand and said it was worth killing for. I can only assume his sister wants the same." No sooner had Sara spoken those words, Davies ran out of the room. Liam Boylan had paid a price for silence.

Davies returned to the FBI field Office and told the team about the recipes and why they were important. As he finished, an analyst came running into his office. "Agent Davies, I think I have a huge lead."

"Okay. Slow down and explain?"

"Yes, sir." She looked around the room as all eyes were now on her. "I have been combing the dark web, trying to find the IP address Boylan sent the extensive file to. No luck there, but while I was looking, someone was watching me. A hacker out of Yemen by the code name, Aladdin. He has since contacted me personally. He knows I'm with the FBI, and I know he is with the United Brotherhood of Islam, a small terrorist organization. Here's the thing. Aladdin is actually a guy named Gilad Qasim. Qasim says he knows a Scottish hacker, a really famous guy in geek circles, codenamed Beithir. That's pronounced, Bee-thee-uh, and it refers to the mythical Scottish dragon. Qasim says the guy's real name is Angus Adair."

"Okay, and who is Angus Adair?"

"He is a senior analyst working for a private company owned by Bridget Drummond."

Davies was on the edge of seat now as he asked, "Okay, but a hacker within a terrorist organization is hardly trustworthy."

"Right, I know, but he says he can provide proof that Angus Adair is behind the computerized voice that Harley Sykes referred to, and we speculate Liam Boylan and Jessica Estrada have also heard. And this morning, someone else tracked me."

"Who?"

"None other than Angus Adair."

"Okay, go for it." This was finally coming together, Davies thought as she left the room.

An FBI field agent in the UK met with his contact at MI5 and discussed the information that Davies from America had provided them about Angus Adair. The same information received from UBOI hacker, Qasim. The database at MI5 had much on Adair, as he had been in and out of trouble for his hacking skills since he was in grade school. They had asked for and awaited approval to apprehend him for questioning.

At that moment, the Home Secretary Jocelyn Holmes, herself, was pondering the decision. A decision that had reached her because of the exploits from the year earlier and specifically, the disastrous raid on the Drummond residence. Holmes had almost resigned over the incident, and there were those that still felt she should have. She was therefore not altogether pleased to start another round with the sister, but the proof in front of her was solid. In the end, she allowed them to approach Adair, but only at his own residence, not the Drummond residence or MDE Enterprises.

Jason was sitting having a beer at his guest house overlooking Lake Washington when his cell rang. It was his dad. He considered not answering, but assumed his dad would never call unless it was important. It's not like they were buddies.

"Dad."

"That's sir to you, boy."

Jason ignored him as usual. "Did you find anything?" They had been trying to locate information regarding the army doctor at the center of all this, Dr. Miles McMillan. DARPA couldn't locate anyone with that name and Harley Sykes had attempted to call in a few favors with his friends within the Military Police.

"Nothing. There is no such person in the army, so while he said that he was Army, he was not. Further, we can't find a civilian doctor of the same name either. What did DARPA say?"

"Dr. Dubois assumed someone had vetted him given that they presented him to her, but they also never ran a background check in part because there was never a formal grant. I can only assume he was likely a Cadieux MT employee. I'll give all this to Davies, adding another wrinkle to an already complex set of events. Thanks for trying just the same."

"Any news regarding De Vires?"

"Davies hopes that Liam Boylan was led to believe Dann was dead to shake him down for money like they did to you, but I'm not aware that they have any leads on his whereabouts." Jason explained the recipes angle with CSC and that the FBI had located a hacker in Scotland, a guy named Angus Adair. They believe he was behind the computerized voice. When Jason mentioned his name, he said, "Dad, don't get any ideas. The FBI is working with MI5, and they'll get this guy."

"You're getting soft, boy. I have a question. When you were in Boston, what was the name of the guy who they shot up trying to get Sara's research data?"

"His name is Richard Chase. He runs a private security company called Fortitude. Why?"

"I may need some help. Thanks," and the call ended. Jason could only imagine what his dad was thinking at that moment and regretted saying anything.

Richard "Rottweiler" Chase was, in many ways, Harley Sykes equal but a much more rounded person. He had started his career as a Navy Seal but was wounded in action. When he was discharged, he used his knowledge and contacts to start a private security company in Kalispel, Montana, called Fortitude Security. They specialized in providing security to high wealth clients. His son Nathan was in his final year at MIT and had been a lab assistant to Sara when she was there. It was that relationship that caused Richard to help Sara when Maximillian

Drummond was after her information. Sitting there in his cabin, he was a bit surprised when his house phone rang. Nobody called that number. He answered, "Chase."

"Mr. Chase, we have not met, but we know of one another. This is Sergeant Major Harley Sykes calling."

"Well, it is an honor, sir. I know your son as well. Good man."

Harley ignored the comment and said, "I understand you played a significant role in helping Sara Ricci when Maximillian Drummond was after her."

"That is kind to say, but truth be told, his security team raided my house; a house my son and I built with our two hands, and they put hundreds of bullet holes in it. My efforts behind the scenes were more about payback."

"That's why I'm calling. I find myself in a similar circumstance." And Sykes told Chase of the events regarding Bridget Drummond.

43

The Burgundy colored Cadieux MT van left the shipping dock in haste for an animal trials laboratory seventy kilometers northeast in Trois Rivières. Cadieux MT had contracted them to begin animal trials on the ten variants of the new nanobot line, the original seven, plus the three new military bots they had fast-tracked. The team at Cadieux MT had produced one thousand controlled samples of each design, and this was a critical step before human trials could be considered. Although Cadieux MT had their own research facilities, they were using an outside lab to provide an arm's length to the effort. This saved time with regulators but was also a necessity because they had a capacity problem given there were so many equally important projects already underway.

The van drove out of sight as a heavyset quality control engineer was heading down the stairs to the temperature-controlled room where the prototypes had been held. He signed in, suited up in biohazard outerwear, and walked into an air-tight chamber. He hit the activate button, which purified the air and brought it to room temperature. When the door opened, it was a like atmosphere to the room it led to. The red light turned green, and the door swung open as he walked in. At first he looked around, trying to get his bearings. The room was not that large, so it wasn't like he had to search very far. He went to the intercom and called the technician outside, "Randy, where are the samples for U-18 though U-27? The pallet was right here."

"It's gone. It shipped to the lab like a half hour ago."

"What? That's not possible. It was on a biohazard hold order. I was here to pull U-23, something happened to it. Alert the Hazard Team and get that van back here." As he ran back into the inner chamber to repeat the process to get out.

Although they had a Hazard Team for situations just like this, anytime that they were activated, it was a hit to the integrity of the facility as a whole. This was a major breach and heads were going to roll.

Within an hour, what they thought was a problem had become a full-blown crisis. The van containing the ten variants, including U-23, was not responding. Montreal Police Service had been notified, and officers traveled the entire seventy kilometer stretch of highway between Cadieux MT and the lab in Trois Rivières with no sign of the van or the driver. The onboard tracking beacon was not sending a signal, meaning it was faulty or someone had removed it. Initial thoughts were that someone had stolen the entire batch of samples, including a possibly deadly version of U-23.

On the Isle of Skye, the freezing rain was blowing sideways as a cold front had come in quickly and was especially strong at the bluff where the residence was located. Inside, one could barely notice but for the sound of the sleet hitting the massive windows, but they had been built to withstand any weather. It was hardly a concern for Bridget as she sat at her desk in the study. The room once had the décor of gentlemen's club, with dark paneling of rich woods and big oversized leather chairs. It had been the only room in the otherwise modern house to have such warmth and charm, but Bridget never got it. It didn't fit the rest of the house or her taste, so after the raid; she rebuilt it in a tastefully done, modern design.

Bridget was happy with the goings on at Cadieux MT, and her preparation to avenge her brother's death. She felt empowered and realized this was what Maximillian must have felt like every day. How amazing to have such power? This called for a drink, but she held off for now and instead summoned Rex Williams.

Williams entered the room shortly after, his office just one floor below, and sat with Bridget at a conference table. Next to them was a single box containing twenty tubes with thirty samples each of the U-23 variant which they had stolen from Cadieux MT in Montreal and flown to Scotland.

Once received, they needed to convert the nanobots from one that brought medicine to one that ate healthy cells. What they needed was a weapon!

To test the new DNA program, they used an engineer to infiltrate Cadieux MT and program a few nanobots to alter their behavior. The altered nanobots were monitored, and the new DNA coding had been successful. The engineer had since been eliminated, but using a colleague of Williams from his past, they had sent samples to a company that had the skill to reprogram the DNA strands. Within a week, all been reprogrammed into the deadly variant. Deadly by design.

Williams was seeking approval for the plan to right the wrongs against Maximillian. "Ms. Drummond, the central idea, is to approach the victims in close quarters and release the nanobots using a tiny micropipette. It's a small syringe with an injector."

"And they won't feel this?"

"There is a risk, but we'll bump into each other and that will be felt over the small prink from the small needle. I think the larger risk is getting close enough to the victims."

"And there is no other way?"

"Not in the time frame we have."

"The priority targets are those that were directly involved. The secondary targets you may use your discretion and if the risk is too high, you can avoid them."

"Very good Ms. Drummond." As Williams took the box containing the changed nanobots and left the room. As he walked out, Angus Adair came in and asked, "Ms. Drummond, do you have a minute?"

"Angus, what can I do for you?"

"I have a situation… which could be a problem. Several sources are looking for information on Cadieux MT shareholders."

"And that means what?" Bridget replied, staring back at him, wishing she had poured her wine first.

"Someone is looking at previous Cadieux MT stock trades. There are two independent sources looking, one related to a computer at Versilant Nanotechnologies and another, is related to the FBI."

"And they can see this?"

"Not easily, but yes. It has nothing to do with us but could show the names of the shareholders and show the in and out transactions."

"So, a bunch of geeks at Versilant and the FBI have uncovered the blackmail scheme related to Sykes, Boylan, and Estrada."

"Not the blackmail, but possibly the trades."

"But they can't tie it to you or us."

"Unlikely."

"Angus. They can't, or they might?" she barked.

"They might." As Angus looked down at the ground, unable to contact Bridget's gaze.

"You have twenty-four hours to solve this. The consequence of failure is not an option. I trust you, understand?" Angus did not have to be told to take his leave, nor that he would be dead if he couldn't stop this. He left, and Bridget immediately poured a glass of wine and informed Williams of the breach.

44

Whidbey Island, Washington

Nineteen-days missing. The air was cool and contained a great deal of moisture from the marine layer that had saturated Community Park off Route 525 on Whidbey Island, seventy miles northwest of Seattle proper. Dann De Vires awoke and, with some effort, shielded his eyes with his arm. It wasn't bright, but he was still not accustomed to any light. Happy just to be alive, he immediately wondered where he was. He tried to raise himself and discovered he was on a park bench in the middle of a large green space. And he was free.

A couple was walking towards him with their dog, but seeing him, they immediately headed off the concrete walkway and onto the greenbelt to avoid him. Sitting up, he was highly disoriented as he watched the couple going across the grass, wishing he had said something to them. He knew he needed help.

As he watched them walk further away, two police officers on bikes had pulled up to the couple as they were pointing back towards him. He waved his hands and tried to yell, but only a weak *Help me,* came out. The bikes were now on the path coming towards him and were soon there.

"Please help me." Dann pleaded.

"Sir, you can't sleep in the park. You need to move on." One of them replied before adding under his breath, "Man, this one really stinks."

"You don't understand. My name is Dann De Vires, and someone has kidnapped me. You have been looking for me, I'm sure of it. Can I use your cell phone to call my wife?"

Both police officers laughed, and one tapped his chest mic and alerted a patrol unit to their location. "Just relax, friend. We'll get you some help."

Dann tried to stand now highly agitated and yelled, "Listen to me. I'm Dann De Vires, and someone has held me captive for over three weeks. I'm not some bum."

"Sure buddy, we get that. Just a few more minutes." As a police SUV made its way along the concrete bike path, it stopped and one of the bike police officers went over to talk to the driver. "This one's a beauty. Says someone has kidnapped him."

"He looks terrible. Did he give a name?"

"Yeah, something foreign, like De Beers, maybe De Veers. First name might be Dan or Van. By the way, your car is going to need some serious air freshener after this one gets out."

The officer laughed sadly as he typed in the name. The screen changed, and he said, "Holly shit," as he called it in. Feeling foolish, all officers were now doing all they could to help the man on the bench and within thirty minutes, two additional cruisers were on scene. An EMT arrived and an FBI helicopter settled down into the park center. Agent

Davies jumped out and jogged over to the police and a man wrapped in a blanket on the park bench.

"Sir, are you Dann De Vires?"

"Yes, they kidnapped me."

"Mr. De Vires, we know all about it. I'm Agent Davies with the FBI and cannot tell you how happy I am to find you alive. Let's get you to a hospital." Davies turned and signaled for one of the EMTs to help get De Vires into the helicopter to take him to Seattle. They would be at the University of Washington Medical Center in fifteen minutes.

When they arrived at the hospital, Davies called Susan and told her they had him, and he was in expert hands. Susan was in hysterics as she ran out of the office, screaming they had found Dann alive. Sara and Jason came out of the conference room, and they immediately headed for the hospital as the cheers from the Versilant team faded into the background.

Four hours later, a clean but weak De Vires was in a comfortable bed with warmed blankets and two IVs providing much need nutrients and fluids. Other than being 16 pounds lighter and severely low on minerals, he was physically doing well, although his mental state was a different story.

The FBI had interviewed him regarding the cabin and Davies had brought him up to speed on the Boylan's role in this, as Dann had told Davies about Lillian's perfume. De Vires learned of her passing and the assumption that she was likely on her way back to him to let him go.

They could not explain who drugged him and brought him to Whidbey Island, nor whether Liam Boylan had taken him originally, but the assumption was that he had. His whereabouts were still unknown, although they had located his SUV in the Montana wilderness. They assumed him dead and likely by his own hand.

De Vires explained he had met Harley Sykes just before the abduction. He was trying to understand the merger between Versilant and Cadieux MT. On hearing that, Davies told him the story and that they knew Sykes was not involved in his disappearance.

Sara and Jason could not see him, but Susan was there, relieved, scared, angry, but overall thrilled he was alive. More than once, she had imagined trying to run the business and raise the twins alone, and it scared the crap out of her. She was equally concerned now, as this would affect them for years. As Davies prepared to leave, he said, "De Vires, you have some talented people working for you. They helped us immensely with the complications of this case. We'll talk again, but for now, get some rest and welcome back!"

45

Inverness, Scotland

The dark blue MDE helicopter lifted slowly into the air and momentarily hovered before the nose tilted down and it moved forward on its return to London. The pilot had just dropped off Rex Williams in Inverness, who, with two of his team, would board a private jet in less than an hour. They were heading to Washington, D.C., with several small vials of his special cargo.

Williams opened his jacket and took out a small sheet of paper. These were the targets in random order, as he would base the confrontation on availability and timing to get to them rather than a predetermined design.

Jeremy Hicks, Former Director of the Department of Homeland Security, Washington D.C. Supplied intel to the SIS.

Conor Gilkeson, former Chief Constable of Police of Scotland. Organized the raid.

Cameron Halladay, former Raid Commander, Police Scotland. Led the raid.

Giles Taylor, the Assistant Director of the SIS. Collaborated with the US to provide intel, which led to the approval of the raid and the assault on Heard island

Dr. Sara Ricci, Know it all bitch who killed Maximillian.

Jocelyn Holmes, Home Secretary of the UK. Authorized the raid and the assault on Heard island.

Alistair Evans, The Foreign and Commonwealth Secretary. Authorized the assault on Heard island.

Williams knew the list by heart, and, with his team and Angus, they had followed them, studied their habits, and created plans to approach them. For Williams, there were no primary or secondary targets. All were guilty and he or his teams would approach them. He took a lighter and, holding the paper over his plate, and burned the list.

The next morning, dressed like many other dads, Williams stood on the sidelines of a soccer field in the suburbs of Washington D.C., Deer Park Heights. He did not have a child playing in the game. This was simply the location of the first target.

The field was close to the Department of Homeland Security at St. Elizabeth's Hospital and Jeremy Hicks, the former director of the DHS, was here, cheering on his grandson just as William's intelligence had suggested. This was how Hicks spent his weekends now after being forced out of the DHS following the circumstances of a joint, DHS/CIA attempt to snare Maximillian Drummond that went wrong. Hicks missed the action and knew this was the political price he paid for getting too involved in what was ultimately a UK problem.

Hicks knew most of the parents and many of the grandparents of the kids as a large man standing near him leaned over and asked which one was his. Jeremy pointed to a blond boy running across the field and said, "That little ball of fire is my grandson." At that moment, the boy tripped and went down hard. Hicks flinched but softened as the boy got up and the man patted him on the back rather hard. His hand cupped over his mouth, the large man placed his other on Hicks' shoulder and yelled over the cheers on the goal that had just occurred. "What a great effort!"

Hicks nodded, making sure his grandson was okay and turned to ask the guy about his child, but he was walking away, talking on his cell phone. He thought nothing of it as he scratched his neck.

Hicks awoke just after 3:00 a.m., feeling weak and disoriented. He knew immediately whatever was happening was bad and assumed the worst. He awoke his wife, who noticed he was out of breath and sweating. She did not hesitate to call 911, assuming a heart attack and forty-five minutes later, former DHS director Jeremy Hicks was in the hospital unresponsive. The emergency room didn't know what was happening, but he was slowly dying.

In Seattle, two days later, Sara and Jason were at the University of Washington Library researching the biology problem from the mutated nanobot. They had been at it for an hour, and neither were having much luck. Sara had considered just asking her friend Amy back in Italy, but it was just before 1:00 a.m. in Rome.

Williams, dressed now in a comfortable suit, was casually walking towards them. His plan was to ask about a book Sara had on the table. He was just two feet away when Sara unexpectedly jumped up to look for another book. Williams was so close; he lost his balance as he tried to avoid slamming into her and instead fell onto Jason's shoulder, using the device on the side of his neck. He quickly righted himself, pushing off the chair and apologized. "Sorry, I was so wrapped up in what I was thinking I wasn't paying attention," he said to Jason. Sara, who was now a few feet away, turned, as Jason said, "No Problem," and gave a thumbs up. She continued into the stacks.

Jason went back to reading and glanced at the back of the large man as he walked out. *Big guy. . . former military,* he thought silently.

After a nice dinner, Jason and Sara had returned to his house, and he was already feeling flushed. As he began to sweat, Sara asked if he was okay. Jason assumed it was the wine, as this sometimes happened from the sulfides. Within fifteen minutes, however, he became concerned and told Sara they needed to get to a hospital. Alarmed, she didn't hesitate to take this seriously. Jason was certainly not the type to whine. When they arrived, he was not doing well and Sara ran in, asking for help to get him out of the truck. The emergency room staff ran out to the truck to get him into a wheelchair when suddenly his vitals dropped. Nobody seemed to understand what was happening. Even hours later, they only knew he was unresponsive and slowly dying.

Williams had failed. Sara was the target, but he had infected the boyfriend instead. It was okay. He had been on the island as well, but he needed to rethink Sara, although right now, he had to return to the UK.

In Fife, Scotland, at the Ceres Inn, the former Chief Constable of Police of Scotland, Conor Gilkeson sat having a local ale with Cameron Halladay. Halladay and his commander, Gilkeson, had been sacked after the raid on the residence. Gilkeson and Halladay were more than pleased that Drummond was dead, but both wished they could have killed him themselves. Their days were now spent, more often than not, having a pint, or three, and bitching about the government.

Halladay raised his glass, gesturing for another, when one of William's lieutenants, dressed in a rugby uniform, approached the bar, and squeezed between Gilkeson and Halladay. Asking the bartender for a pint, he turned to Gilkeson, patted him on the shoulder hard, close to his neck, and apologized for the intrusion. He changed syringes with his right hand and did the same to Halladay. The jab had released the nanobots, but both waved it off, not understanding or caring, as their new mate had just bought them a round for their troubles. No sooner had the beers been delivered; they went back to their complaining. The rugby player was already halfway down the street.

Hours later, Gilkeson and Halladay were at their respective homes when the symptoms developed. Halladay woke with a start and his wife called 999 in alarm to get emergency services. Once they got Halladay to the hospital, the emergency room staff had no idea what was wrong with him, except his vitals were failing.

Gilkeson, who lived alone having divorced years ago, felt flush with the sweats, and soon became lethargic. He thought he could tough it out, but was soon unresponsive. It would be some time before anyone found him.

Giles Taylor, Assistant Chief of SIS, formerly MI6, arrived by car with his wife of thirty-one years, and two security men. One of them parked the car, and the other joined them as they entered an older restaurant in the SoHo district of London. The Taylors rarely came down to SoHo, but his wife wanted a change of pace, and, despite the risks, Taylor was a shadow. A man of enormous power, but nobody knew who he was. For Williams, this would be harder to pull off, as Taylor never went to the same place and had no preset schedule. His team designed everything he did with security in mind.

Tonight, however, Williams was up to the challenge, with an insider tip and a team of three. They concluded the only opportunity to get that close to him was when they left the restaurant to retrieve the car. Williams was at the bar an hour later when he saw Taylor pay the check as one of his security left to get the car. Williams rose and signaled one of his team, an attractive woman who was easily stronger than most men. Once they exited the restaurant, she approached the second security man for Taylor and feigned for a light as she placed a cigarette in her mouth. He momentarily stopped and as he reached into his jacket to get a lighter, with Taylor standing five feet away. Another of Williams' team approached Taylor, pretending to await his own car, and asked Taylor if the meal was good. Taylor, holding his wife at the waist, responded yes, but the man was apparently hard of hearing and motioned cupping his ear. He had not heard him. He moved closer and placed his hand on his shoulder, close to his neck and Taylor repeated the comment. The man nodded and said he had been at the bistro next door but wanted to try it there someday. They both waited as Taylor rubbed his neck and soon his car arrived and was off. Williams and his team all walked away separately.

Taylor would show symptoms within three hours but assumed indigestion when, six hours later, he laid unresponsive in the emergency room at St. Bartholomew's Hospital.

After three attempts during the week, it proved too difficult to get close enough to the Home Secretary Jocelyn Holmes or Alistair Evans, the Foreign and Commonwealth Secretary, giving Williams pause. It was not worth the risk as yet, but he would get to them in time. His concentration was now Dr. Sara Ricci.

46

South Beacon Hill, Washington

The Versilant team had been busy trying to understand the changed behavior of the U-23 military nanobot, that was only eating healthy cells. Publicly, the Cadieux MT team said that human error likely caused an unexpected change, possibly contamination, but internally, they readily accepted that this could only happen by reprogramming the DNA strands. The problem now was that they didn't have the production units to test. They had been stolen.

Sara had not wanted to leave the hospital, but with nothing to do, she wanted to better understand her theory. When she finally got to Versilant, she got the bioengineering team together and told them what she was thinking. "Guys, hear me out. We located a few samples of variant U-23 that's doing the opposite of its design. If I have heard you correctly, the body would view that nanobot as a natural killer cell, and phagocytes would trigger the body's innate autoimmune system. I'm thinking that Jason was exposed to one of the contaminated U-23 bots."

"Sara, we have protocols to avoid that, but I guess it's possible." One bioengineer replied.

"So, it's not a wild thought?" Sara countered.

"No, but if that's the case, there have to be samples missing," he replied.

"Okay. Given that this could explain Jason's symptoms, first, let's make sure we have all the samples. Second, the electromagnetic catalysts we applied to drive the nanobot are still there. Magnetism still affects it, unlike normal cells. My thought is this. Even though the original drive system is not yet developed, what if a dialysis type machine could pull blood out. As it does, the cells pass it through a side chamber where a magnet could pull the nanobots out of the bloodstream?"

The bioengineer nodded and said, "It could work, I suspect. We could create a wider tube with the magnet to the side so it could pull them in. We would have to design some kind of check valve to keep them from returning. But yeah, maybe."

How many samples of the altered bots do we have?

"We found three. We can mix them with human blood and try it."

"Let's use just one and save the other two as evidence just in case." Sara added cautiously. "By the way, how many units do we have in total?"

"We have one-hundred-fifty. Fifty from the Beta prototypes and one-hundred from production." The team broke into subgroups and tried to stay focused, knowing they might be able to save Jason's life. By the next afternoon, having worked through the night, they had a crude but effective setup and, using one pint of blood and one altered U-23 nanobot, they cycled the blood past the magnet. They had to adjust the blood flow and magnetic strengths several times until they could capture the nanobot. Once they did, they repeated the same test thirty times and got the same result. Each time, it located and pulled the nanobot to the magnet. You could only confirm this under a powerful microscope, but one engineer made a crude magnetic counter.

Sara informed Dann, who then called agent Davies and told him about their theory that Jason might have been exposed to one or more nanobots. And that there might be a way to pull them out of his body. Davies immediately contacted the Special Agent in Charge (SAIC) in Seattle, Ethan Clarke, who immediately contacted the CDC.

47

South Beacon Hill, Washington

It wasn't six hours later when everything fell apart at once. While Sara and the Versilant team had thought they were helping Jason, what really happened was that the FBI and the CDC took the same information they had and concluded that this was all part of a terrorist plot.

They immediately placed Jason into a guarded biohazard unit and the CDC sent an entire team both to the hospital and then to Versilant. As soon as they saw the data from the original nanobot design and the findings the team had uncovered about the suspected contamination or reprogramming, the CDC agreed this likely caused Jason's condition. The Versilant team was now in the conference room with the FBI, who was not allowing them to leave. The CDC also took control of their research and the entire company in less than an hour to a bewildered Dann and Susan De Vires.

The lead scientist from the CDC was a very tall man with an enormous frame. Dr. Mikhail Lebedov walked into the room, commanding authority as he did so. He placed his notebook on the table and sat and scanned the room before he focused on Sara. "Dr. Ricci, what is your relationship with this program?" His deep Russian accent made his loud voice sound ominous.

"I'm a paid consultant."

"Consulting what? You are a physicist, correct?"

"Yes. I was assisting the team in the locomotion of the larger nanobots using electromagnetism." Sara replied nervously.

"And what was your role in the development of the variant U-23?"

"Versilant nor I had anything to do with that design or creation. They were made in Canada at Cadieux MT using research from a historical program. Our role was to develop a nano skeleton to add strength and an electromagnetic catalyst to provide controlled movement."

"How many samples did Versilant receive from Cadieux MT?"

"I believe they gave us a total of one-hundred-fifty units."

"You know, or you believe?"

"A figure of speech. I know."

"And you have controlled these units?"

A bioengineer answered but was cut off by the Lebedov, "I was not talking to you." He looked back at Sara and repeated the question. The bioengineer mouthed, *what a dick,* as Sara answered, "Yes, we have such records."

"But seven hours ago, you told the FBI that Mr. Sykes might have ingested one or more of these. That implies you are missing some of your controlled samples."

Sara looked at him oddly and said, "Dr. Lebedov, I never said he was infected here, nor has anyone else. Do you always jump to conclusions?"

Dr. Lebedov glanced up and gave Sara a nasty look when the young bioengineer, now smiling at her comment, stood and added. "All one-hundred-fifty nanobots are present and accounted for. They came in two sample sets. The first fifty were beta prototypes and the next one hundred were production units received nine days apart. The first fifty act as designed and have attacked no healthy cells. Of the production units, there were three out of the one hundred that exhibited the changed behavior. We have them isolated and protected."

Sara nodded as Dr. Lebedov, looking at the bioengineer now, replied, "And to what do you attribute the cause that all perform as designed, but for three?"

"The team at Cadieux MT originally said this might be contamination," the bioengineer said and then paused.

"But..." Dr. Lebedov replied with a smirk.

"I think they have been reprogramed by accident. These DNA strands must be told what to do."

"And you can program them here in Versilant?"

"Here no. These were all made in Canada, and we don't even have a DNA sequencer on site." The bioengineer said matter-of-factly.

"But you can purchase one on Amazon for what, three hundred dollars?" Dr. Lebedov replied harshly before adding, "Tell me. In your professional opinion, is it a simple process to reprogram these DNA based nanobots?"

The bioengineer looked nervously at the Dr. Lebedov seated next to the two FBI agents. "The three hundred dollar unit won't achieve this, but to your question, reprogramming is easy, but knowing the revised program set is not."

"So, this is not an accident even though you have said it was." Lebedov said coldly.

The young bioengineer jumped up and yelled, "I didn't say that. I said reprogramming is easy, but knowing the revised program set is not. This is not accidental, someone did this on purpose."

Dr. Lebedov looked at De Vires and shouted, "And why the hell didn't you alert the FBI or CDC the minute you found this weapon?"

SAIC Clarke jumped in. "Dr. Lebedov, Mr. De Vires, was at the time being held captive for still unknown reasons. The Versilant team informed Cadieux MT and the FBI within twenty-four hours of the initial find. We just didn't know what it meant until Dr. Ricci made the connection to Jason Sykes' condition."

"Sloppy protocols! All one-hundred-fifty U-23 variants are now the property of the CDC. We will need statements from each of you separately starting now. No one leaves until they're done," as he glanced angrily over to SAIC Clarke and Agent Davies.

Sara was unaffected by the volley and asked, "Dr. Lebedov, what about Jason? What about our idea of saving him?" The room was silent now, as all eyes were on him.

"Dr. Ricci, you are perhaps too close to this to understand what has happened. We are not dealing with a contaminated nanobot. We are dealing with a man-made weapon, purposely placed inside the body of former DARPA employee, Jason Sykes."

The room gasped as he continued. "Our priority is to insure we have these weapons secured and accounted for. The second priority is to understand precisely how they work and how they are administered. And the third priority is to understand every person who has touched any of the production units. One of you may be a potential murderer."

"Have you lost your fucking mind? Murderers? And what, you're suggesting that learning from his reaction to the nanobot is more important than saving him?" Sara said to a shocked room of Versilant staff.

"Dr. Ricci, we are not here to be understood by you and I find it interesting that you, in particular, are even involved. That you made the connection and are speaking the loudest. I would dare say you are most likely at the heart of this."

As he said that, Clarke stood and said, "Dr. Lebedov, that is enough."

Lebedov glanced around the room to the look of horror on everyone's face and calmed as he said, "Our charter is significantly beyond Mr. Sykes. I know he is your colleague, and it is my hope we can accomplish both, but simply stated that is not why we're here." He then turned to his own team. "Tanner, Bodie, stay here. You know the drill. The rest of you, come with me." He did not say it aloud, but they were off to Cadieux MT in Montreal.

There was a collective gasp in the room, and Sara burst into tears. She tried again to get anyone to listen, but they simply left the room without answering. Clarke and Davies were sympathetic, but this was well outside of their control now. The two-remaining people with CDC paired with the FBI and interviewed with everyone on the team and they were especially hard on Dann, Susan, and Sara, but did not explain why.

The skies in Montreal were overcast and had been for the past week. From his perch atop the headquarters of Cadieux MT, Remy Cadieux looked down at the street below. Even through the fog, one could not escape the view of four Royal Canadian Mounted Police (RMCP) vehicles effectively blocking the traffic in and out of the Cadieux building. Members of the Public Health Agency of Canada (PHAC) had descended into Cadieux MT with blinding speed, and the RMCP was there to provide control and protection. The CDC plane would land in less than ten minutes and scientists with the PHAC had already begun the same type of questioning that had taken place in Versilant.

Remy had gone downstairs to meet them and in a conference room they were told of the likely infection of an American, Jason Sykes. The CDC suspected a nanobot of Cadieux MT design had infected him and they would have confirmation in a few days. Remy told them of the program and of the design, and that Versilant had discovered the change in behavior and assured the PHAC that Cadieux MT would offer their complete cooperation.

Dr. Veronica Robbins, Deputy in Charge for PHAC, was an unassuming woman, but her eyes suggested caution. She addressed Remy, "Monsieur, please assemble the entire team working on this project and take me to them."

"They are gathered and in the conference room next to us, Dr. Robbins."

Robbins said nothing. She just rose and walked in that direction. She entered the room, and the speed and efficiency of her movements told the various engineers and lab assistants to sit down and await instruction. "Who is in charge here?" She barked.

Henri Cadieux stood and replied, "I am Henri Cadieux the COO of Cadieux MT. I am running this development and this team. How can we help you?"

"Monsieur, I am surprised the COO of a billion-dollar organization would run such an insignificant program."

"And you are here because it is insignificant, Dr. Robbins?"

"Ah, yes, of course. So, you have been in charge since the beginning, then?"

"Yes. Besides the seven designs we're building with our partner, Versilant Nanotechnologies in Seattle, three military designs were added and given secrecy and fast track status, I took control myself."

"And why did these designs require a fast track?"

"To meet the timeline of the other seven so they could launch into trials as a family of products."

Just as she spoke, the CDC team arrived, and Dr. Robbins met briefly with Dr. Lebedov privately outside the tense room. When they returned, she continued. "Who has the log of the U-23 population?"

An older engineer stood and said, "I do, Dr. Robbins."

"And you can account for them all?"

The engineer said nothing, clearly looking for a lifeline when Henri Cadieux spoke. "The entire population of production units for all ten products including, U-23, are missing and may have been stolen on Tuesday of last week. There were exactly one thousand of each design in the van that is still missing. Besides those, there are two-hundred-fifty production samples, two-hundred-seventy-seven beta prototypes, and fifty-five alpha prototypes here at Cadieux. I sent fifty beta samples and one-hundred production samples to Versilant Nanotechnologies in Seattle. An additional eleven hundred and seventeen have been destroyed since the program's inception." He handed her a stack of destruction certificates and a list of each bot population by ID number and lot number.

"I am aware of the theft, Monsieur. Therefore, that is the entire population?"

"Yes."

"According to CDC information, you believe that the behavior modification to the nanobot results from contamination." Dr. Robbins asked humorously.

Henri stiffened and replied, "No, Dr. Robbins. We initially considered that, but given all affected bots are operating in the same manner and have the same program, we have confirmed that the DNA strands were reprogrammed."

"Versilant says they have three affected bots. How many have been located here?"

"We have located one. Someone has reprogrammed four."

"Do you have a complete list of those allowed to use the DNA sequencing device?"

"We do."

"Are all employees allowed present?"

"Yes."

"Gather them please and let us proceed to a quiet and secure room." She rose and two RCMP officers rose with her. The four engineers followed, clearly nervous. They went into another room and were interrogated for over an hour as the PHAC compared their comments to the memory of the DNA programming device that recorded every transaction that the device attempted. It took just under two hours to locate four transactions that were not done by one of the four engineers present.

Dr. Robbins asked the obvious question. "Who is the employee with badge number 0007094?"

Henri Cadieux looked perplexed and said that person was not on the project team. He walked over to a computer and keyed in the employee number and the name that came up was Stephanie Carlisle. He thought back, trying to recall her as Dr. Robbins and Dr. Lebedov stared at him. Even the RCMP officer waited for his reply.

"Monsieur, have you located this person?"

"Yes. Dr. Robbins. It was a young girl we hired to do clinical studies. She was here for a few weeks and then suddenly never returned to work. Her name was Stephanie Carlisle."

"How could she access the DNA sequencer if she wasn't part of the team? I assume only certain employees have access."

"That is true. I cannot explain this. I will have Human Resources pull her information." Over the next hour, the limited information came in of one Stephanie Carlisle and it did not take long to establish that there was no such person living in Canada. Her application was all fabricated. They had a picture of her, and the RCMP took it as evidence.

At the PHAC headquarters later that evening, Dr. Robbins and Dr. Lebedov discussed the results of the day in private.

"CDC has confirmed that Jason Sykes has in his body an unknown number of nanobots. They isolated and removed one."

"How did they extract it?"

"As Dr. Ricci suggested, they lured it and removed it using a magnet."

"Good to know. So, although the project was well maintained and approached using proven methods, at some point, their controls failed and allowed this Carlisle person to alter the program. But why only four units?"

Dr. Lebedov shrugged his shoulders and then with a look of concern replied, "We can only assume that they reprogramed them to allow the teams to find them and report. When they did, they had confirmation that it worked. If they have such methods to access data with Cadieux MT, it stands to reason, they could create access for her in the DNA Sequencer. I doubt Cadieux MT knew any of this."

"So, the terrorists used them from day one?"

"That's my guess. With one hundred percent of the units accounted for, including the four that were reprogramed, I suspect the terrorists reprogrammed the stolen units away from here. They targeted Sykes somewhere else."

"We need to open the net to see if others have the same symptoms. Mr. Sykes might not be alone."

"God help us." Lebedov replied.

48

Harley Sykes was looking out the window from his home office overlooking Lake Lowell. It wasn't the most attractive waterfront property, as this large man-made lake was almost void of trees, but it suited his needs just fine. Using contacts from his past, he had learned of Jason's illness and the fact that the hospital staff was unclear about what was wrong with him. Annabel made him so miserable asking for details, he finally found the number, and called the women Jason had been seeing to find out what was going on. He vaguely knew of her, and dialed Sara's number on a speakerphone, and she answered, "Hello, this is Sara?"

"Sara, we don't know each other formally, but I'm Sergeant Major Harley Sykes. I'm… Jason's father."

Sara paused, never expecting a call from him, although given the circumstance, it made sense. "Um, yes. What can I do for you, sir?" She was unsure how else to address him.

"I've heard the boy is ill, seriously ill."

Sara wasn't sure what to say. She knew the relationship between Jason and his parents was abnormal and, in her view, unhealthy, but knew nothing about them. At least nothing good. She assumed he wanted an update and asked the Versilant team to please excuse her, and she walked out of the lab and into a hallway. "Yes, that is true. I am unaccustomed to your army, but do I address you as Major or Mister Sykes?"

"It is Sergeant Major, but not important. You are a civilian and can refer to me as Mister Sykes or Harley, if you prefer."

"Fine, and thank you, Mr. Sykes. Jason is in intensive care in a special biohazard room, and his vitals continue to deteriorate. They are struggling to save him."

"Biohazard unit?"

"Yes, it is a standard precaution given what we know."

"And based on what you know, is his condition irreversible."

"I'm not a medical doctor and cannot answer that directly. I can say that the body will only tolerate a loss of so many healthy cells before it gets overwhelmed and shuts down."

"And this loss is being done by a virus, hence the biohazard unit?"

Unclear how much she could say or not say, she elected to tell him what she knew, given who he was. "Well, not actually. Our working theory is that he was exposed to a military nanobot. It is inside his body attacking his heathy cells."

"Sara. Was this accidental or did someone try to kill him?"

The comment shocked Sara, and she reacted. "What?"

"Given your knowledge of this last year and his former career, I believe you understand my question."

Still stunned, she answered, "Um… well, yes, perhaps. I know the FBI and CDC believe this nanobot could be a terrorist weapon. Given that you came to the same conclusion, do you think this was intentional?"

"Yes. I also think it is probable that you were the intended victim. The boy just got in the way."

"Mr. Sykes, I don't know you, but his name is Jason, not 'boy'. When you address him personally, you may do as you please, but when you talk to me about him, please use his given name."

"Sara, you are correct. We don't know each other, so I will remind you, I do not take orders from you. Are we clear?"

"And I'm not one of your subordinates, Mr. Sykes… Are we clear?" Sara replied in a commanding tone.

There was silence on the other end of the phone as Annabel looked at Harley and said, "Well, you handled that well, as usual," as she leaned over and grabbed his phone. "Sara, this is Annabel Sykes. I'm Jason's mother. I'm so glad he has found someone."

"Oh, Mrs. Sykes. Hello, I'm Sara, Sara Ricci. Listen, this might come off the wrong way, but Jason is a very private person and will barely talk about either of you. Based on what he has said, you are no better than your husband for allowing Jason to be treated as he was. You have no idea what a good man your son is and likely has always been. And at this minute, he is dying." Sara cried despite trying to keep it together.

"Yes, well, perhaps you believe you know our past. I lived it and it is doubtful we'll solve that on this call. We are, however, trying to understand his condition. If I heard this right, it's about a nanobot. Isn't there something you and Versilant can do? Isn't this what you do?" Annabel said, pleading.

Sara regained her composure and replied, "Possibly. The nanobot, we suspect, is a military version that our partner Cadieux MT has developed, but we believe someone altered it and Jason was infected. We are working with the CDC to get approval to try an experiment on Jason to save him, but we're not getting much help."

"Why the hell not?" barked Annabel.

Sara explained the terrorist angle, and, after a brief pause, Annabel said, "What can we do? We can't be expected to just wait here for him to die?"

Sara was at the end of her emotional rope and only replied, "I'm doing all that I can, but my advice to you is this. Come to Seattle and give the hospital approval to use our experiment once we get approval from CDC. It is a long shot, given it is doubtful he'll survive if the approval takes much longer, but it may be the only way to save him if they agree." Sara didn't wait for a reply. She hung up and burst into tears.

Annabel was in shock, but she also understood and felt for Sara, even though she knew little of her. She handed Harley back his phone and said, as a command, not a request. "I'm driving to Seattle. I leave in ten minutes. You're with me or you're not," as she walked to the bedroom to pack.

Minutes later, without a word spoken, Annabel and Harley Sykes were on their way to the University of Washington hospital. When they arrived, they were taken to the biohazard floor but not allowed to enter.

There was a small window, and they could see him surrounded by tubes and machines. If Harley was troubled, he said nothing, nor did he show any emotion at all. Annabel, on the other hand, was a visual wreck. The staff did what they could to tell them what they knew, and that the prognosis was poor. They also provided the paperwork to perform the experimental treatment once the CDC allowed it. If they allowed it.

The following day, the CDC called Clarke and Davies and confirmed that they found a nanobot inside Jason. Davies then told Dann and Susan De Vires. He also made clear, this had not occurred at Versilant, or Cadieux MT. Davies said nothing of the possible sabotage, but Dann already knew this from word out of the Cadieux MT Team.

When Dann tried to find out when they might approve the special treatment for Jason, Davies frowned and said there was nothing he or the hospital could do. Everything about this situation was being run by the CDC. Davies left and Dann went looking for Sara finding her in the lab. As he approached her, her physical appearance was haunting. Her eyes were swollen and red, and her smile was nowhere to be found. He suspected she had not eaten or slept for some time.

"Sara, how are you? I'm sorry, that was stupid. Of course, you're not doing well."

"Dann, you have been through your own ordeal. You don't need to listen to me."

"Sara please. We're all in this together."

"I just don't understand how they could just let him die for science. And I'm a fucking scientist," she blurted out as the tears came again. De Vires told her about the confirmation from the CDC that her assumption was correct. A nanobot had affected him. They even used her method to find and extract it. He also told her about the PHAC/CDC assault on Cadieux MT.

Sara sniffed and said to him, "I had a brief conversation with Jason's parents yesterday. They're coming here to Seattle, but his dad suggested I was the intended target. Jason just got in the way."

"Sara, he is a solider and a real bastard as I know him. Don't let him get into your head. He is just a bitter guy who is dysfunctional outside of the army."

"Thank you, but I actually think he's right. Someone reprogramed the DNA strands and was trying to kill me, and I think I know exactly when it happened. I'm sorry, I have to talk to agent Davies."

49

Montreal, Canada

Gustave Cadieux sat in the boardroom with Remy, Henri, and several of the executive staff. The commotion around the combined PHAC and CDC visit had sent ripples through the investment community. Remy had held a press conference to discuss a technical glitch that attracted the attention of the PHAC and that the company was cooperating to the fullest extent possible. And that there was no threat or danger to employees or residents near Cadieux MT.

Of course, there was no mention of the nanobot and the assumed theft, but everyone in the room knew at some point, this would get out. The issue right now was that the PHAC intrusion on the business with several CDC members on hand. This had driven down the stock price three percent on the day of the visits and an additional eleven percent since. Remy's message had not reassured the market.

Gustave got everyone's attention. "Dammit, we have to do something bold, something decisive."

Remy responded, "Dad, the PHAC and the CDC do not want this to get out any more than we do. We need to relax and see where the investigation leads before we take a dramatic action of any kind."

"You idiot. They'll do whatever serves the public interest and to them, and possibly our reality, is that the stolen units are now weapons. Weapons we made in this facility. If that gets out, it will be too late to say anything."

"We have but four unaccounted transactions in the sequencer that are under review. Whatever happens to the thousand production units did not happen here." Remy said, trying to reassure himself.

"Will anyone care?" Henri added.

"Perhaps not." Remy admitted, in frustration.

Gustave was furious now. "Remy, I'm firing you to put a lid on this since these designs and the fast track were all the idea of you and that damn girlfriend of yours. You said I didn't have the backing. Well, you little shit, I bet I have it now," as he got up and headed to the door.

Cinead Vass, their attorney, blurted. "Gustav, I would caution you not to do that. It will imply we did something wrong and actually make things worse."

"Cinead, I understand what you are saying, but once the terrorists act, it will be too late for us to respond. I'm going on the offensive." Gustave turned and walked out, leaving the room silent.

Dr. Lebedov and Dr. Robbins sat with SAIC Clarke at the FBI field office in Seattle, and he was speaking. "When I received your initial call, I wasn't sure what to expect, but this is what we have from the CIA, Interpol, and MI5. Worldwide, we have encountered five patients in the same medical state as Jason Sykes. In America, we have a former director of the DHS Jeremy Hicks, and former DARPA employee Jason Sykes, which you were aware. In the UK, we have assistant director to the SIS, Giles Taylor, former Police Scotland Constable, Conor Gilkeson, and former commander who worked for Gilkeson, Cameron Halladay. Gilkeson has since passed. All others are in intensive care."

"Is there any connection to this group of individuals?" Dr. Robbins asked.

"Yes. They all relate to events last year in which United States and United Kingdom intelligence tried to apprehend the head of security and the CEO, for MDE Enterprises. As I understand it, Hicks and Taylor were leading the hunt. Gilkeson and Halladay attempted an ill-fated raid that killed many and almost killed the CEO's sister, Bridget Drummond. Sykes was a DARPA liaison to Ms. Sara Ricci, a PhD student at MIT during that time. Apparently, the CEO, Maximillian Drummond, wanted her inventions and when he couldn't do so conventionally, he kidnapped her and held her hostage on an island in the Southern Sea. A raid on the island where Sykes was present was part of a joint UK/US team that rescued Ricci and killed Drummond and the security head Adkin."

Both scientists looked at each other, not understanding the young Dr. Ricci was really at the center of this. Dr. Lebedov looked stunned. "So, this is about revenge?"

Anderson replied, "It appears to be. The sister, Bridget Drummond, is at present, the largest single shareholder of Cadieux MT, and it was she who urged the joint venture with Versilant Nanotechnologies. She also promoted the fast-track nanobots, one of which is thought to be the weapon of the U-23 variant. We cannot rule out that the Cadieux CEO may also be involved."

Dr. Robbins asked, "Are there any other potential victims?"

Clarke looked down and replied, "Yes, possibly. According to the CIA, the UK Home Secretary Jocelyn Holmes, and the Foreign and Commonwealth Secretary Alistair Evans were also involved in the approval process, but I suspect they make much more difficult targets."

"What is our focus, given the likelihood this is purely retaliatory and not a mass terrorist attack?" Dr. Lebedov replied.

"Dr. Lebedov, Dr. Robbins. I have authority to ask you both to do whatever is required to save the lives of those involved. We have the best chance we'll ever have to take down Bridget Drummond, but not if she kills off everyone that was directly involved."

"Understood. We may have a method." Lebedov said with confidence.

Dann De Vires received the call at close to 4:00 p.m., and after listening, he realized it was going to be another late night. The CDC was on their way with the FBI and the Deputy Director of the PHAC. They had asked him to assure that Dr. Ricci was available. He walked down to the lab and motioned for Sara.

"Sara, I just got a call from Ethan Clarke, and he is on the way with the CDC and PHAC. There has been a development."

"Like what?" Sara replied.

"I have no idea. They just said we were to make ourselves available to them, but this doesn't sound good."

"No, it probably isn't."

They arrived not ten minutes later, and all poured into the conference room. Dr. Lebedov took command. "Dr. Ricci, explain your process to extract the nanobots."

Sara was shocked, but explained how they had done it and mentioned they had built a unit in advance if approval could be obtained.

Dr. Lebedov said tersely, "Please get the unit and whoever can run it and work with hospital staff. We are heading there now."

Sara didn't need to be told twice as she ran out of the room. She grabbed the young tech that had built the unit and with him; they loaded the already sterilized unit into Jason's 4-Runner and headed for the hospital.

50

Sara and the tech ran into the hospital to find they had been expected. A doctor and two nurses met them at the door, and they were soon heading to the elevator to go down to the biohazard room. Sara could barely breathe, but knew she needed to keep it together. She had to be part of this, not just an observer.

No sooner had they entered a side room next to Jason when the two FBI agents arrived with Dr. Lebedov of the CDC, and Dr. Veronica Robbins of the PHAC. The hospital staff had approved the unit, and it was being put into place. Sara glanced into Jason's room and could see through it saw a small window on the opposite side of the room. In the center of the window was the sad face of an older woman that she assumed must be Annabel Sykes. She asked if they could excuse her for just a minute.

Dr. Lebedov, poster child of sadism, responded, "You have three minutes. Nothing outside of saving Jason Sykes is your concern."

"You could have saved him three days ago, asshole, don't talk to me about timelines," Sara barked and ran out the door into the hallway. Harley Sykes was stoic and unmoving as she walked down the hall towards them. He was the stereotype of the army in Sara's mind. Tall, standing stiff-straight, crewcut hair, topping a face and jaw that appeared chiseled from stone. Annabel, in contrast, was a very attractive woman, but standing entirely in his shadow. Sara immediately felt sorry for her when she suddenly turned toward her and asked, "Sara…?"

Sara replied, "Yes," and held out her hand. Annabel grabbed her hand and pulled her in for a hug, which Sara allowed, and they both cried. As if she were trying to right years of wrong, Annabel held onto Sara for such longer than expected. "I knew you were beautiful, but in person, the pictures in the paper did not do you justice. Jason is a very lucky man."

"Papers? What papers?" Sara asked, not understanding.

"Although I do not speak to him often, I follow Jason in every way I can. After all that nasty business on that island last year, your story made the international papers."

"I see. Yes, well, that is behind us."

Harley leaned over and said, "Are you sure Dr. Ricci? I believe this is all about Bridget Drummond."

Sara was trying so hard not to consider the obvious. Hearing the words directly made it seem so likely. "That is unfortunately possible, Mr. Sykes, and the FBI is working on that. Listen, I have just a minute. I got CDC approval to use our invention to remove the nanobots. We start in less than fifteen minutes, and it will take about five hours. I'll come out as soon as it's over, okay? We're going to save him. I promise." She squeezed Annabel's hand and turned and ran off.

It took just ten minutes to get the machine verified and validated. One of the Versilant bioengineers was in the room with Sara monitoring the machine and the medical staff was ready. All were in biohazard suits with respiration masks. There was ample security, which included an FBI agent outside the room, and from what Sara could tell, they had locked down the entire floor.

At 6:21 p.m., they attached the unit to Jason. With the Sykes consent and the CDC approval, doctors had performed a minor surgery to install a vascular entrance point and exit point into Jason's body earlier in the day. Jason was unresponsive during this procedure, as he had been for four days before that. They had him on blood thinners, and soon a pump would take blood from the exit point they had installed. This wasn't dialysis, so there was no need for a dialyzer, but the slow pumping action would take blood straight to the magnetic unit that would capture the nanobots. The remaining blood would head to the entrance access point and back into his body.

Shortly before midnight, the doctor looked over at the nurse and Versilant technician and motioned to stop the unit. Nurses came over and took control of the process. Sara asked the obvious question, "Doctor, what do you think?"

He looked over at the tech and asked, "How many did it locate?"

He replied, "We'll have to double check under a microscope, but the counter says twelve. None in the last hour."

The doctor looked over at the monitors and said, "He was near death, so this will not be a sudden recovery, but his vitals are holding. We

need to let his body sort this out, but if you got them all, he'll make it."
The room did a subtle clap, and through the glass window, Harley and
Annabel Sykes were staring and knew this was a good sign. Sara looked
directly at Harley, who looked misty eyed. He saw her and gave her a
thumbs up; probably the sincerest gesture you would ever get out of him.

51

Harley Sykes walked briskly off the military transport plane with a small duffle bag at a US airfield in Ireland. After making several calls, he hitched a ride. He spoke to no one, and no one spoke to him as he met a contact that Richard Chase had arranged, and they drove in near silence to Broadford on the Isle of Skye. He knew there was nothing he could do for Jason at the moment, and he appeared to be on the mend, so he elected to take care of some unfinished business.

Fortitude Security had helped him get intel on Angus Adair and although Sykes had offered to pay for the services, Chase had done it gratis. That was because Adair had supplied the intel the MDE Security team has used to get to his and Sara's data the year before. As payback, Chase had also offered to get a team together, but Sykes wanted to confront Adair alone.

Thanks to the intel Chase provided, Sykes knew that the Security Service, also known as MI5 or the Military Intelligence, Section 5, was also watching Adair. It would not be good if MI5 found Sykes on UK soil, and certainly not with their suspect. It took his trained eye less than twenty minutes to determine where the MI5 agent was located, and that allowed him access to the east side of the small house.

At close to ten that evening, the house was dark when Angus drove into the driveway from a long and unnerving day at the residence, forty kilometers up the A87 highway. Entering the house, he grabbed a beer and a bag of crisps, and systematically turned on three computers attached to six monitors. While he could not stop the Versilant team and the FBI, he had a bigger issue. He had evidence, the terrorist hacker, Aladdin, that had traced him the year before might have done so again. He was going to try one last thing before implementing his escape plan to avoid death by Drummond's security team.

As the computers booted, he set down the bag of crisps when a sound to his right startled him. He gasped when a figure in the darkness said, "Good evening. If you so much as touch that keyboard, you will die instantly." Angus could only see the shape of a man, but summoned the courage to ask, "Who… who are you? What do you want?" He assumed Bridget was having him executed.

Sykes said, "I told you I would kill you, and I meant it."

His eidetic memory flashed to the call. The army guy who said someday he would kill him and said calmly, "We can work something out. I have money."

"Yes, you do… And some of it is mine." Sykes replied, as he had silently walked behind Adair, who had both hands on the edge of the table, as if to approach the keyboard. Harley, using the butt of his gun, brought it down quickly, immediately breaking two of Adair's fingers.

With his other hand, Sykes expertly held a hand around Adair's mouth to capture the scream. "It would be wrong to alert the MI5 agent who has been monitoring you so early in our evening." Adair, in pain, asked, "What the fuck? Why did you do that? What MI5 agent. Where?"

"You, my pathetic piece of shit, do not get to ask questions." As he expertly pulled a gag over Adair's head and into his mouth, cinching it tight. "Using your good hand, please transfer the one million you took from me back into my account. Each minute that is not done, I will break another of your fingers, meaning you have eight minutes left. Starting now." He then placed a piece of paper next to the keyboard that contained his routing information. Adair wasted no time, as he transferred the amount in less than three minutes.

Angus Adair had fucked with people via his computer his whole life, but had never been on the sharp end of the stick, and was terrified. When he was done, Harley asked, "What is the relationship between the blackmail, the Cadieux stock and nanobot your boss has used to infect my son?"

He loosened the gag just enough to allow Adair's words to be heard, prepared to cinch it back if he screamed. "I can't reveal that. I would be dead before tomorrow morning."

"Young man, you don't seem to understand. This is not about my money. That was just the right thing to do. I told you I was going to kill you and I am. No one threatens me or my family and gets away with it. What you are negotiating now is how you will die. Slow and painful, or fast and easy." Angus was crying now as he again shook his head as if to say, *I Can't.*

As the gag was cinched, the butt of the gun came down and two more fingers were shattered on his other hand. He screamed into the gag, but it was muted, and the MI5 agent, over two-hundred yards away, didn't hear a thing. Adair had no tolerance for pain and was almost ready to pass out. He yelled to Sykes, "Please stop. I'll tell you anything, just don't kill me, please."

"I'm listening," was all he got back in reply. Angus Adair told him what had happened and added, "How do you know about me? Nobody knows about me?"

"Well, apparently you're not the only smart person in the world." He didn't tell him about Aladdin and the fact he had given the FBI proof it was Adair behind the computerized voice and how the Fortitude team found him.

"How is MI5 involved?"

Sykes thought for a moment and replied, "That is your problem, not mine. You have helped me, so I'll let you live, but if you ever reveal what happened here, I'll make sure that Drummond's security team knows you betrayed them." Harley zip-tied his hands and legs to the chair as he walked back towards the rear door and left. It had been a while. That felt good, he thought, although he should have just killed him and done the world a favor. Using the extraction plan Chase had created for him, he was on his way out of the country in less than two hours.

The following morning, MI5 finally received the warrant and order to arrest Angus Adair. There had been no activity outside his home, and they knew he had arrived but had not left. Agents came to the door with two officers from Police Scotland and after taking precautions, they knocked and identified themselves. There was no answer, but they heard something and kicked in the door.

Strapped to an ergonomic chair, on the other side of the room from his computers, a gaged Adair, was staring at his computers in a trance. As officers approached him, they noted several fingers of both hands were bloody and fractured in several places. Someone had got to him. Adair, tied tight to the chair, could not hit the kill switch that would render his data useless. While the screens on standby were password protected, it might not be good enough to save him, or Bridget Drummond. The British equivalent of the NSA, the Government Communications Headquarters, or GCHQ, were going to have a field day.

As he was being led to an EMT van by Police and an MI5 agent, Rex Williams rounded the corner and drove past slowly. Bridget had sent Williams to kill Adair after two days of not hearing from him. After their last encounter, she assumed he was doing something that would not benefit her. Right idea, bad timing, as they were obviously too late. Williams would have to take care of this once Adair was in prison. He left to discuss options with Bridget, although Adair's infamous computers were another matter.

52

Montreal, Canada

Remy sat in his Land Rover as he watched the MDE Gulfstream coming towards him. He wasn't sure why he agreed to meet her. He knew Bridget was bad news, but she had a hold on him. Part of that was her looks and her confidence. But also, she had the type of control over things he wished he had and everyone that encountered her was momentarily star struck. He wanted that kind of presence, but knew it wasn't an act. It came from within. He also knew he needed her. She was likely the only one that could get rid of his dad, but he wondered. What would it be like to have Bridget as a boss? Did anyone actually survive such a woman?

The plane had stopped, and Bridget walked down the air stairs with the look of a Hollywood scarlet. The perfect dress, the matching purse, and belt. She noted Remy's car and both she and Rex Williams headed towards it. Remy got out to open her door as Rex, walking in front of her now, checked the car interior before heading back to a second car he would drive and follow them. He didn't like this arrangement, but Bridget had insisted. As Bridget climbed in the car, Remy longingly admired her long legs. He went back around to the driver's door, and they drove off.

The purpose of this visit was the Cadieux stock price, and what Bridget considered an inadequate response to the events that had happened. It was almost as if she forgot she was behind it all. They arrived at Cadieux MT and went directly to Remy's office when Bridget asked, "How is dear old dad?"

"I'm surprised you're not telling me." She did not reply, and Remy, not understanding she no longer had Angus, continued, "He's the same. He is threatening to fire me as a gesture of goodwill to the markets."

"Well, that would require my approval, which I am not likely to give. How bad is it?"

"Bad. The PHAC, the Canadian equivalent of the CDC, has all but shut us down over the loss of the production units. A Cadieux MT employee not on the team, and not allowed to use the DNA Sequencer, reprogrammed the bots, and disappeared. As if that didn't do enough damage, one or more of the reprogramed bots has affected one of the Versilant team members, and the United States and Canada are viewing this as a terrorist act."

"Who was infected?" Bridget asked, knowing full well it was the little bitch, Sara Ricci.

Remy replied, "The leader from Versilant, Jason Sykes. He was dying, but the Italian gal, Dr. Ricci, may have saved him. I think they are trying out her invention as we speak under top security."

Bridget was without words as she processed what she was hearing. Rex Williams had said nothing about Jason Sykes. Did he miss Sara and get him accidentally, or was he doing his own thing? This was not good as she asked, "What do you mean, save him? Is that even possible?"

"I believe so. The original nanobot contained an electromagnetic catalyst to allow doctors to drive the nanobot. Dr. Ricci repurposed a dialysis machine to use a magnet to pull the nanobots out."

Bridget held back her first reaction and replied, "So, this is good news for Cadieux. He'll be saved and the stock will go back up."

Remy looked over at Bridget and said, "Sadly, no. First, nobody even knows he was infected. Second, losing the production units puts Cadieux at the headline of any terrorist story. If they are used to harm others, it will be years before we can weather this, I'm afraid." Bridget realized there were elements of this plan she had not thought through. Regrouping, she said, "Send your plane down to get Dr. Ricci. We need to thank her in person and make a big deal out of him being saved."

"Bridget, that will not help us."

"It will help the team and me." She replied with an icy stare.

Remy's first thought was the warning from Jason Sykes, and he wondered if this was real or an act. She couldn't be that brazen, could she? He noted the time and, given he was three hours ahead, he reluctantly called Sara, with Bridget watching his every move. She picked up on the third ring. "Monsieur?"

"Yes, Dr. Ricci. Was the surgery with Jason a success? The team here is eager to know."

"It will be a long recovery, but yes, we retrieved a dozen nanobots from his system, and his vitals are stable. His body has to replace the lost cells, but early signs are hopeful. Thank you for asking."

"Dr. Ricci, this is fantastic news to an otherwise horrible week. I'm sending the plane down to pick you up and bring you here for a quick party on your invention and the progress to save Jason. It will land in two hours. Please tell me you can make it."

Alarmed, given the New York incident, she replied, "Monsieur, I appreciate the gesture but there is no chance to leave even if for a short time."

"Dr. Ricci, the team here is devastated. The PHAC was rougher on us than the CDC was on Versilant, and all seems lost after so much work. With Dann's abduction and then Jason, it has been difficult to keep the spirit alive here. I was hoping you would give the team a pick-me-up. You know, a good news story for a change."

Sara didn't want to, but the team there really was great and if she could help them, she would, so she reluctantly said, "Okay, I'll come, but only until tomorrow."

"Thank you. It is a wonderful thing you're doing for the team. I'll text you the flight info. Thanks." As he clicked off, Bridget looked at him from across the room. "What a good little liar you are. I'll have to remember that."

The Cadieux jet landed at Renton and a hired car had picked up Sara and took her to the plane. Given her short time in Canada, she had not intended to tell anyone about the trip, but Jason's mom, Annabel, had called, asking if Sara could join them for dinner. She had told her of the trip and asked if they could go out the following night instead. Sara boarded the private plane, and a hostess prepared her an excellent glass of 2015, David Arthur 1147 Cabernet.

Despite the distance, the plane was exceptionally fast, and Sara arrived just before 6:00 p.m., Montreal time. A car took her directly to the company and as she entered, Remy was there to meet her.

"Dr. Ricci, it is good to see you again. I have the team assembled, please this way." They walked to a conference room, and it erupted in cheers as the door opened. Sara was shocked but immediately felt happy, and for the next couple of hours, they partied and talked of the future, everyone trying to keep it positive. It was just after 9:00 p.m. when Remy said her car was there to take her to her hotel, and she got in as Remy and the team waved goodbye. The hotel was nearby, and she exited the warm car with her small bag and went to the reception to find that they had reserved a nice suite for her.

Sara took the elevator to the eighth floor, pleased the night had gone well. Jason was convinced that Remy had lured them to New York for Bridget to harm, but Sara just didn't think he was that type of guy, although she had been nervous about coming here. Thank goodness there had been no reason for concern.

She found her room and opened the door with her key. It was weird to use old fashion key, but it added a touch of class to the hotel, certainly something she could not afford. She opened the door and turned on the entry lights. The room was charming and quite large, a sitting area with a bar in the center, a bedroom area to the right, and an office or den like room to the left. She put down her bag and purse and considered having one last glass of wine before she called it a night. As she rounded the corner to the bar, a voice startled her.

"I know you like red wine, so I poured you a glass. Please don't be alarmed, come have a drink with me."

Sara spun around and would never forget those eyes looking at her now, the same way as they had the night in New York. That was the only time she had seen Bridget Drummond, who was walking towards her now, holding a glass of wine in one hand and offering Sara a glass in the other. The surprise lasted but a second before Sara yelled, "Get the hell out of my room now or I'll call security."

Bridget held out the glass of red and smiled. "That will not be necessary, my dear. Security is already here." Rex Williams walked in, nodded, and then walked back out to the office room.

"I meant hotel security Ms. Drummond."

"Yes, I know," she smiled, "But as I am paying for the room, you are my guest, and we already have security. All over the hotel, I might add." She smirked a look of confidence and once again held out the glass.

Sara took it and resigned herself to say, "Why in the hell can't you just leave me alone?"

"Well, you know the reason, my dear. It is only fair."

"Fair? Your brother almost killed me twice. He had my office searched and stole my data. He almost killed my assistant's father and most recently you almost killed my boyfriend."

"The opportune word here is 'almost', Dr. Ricci. You, on the other hand, didn't almost kill my brother, you actually killed him. Like I said, fair is fair."

Sara sat down, dejected, and wondering what was coming next. She elected to face this head on, "So what now?" as she put down the wineglass untouched, no longer interested.

Bridget liked she was feisty. "I'm not sure. At some point, you will die. When and how is still unknown, but please, have your wine. It might be the last for you, I'm afraid."

53

Rex Williams avoided notice as the three of them went downstairs for the drive over to Cadieux MT. The hotel suite had a semi-private elevator, which was in their favor, and MDE security was everywhere. Williams kept his Glock 19 hidden under his coat, very close to Sara's waist as they walked to and entered the car at the outside valet. Bridget went in first, Sara next and Rex climbed in next to her. The driver took off and soon they entered the Cadieux headquarters, which was empty. The front security man, on seeing Bridget, quickly ushered them to the elevator. Sara thought about making a scene, but didn't trust Williams. He looked like the type that would kill the innocent guard without a thought.

They exited and went to Bridget's office. It was new and still smelled of glue and solvent. Rex took her to a chair, and Bridget sat behind a large glass desk, perhaps to show Sara that she was in control. Despite the situation, it amazed Sara how exotic and attractive Bridget was. She easily could have been a model, even though she was bat-shit crazy.

"So, you saved Jason. How touching. I meant those nanobots for you."

"Yes, I know. So does the FBI."

"Ah, so smart, Dr. Ricci. You think you know everything, but you actually know very little."

"That is not true. The FBI, MI5 and SIS know everything. You can kill me, but you'll never survive this."

"Such tough talk. No, I think I'll be fine, but you, you will die."

"Only if your security does it. You don't have the courage."

Bridget chuckled as she said, "Yes, Dr. Ricci, keep trying to provoke me. I'll give you credit, you're not a puss... but you're not a villain either." Bridget stood up, and with everything she had, backhanded Sara across the face. Sara was not expecting it, and combined with Bridget's size and strength, she went flying off the chair onto the floor, her head spinning.

"Perhaps now you'll have some respect for your predicament. You are so wrong. Rex was kind enough to save you for me and it is taking everything I have to not kill you." Bridget smiled as she kicked Sara in the ribs as hard as she could, a loud crack omitted and Sara lost her breath, doubling over.

Sara tried to right herself despite the pain, but was having a tough time. Bridget stood above her, waiting for her to rise. On her knees now, Sara tried to swing at her, but barely connected as Bridget hit her again and then kicked her in the stomach, hurting her ribs all the more. Sara screamed and fell back to the floor. Bridget was euphoric, and said loudly, "Rex, bring in a vial of our little friends. I can no longer contain myself."

This was it. Sara was doubled over, knowing they were going to inject her with the deadly nanobots. A minute went by, but Williams did not answer. Suddenly a fresh voice said, "I'm sorry, mademoiselle, but your security man is preoccupied." Bridget turned and stared at Gustave Cadieux, who entered the room to the left where Rex had been. Even Sara looked up.

"Monsieur, so nice to see you, but please leave. This does not concern you, and this is my private office." Bridget said, surprised.

"I'm afraid I cannot do that. You are on my family's property, and anything that happens here is my responsibility."

Bridget was now enraged. "I'm afraid if you stay, there will be repercussions for you," as she headed towards him. In the blink of an eye, a black shape appeared across the room and with a roundhouse, kicked Bridget hard in the face. So hard, she fell to her knees as the dark shape punched her in the head's side, knocking her momentarily unconscious. Sara watched Bridget collapse and stared at the large women in black, wondering who the hell she was when Harley Sykes walked in the side door with Richard "Rottweiler" Chase. "Hello Sara. Mr. Sykes and I were having a chat with Mr. Williams." He straightened his shirt and ran his hand over his face with a towel before handing it to Sykes, who did the same and held it to his bloodied knuckles.

Sykes looked at Sara and said, "Please let me introduce my daughter, First Lieutenant Racheal Sykes." Sara looked over at Racheal and said, "Thank you. I really thought she was going to kill me." Rachael just smiled and Sara looked back at Sykes and Chase and asked, "How did you even know I was here?"

Sykes replied, "When Annabel told me you were coming here, I expected the worse. Gustave and I met several years ago, and I called him. He confirmed my concerns when he said you were here, lured by Remy. I immediately called Chase, who used his contacts to get us all here in time. The rest was a waiting game that I wish had not happened, but it did. Sorry for that. We didn't expect Bridget to get rough."

Chase added, "Hope you're okay."

Bridget had come to and was now righting herself. Her eyes looked like red dots. Rachel Sykes watched her movements and belted her again as Bridget yelled, "You will all pay for this. I'll fucking kill you all."

Gustave said with confidence, "I think not, Ms. Drummond. I made the office exactly to your specifications, but added a few touches of my own." He smiled and pointed to the ceiling as he walked out, and moments later, three RCMP arrived with an FBI field agent. They entered the room and promptly arrested her. The entire room had been recorded.

An EMT tended to Sara, and they eventually helped her onto a gurney. As the EMT wheeled her out, a perplexed Remy Cadieux entered the room with a bottle of Dom Pérignon vintage 2010 and two glasses.

His look was priceless as there was bloodied Bridget in handcuffs being led out by an FBI agent and one RCMP. A second officer was strolling with a handcuffed Rex Williams as Sara, on a gurney, was being pushed out the door by two EMTs. Standing next to another RCMP were his dad and three people dressed in black. He didn't know as he muttered, "What the hell is going on?"

Gustave laughed and replied, "Remy, once again, you are late to the party." A moment later, one of the RCMP officer approached Remy and told him he would need to accompany them for questioning about the attempted murder of Dr. Sara Ricci. Remy tried to argue, but the officer simply said he would be arrested if he did not cooperate, and he too was soon being led out of the office.

54

The following week, sitting in the office of SAIC Ethan Clarke, Agent Trevor Davies outlined what they had uncovered. "So, this was never one case. It was several that all came together, each with its own beginning. Starting with Remy Cadieux, who had lots of ideas, but little money. He thought he could get a contract with DARPA for the nanobots that hastened blood clotting. When it fell through, they touted the company going public through a bioengineer he hired to impersonate an army doctor. There are more than a hundred original investors involving fifty million dollars in cash."

"And these people became the targets of the blackmail scheme?"

"Some. Drummond had a gifted hacker, Angus Adair, who the GCHQ has now confirmed was the actual blackmailer. Although GCHQ has supplied evidence that they had nine targeted, only three were approached. It was Adair who found the initial connection and created the scheme to blackmail early shareholders for insider trading, and force them to sell their shares, which Bridget immediately bought. She wanted to get enough Cadieux MT shares to oust Gustave Cadieux so she could control the company and the son. In a twist of fate, Adair, on his own, shook them down for money, based on dirt he could find or invent. The GCHQ is still going through terabytes of his information."

"Is Adair talking to MI5?"

"Unfortunately, no. He was conveniently killed in a holding cell last week. His computers will have to talk for him."

"They should have expected that and protected him. I presume there is no tie back to Drummond?"

"No, the inmate that killed him is a lifer with nothing to lose. He claims Adair pissed him off and talked down to him, but the GCHQ suspects they will find a money trail to him at some point."

"Where do things stand with Cadieux MT?"

"Remy Cadieux is under investigation by the Canadian Securities Administration for his role in the original stock sales, tax evasion, security fraud, and has to answer for the military nanobot. It is doubtful he was involved in the most serious charges, but he aligned himself to Drummond. That makes him an accessory, allowing her to execute her plan, even facilitating it in hopes she could oust his father, Gustave. Our field office there has already given the RCMP our case files and evidence, and they're hoping Remy can provide key information on Drummond in exchange for a plea deal. In a twist of irony, Gustave Cadieux is back to running the company at eighty-six years old and his first order of business was to fire the son."

"But Drummond remains the company's largest shareholder?"

"True, and her arrest does not change that, but as a wanted criminal, they immediately terminated her as a director, along with Alexandre Arnaud. She had not yet nominated the third board member."

"And so, as we suspected, Liam Boylan was the kidnapper of De Vires but was also being blackmailed by Adair besides Sykes and Estrada from Spain."

"Yes. They located Boylan's body, and he had taken his own life. According to the computer files, they initially threatened Boylan with exposure to using investor funds to purchase his Cadieux MT shares. They forced him to keep De Vires on standby if Sykes or Boylan didn't go along. The head of security for Drummond, Rex Williams, isn't talking as yet, but we believe he pulled De Vires from the cabin to give the illusion he was dead to raise the stakes. We still need to confirm that. Dr. Ricci and Jason gave a description of him to us and MI5, believe it was Williams who infected at least some of the various people with the nanobots."

"And Bridget herself?"

"She is being held in Montreal on charges of attempted murder of Sara Ricci. That will probably stick. The evidence is overwhelming given the testimony of those in her office at Cadieux MT. The recordings from the room itself add to the already strong case, but there is a question if the recordings will be admissible given that the Chairman, Gustave Cadieux, added them without her consent. To the grander charges, the UK is working to extradite her. The information from the hacker, Adair, is incriminating, but solicitors for Drummond have made the case that he was a rogue employee. They'll have her dead to rights if the computer evidence points to her, or if Williams talks."

Clarke replied, "Where are we on the military nanobot? The deadly U-23 variant. I heard they found a vial on Williams?"

"Yes, he had a vial with thirty nanobots and the PHAC have them. That places the altered design on him, and likely Bridget. They have since located the entire stolen cargo for Cadieux MT. Variant U-23 has been isolated."

"Were all affected people saved?"

"The Versilant machine designed by Dr. Ricci saved Sykes, and in less than forty-eight, saved former DHS director Hicks, the SIS assistant director Taylor, and the former commander of Police Scotland. The former constable of Police Scotland died before help could get to him. So, with Dr. Ricci, there are five attempted murder charges and one murder charge pending against Drummond."

"It surprised me to see veterans' Harley Sykes and Richard Chase throughout the case files." Clarke mentioned causally to the raised eyebrow of Davies.

"Yeah, those two are quite a pair. Sykes has been busy likely using Fortitude Security and Richard Chase to help him, but there is no proof of any wrongdoing." He smiled.

"And Sara Ricci?" Clarke asked.

"They have released her from the hospital with three broken ribs, a neck injury, and facial bruising. Her dad arrived in Montreal and is with her now in Seattle. I'm told she is finishing up at Versilant and returning to Italy to teach at Sapienza University in Rome."

"It should be a quieter life for her."

"Only if Drummond is put away for good."

"Well, I hope for her sake that happens. Well, it took a while, Davies, but good work although it will be a year or more before all this is over."

"I know. Don't remind me. We work to get these guys and the lawyers work to undo it all." Davies replied as he took his leave and walked back to his office.

55

Montreal, Canada

Bridget Drummond awoke to the many sounds of the Nova Institution for Women in Truro, Nova Scotia, a mixed security prison. Her solicitors had got her transferred here from a holding center in Montreal pending charges being filed and an extradition request from the United Kingdom. There were expected to be five counts of attempted murder, one count of murder, extortion, blackmail, and kidnapping. She was being held without bail until they brought charges against her.

Inside Nova Institution, there were less than eighty women at that moment, and authorities had kept Bridget separated from others, at least for now. In her small room, she rose, used the commode, and after, washed her hands and face. There was no mirror, so she could only imagine her appearance dressed in the navy-blue shirt and pants they mandated her to wear. She had met with her solicitor Hasina Andrianasolo the previous day, and learned of the pending charges, the extradition request, and that Rex Williams was also being held. The opinion of her many solicitors was that they might avoid the damage caused by Angus Adair, but Williams was another matter. He only took orders from Bridget, and authorities knew this and would pressure him accordingly. That convinced Andrianasolo there was a very high likelihood that Williams would expose all if he thought Bridget would roll over on him. More important at the moment was the fact that gaining access to him was difficult because authorities likely expected an attempt on his life. He was working on a plan, but his primary thoughts were how to help Bridget. Best they could tell, authorities had too much on her to avoid prison time. Even the UK Home Secretary had publicly said Drummond was a menace. And that she would put the weight of her office behind the effort to extradite her and hold her responsible for the many crimes of which she would be soon charged.

After a quick breakfast, they took Bridget to a room to meet Andrianasolo a second time. She watched him closely as he asked how she was and if she needed anything. She did not. Using a verbal code, they had developed from Maximillian's days to speak in public about very serious matters; he informed her of his plan.

On the day of the hearing, Correctional Service Canada was taking no chances. They were holding the extraction hearing at the Nova Institute after they successfully appealed that traveling was not an option for Ms. Drummond. The hearing would therefore take place there at 10:00 a.m., in a conference room of the administration building, which was in the facility's front.

From James Street, the main building looked a lot like a medical clinic or a retirement home. This frontal area was not for inmate housing but was an area for administrative, medical staff, the visitors' lounge, and food preparation. On the grounds behind that were five large two-story buildings that housed up to one hundred women with consideration for minimum to maximum security. The yard contained various workout and work-related areas, with a large dirt common area in the center. Retrieved at considerable expense, Andrianasolo had insider information. The staff would bring Drummond to the front twenty minutes before the hearing start. It included a video component with the UK and so the meeting time was fixed and as expected, a woman guard appeared in front of her dormitory at 9:38 a.m. They had brought Bridget downstairs to a small room before the exit door, where she was transferred from the interior guard to the exterior guard. The latter handcuffed herself to Drummond. In addition, there were two others. One standing outside the dormitory and one standing outside the building they were going towards as they started to walk.

In the distance, a helicopter could be heard, but no one had noticed it except Drummond. It was coming in quick and soon the guard walking with her heard the noise and walked faster, pulling Drummond with her. Drummond resisted slowing her down, saying nothing as her nerves strained at the thought of pulling this off. The guard was pulling hard now, and all three guards could now see the helicopter gunship that was coming down into the grounds so fast it seemed as if it would crash. A second helicopter had come in from a separate angle and was landing closest to Drummond as the gunship, with its powerful rotors, turned the dirt area into a dust bowl.

The side of the gunship was open, and two flash-bang grenades were tossed down near the two guards. As they flashed, both guards fell to the ground, stunned, holding their ears as if it would help the sudden pain and disorientation. Into the dust cloud, a soldier jumped down to the ground, somersaulted on impact, and then raced to the guard holding Drummond. He shot her with a taser before she could aim her sidearm, which was already out, the safety off. He immediately cut the cuffs and hustled Bridget into the second helicopter, and it took off without hesitation. As Bridget jumped in the helicopter, her own ears ringing, she reached for her small platinum vial around her neck, but, of course, it wasn't there. They had confiscated it. Were the bullet fragments it contained good luck or an omen?

Guards had poured out of the facility which held little tactical armament, but everything they had was being fired towards the gunship that had been built to handle small arms fire all day long. Without penetration or damage, the pilot lowered and tilted the rotors to create even more dust and then reversed, shooting the helicopter straight up as it quickly angled and took off. When the dust settled, three guards had minor injuries and Bridget Drummond was gone.

Rex Williams spent his first three nights in an isolated holding area for the RCMP off of Boul Dorchester, outside of Montreal in Westmount. Given the extradition request and reported crimes, they transferred him to the Regional Reception Center, which is located on the grounds of the

Ste-Anne-des-Plaines Institution. It was a Canadian federal prison for men that includes a super-max wing.

The RCMP and the local FBI had already concluded that Williams needed to be protected. Everyone was aware of an attempt to kill him or try to rescue him, as he was the key to taking down Bridget Drummond. For this very reason, they had tried to get him into the super-max wing, but because he was not yet formally sentenced, the request was denied. Williams sat in his cell wondering about his fate. He had already talked with Andrianasolo, and knew Bridget was backing him. He also knew she would throw him under the bus in a second if it helped her case, but he had a surprise for her if that happened.

At 9:50 a.m., his solicitor had arrived and needed a few words. Other than this request, they had confined him to quarters for safety. He agreed to see him, and the process took him to the visitor's area. There were two guards with him, and he wore a foot brace connected to his handcuffs, which were connected to them, one on either side. An inmate was coming towards them, and the guards went into action. Another guard entered the area outside of the visitor's area to confront the inmate as the two attached to Williams yelled, pulled their sidearms and prepared for a confrontation. Meanwhile, a second inmate walked out of the visitor's area with his guard in front of him, who having just walked into the crowded hall, was trying to find out what the commotion was about.

It took just a second for that second inmate to jump sideways and in the confusion, shove a prison made shiv, made from a long-forgotten screwdriver, into Williams ribcage and up into his heart. The inmate knew what he was doing as the officer attached to Williams fired, killing the inmate instantly. All attempts were made to save Williams, but he was gone. Word of his execution traveled to the RCMP and Correctional Service Canada at the same time word was coming back that Drummond had escaped.

It had been a terrible day for law enforcement… and an even worse day for Sara Ricci.

56

After two days in the basement biohazard room as a precaution, a porter wheeled Jason upstairs into a standard single room. His vitals were improving and the doctors, with CDC blessing, had allowed the move, although he remained under guard from local police. He was groggy but awake.

Standing together in a single room with him for the first time in over thirteen years was the entire Sykes family. Annabel and Rachael were next to Jason's bed, and Harley was standing off to one side. Jason looked up, saw his mom and sister, and smiled. Seeing them surprised him as he didn't know why they were here; unaware of how close to death he had been. When his eyes connected with his dad, he was even more shocked, but noticed some bruising and cuts on his face. As an icebreaker, he said, "How's the other guy?"

Harley chucked and answered, "Worse. Welcome back."

"How long have I been here?"

"Just over a week. Someone tried to infect Sara with one of the altered nanobots and got you instead."

"What? Is she okay?" he said, concerned.

"She's good."

Jason's mind immediately went back to the library and pictured the soldier that bumped him. That had to be it. "I think I remember the guy that did it."

Harley looked at his knuckles, still swollen and red, and said, "Sara recalled the same encounter and gave the description to the FBI. It matched the head of security for MDE Enterprises. Former Royal Marine named Rex Williams. Richard Chase and I formally introduced ourselves to him." Jason wasn't sure what that meant, but smiled. At that moment, he suddenly realized Sara wasn't there. He looked at his mom and asked, "Dad said Sara is okay. Has she been here?"

Annabel answered, "Sara has been here the entire time. She even made the machine that saved you. We're so grateful to her. She is a gifted woman and tough, too. You should have seen her with the CDC people."

"Yeah, she can be scary." He closed his eyes for a moment and then reopened them and said sadly, "So she went back to Italy?"

Harley had not moved but said from the window, "No. She's outside with her dad. She was just giving us a chance to see you first. Listen, when she comes in, don't overreact, she had a brief run in with that Scottish bitch and got a little banged up, but she'll be fine," as he waved to the door.

Jason rose so quickly he got the spins, and an alarm went off, prompting a nurse to rush in and almost knock Sara over. All was fine, and the nurse left apologetically after resetting his GVS monitor. Jason looked at Sara and noticed her awkward walk, rigid stance, and bruised face. He looked at her dad, Giovanni, his face one of worry and concern. Jason smiled at his him and said hello. They had only met once before, and Giovanni said softly, "Hello Jason. It is good to see you on the mend, as they say." Jason nodded and looked at Sara, who had approached the bed before asking, "Is it as bad as it looks?"

"Only my ribs, all else is of no concern," as she held her side.

"So, are you going to tell me what happened?"

Sara bent down and kissed him, and then replied, "Bridget made her move after they accidentally infected you instead of me. Your dad, Mr. Chase, and Rachael saved me." Sara chuckled as she continued, "Rachael really beat the crap out of her. I must admit, it was fun once we got to that point," as she smiled and looked over at Rachael and Harley. "That is one troubled woman, but she's in jail and hopefully they have enough to put her away for a long time. I sincerely doubt it, but it's a start."

Jason mouthed a thank you to his dad and sister before he asked Sara, "So I hear you saved me."

"I did. A couple more times and we might just be even."

"Well, thanks."

"I'm just glad it's over. You have no idea how close you came to dying."

"The military nanobots were deliberately altered?"

"Yes. Bridget had them reprogrammed and her security team went after me and those that were involved in the raid on her residence. She came very close to killing us all."

Jason looked at his dad and said snarky, "You must have been heartbroken."

The room got silent and Annabel, sensing Harley was going to go off, rose to calm him, but he didn't move. He looked down and simply said, "I was. Glad you're still with us." With the entire room expecting a blow up, the kindness caught everyone by surprise. Even Giovanni sensed this had been a big moment and smiled at Sara, who was smiling back at him.

"Thank you, sir." Jason mumbled out of respect.

Harley just nodded when FBI Agent Davies walked into the room. His look of concern was all anyone needed to wipe the smiles from their faces. Harley was closest to him and asked, "Oh shit, what happened?"

Davies was not expecting a room full of people and was hesitant to talk when Sara's eyes met his and she asked, "It's about her, isn't it?"

Davies looked down and then said to Sara as if she were the only one in the room, "I'm afraid so. We just got word that this morning from Quebec. An inmate killed Rex Williams while he was going to see his solicitor. At about the same time, Drummond escaped from the Nova Institute for Women, where they were holding her moments before her extradition hearing. The efforts to protect Williams, a known risk, were not good enough and nobody expected a military style gunship to enter the compound in broad daylight and snatch Drummond out. Thankfully, nobody was seriously hurt in the attempt."

Harley looked over and said, "You'll need to get this young lady some serious protection." Looking now towards Sara.

Giovanni was holding Sara as she trembled and said forcefully, "Agent Davies, that will not be necessary. I'm taking my daughter somewhere safe, and she will never return to America again if I have my way." He looked around the room and met everyone's eye as he then added, "It will be best if nobody knows where we are until they have dealt with this."

Harley looked at him and replied, "I understand your instincts, Mr. Ricci, but if this woman could kill a man in prison and then get broken out herself, you are just no match for her."

"Then I will die trying, Mr. Sykes. Sara is all I have."

"Fine. At least take Jason with you. The three of you hunker down somewhere and we'll work things from this side."

Davies had no idea what Harley was thinking, but he knew he didn't like it. "Listen, I understand you have all been through a lot, but you're going to have to leave this to the professionals. Nobody is going anywhere just yet."

Harley glanced at him sideways and said, "Davies, I have no issue with the FBI, but we handed you Williams and Drummond on a platter. Now one is dead, the case against Drummond weaker, and she's on the run. No, the 'professionals' have done more than enough, thank you." He looked over at Jason and said, "I'll talk to the doctor and see when you can travel." He then looked at Giovanni and said, "You and Sara go somewhere quiet and figure out a place where you can stay hidden. I have money if you need it. I'll call Gustave Cadieux and see if we can borrow his plane. Let's regroup at fourteen hundred." Davies knew he had lost control as the room cleared.

The air was crisp following the storms of the night before as the research vessel, RV *Bjørn Østberg* motored into the North Sea from Nova Scotia. Bridget had left her stateroom and shuffled into the galley to make some tea. It had taken over forty hours to escape Nova Scotia and get here after her dramatic rescue.

Bridget, thanks to Maximillian's insistence, always had an escape plan. She arrogantly never thought she would need it, but such is the reason for planning. She had grossly underestimated Sara Ricci and her base of friendships, just as her brother had. That left her vulnerable, and they caught her in the act as she momentarily lost control of herself. In time, Gustave Cadieux and Harley Sykes would die along with Sykes' daughter Rachael. But that was for a later date. When they least expected it.

Hasina Andrianasolo had, at Bridget's request, promoted one of her security team, Brody Gallagher, to head her security detail. His original assignment was only to remove the threat of Rex Williams, but Andrianasolo had further suggested she consider an escape, given the strength of the case against her. He and Gallagher had created a plan to time the two events together.

After they broke her out, the gunship and her helicopter had flown southeast approximately one-hundred-twenty kilometers off the coast of

Nova Scotia, where they offloaded her and the attack team onto the research vessel. After they relieved both helicopters of their passengers, pilots scuttled both aircraft at sea and the ship was on its way to Gothenburg, Sweden. Gallagher had insisted she head to Madagascar, but Bridget simply hated it there and honestly felt it was the most obvious choice and therefore not the one she wanted. The plan was to stay out of sight in Sweden and make her way to Kaani Palm Beach, in the Maldives islands, but she had to think this through. After all, she might just have to stay there for the rest of her life.

Days later, the Ricci team had formed a plan and, following Jason's release from the hospital, Jason, Sara, and her dad headed to Renton airport. Thanks to the kindness of Gustave Cadieux, they would take his private jet to Italy, but not Rome or Milan. They were heading for Lake Garda and, specifically, Limone sul Garda, a quaint community on the north side of the lake. It was there a boyhood friend of Gustave's was a partner in the hotel chain that owned several boutique hotels in the area. The decision to return to Italy was a risk, but they needed to be close to resources that they knew and understood. Giovanni had spent his summers here as a child and knew the area fairly well. Together with the private flights and special access at the hotel, they felt they had the upper hand and prepared to stay hidden for as long as it took.

Back in Idaho, Harley Sykes had spent the first day home using his contacts to locate any news regarding Drummond. His gut told him she would return to Madagascar. According to his intel, authorities in Nova Scotia had a brief radar contact with the second helicopter heading southeast, but the RCMP considered this a diversion tactic. It was assumed it had then headed north to Newfoundland, although there was no evidence to support this.

The RCMP had also contacted Interpol to work with local authorities in England and Scotland to ground the MDE fleet of planes and their mega yacht, the *Princess Alana.* That was an effort to make it harder for her to move, but, of course, Bridget and her team had anticipated all of this.

Meanwhile, Sykes and Chase were making plans to intercept Drummond the moment they found her location.

The Cadieux business jet landed in Verona, Italy without concern, and the three loaded their things into a sprinter van, complements of the Hotel Camilla. It would drive them to Torri del Benaco and ferry them across the lake to Maderno for a drive along the shoreline to Limone sul Garda.

Jason was still weak but managed, and Giovanni was visibly on edge. He calmed once as they arrived at the hotel, knowing that Gustave's friend would be there the following day to greet them and help them with any needs they might have. They were using assumed names, and nothing would trace to them personally. Two panorama rooms next to one another were prearranged for them and they had already sent smart keys to their phones to avoid the reception area all together.

Once they arrived, Sara and her dad ordered a light lunch from room service while Jason went into town to meet a friend. Giovanni suspected he was actually purchasing a weapon but said nothing to Sara and was thankful to have Jason and this protection.

When Jason returned, the wind they had noticed while driving over was stronger coming off of the expanse of Lake Garda or Lago di Garda. It was the largest lake in Italy with over one-hundred-sixty kilometers of shoreline and a maximum depth of over three-tenths of a kilometer. While the view was breathtaking, it was quite cold this time of year, and Sara took refuge inside. After a warm shower, Jason cut up some cheese, salami and opened a bottle of wine he had purchased in town. When Sara came out in her trademark yoga pants and sweatshirt, Jason went in and took a shower himself.

Once they were together, they clinked glasses and said cheers. "Does your dad want to join us?" Jason asked.

"No, he is doing some work in his room. His company understands the situation and they are trying to accommodate him. He doesn't have to work, but I suspect it keeps him busy and he takes it seriously. What about us? How are we going to fill our days?"

"That depends on what my dad finds. I have a call with him in three hours, but I don't suspect he'll have much just yet. We should stay low key until we know more. We can't do anything to bring attention to ourselves."

"Okay, I understand, but I'm going to go mad after just a few days of this, I just know it."

"Sara, there is a genuine reason for all this, so take that into account. By the way, have you spoken to Dr. Ferrera about what has happened?" Jason was referring to the fact that Sara was to teach at Sapienza University that coming Monday.

"I have and told him it could be a few weeks, possibly longer. I gave him more information than I needed to, but wanted him to understand I was not making this up. He understood, but was not thrilled."

Thousands of miles away at Versilant Nanotechnologies, Dann was in his office when Susan called from the front of the building and said an attorney was there and wanted to speak with them both. Susan walked him to Dann's office where he introduced himself. "Hello. My name is William Randolph and I represent the estate of Liam and Lillian Boylan." Susan closed the door, saddened at hearing their names as Dann motioned for Randolph to sit before he asked, "Mr. Randolph, were you their business attorney?"

"No, Mr. De Vires, I was Liam's personal attorney and often advised him on maters relative to CSC as long as it didn't create a conflict of interest."

Dann replied, "I see. We are still very much at a loss for both Lilliar's death and Liam's disappearance. Do you have any news?"

He nodded and looked down as he replied, "Yes, that is why I am here. The FBI located Liam's car in a forest near Lolo, Montana, and last week, his body was located four miles from the trailhead where his car was parked. He had… taken his own life." Both Dann and Susan gasped, but they knew the back story which made it even worse. *Liam killed himself, thinking he had killed Dann.*

"The medical examiner has completed the autopsy, and Mr. Boylan has been declared legally dead."

"That is unfortunate. We had hoped he would resurface after he had time to process everything."

"As his attorney, I am aware now of the circumstance that took him to the wilderness, although I didn't know that when we spoke presumably, hours before he made that unfortunate decision." He reached into his bag and withdrew a series of papers. "Mr. and Mrs. De Vires, the Boylan's had an estate plan and a living trust, but no heirs. There is no family on his side and only distant relatives on hers. Their entire estate was to go to a charitable organization until three days after he went missing. He sent me a signed affidavit and then called me to reiterate his wish that same day. The entire estate, which includes assets of seven-point six million dollars and his company, Cerium Scientific Compounds, is directed in its entirely to Susan De Vires."

Dann and Susan were speechless as Randolph withdrew a letter, which he handed to her. "My further instruction was to give this to you, Mrs. De Vires." She took the letter, opened it, and read it out loud.

Susan,

By now, all has been revealed. I alone am responsible for my actions. While being blackmailed, I made several poor decisions, but give you my promise that I never intentionally meant to harm my only friend and your loving husband. I am forever sorry and will pay the ultimate price, but meanwhile, anything that I had is now yours. I only ask that you move beyond your hatred of me long enough to realize that CSC was my and Lillian's dream. A dream shared by Dann, my only remaining investor. The thought of losing this influenced my actions, but in your capable hands I know you can make them proud. Please do this for them.

Liam

Susan set down the letter and looked at Randolph and asked, "Why would he do this? He did this under a duress that turned out to be false. These people blackmailing him led him to think he killed Dann, but he didn't. He's right. I hate him for what he did to Dann, but this? I don't understand."

"Mrs. De Vires, when Liam called me I knew he was in trouble but did not understand what that was. I alerted the FBI because I felt he might attempt to take his own life. I further urged him to reconsider, but his intentions were very clear, and he followed an appropriate process to change his initial wishes. Regardless of his criminal activity, my responsibility now is to make these wishes known and implement them. Nothing he did changes that regardless of the reason."

"It all seems so wrong. I'm having a tough time getting my head around this." Susan mumbled.

Dann stood and placed his hand on her shoulder before replying, "They were both victims. They both made poor choices, but Lillian had enough. She was coming back to let me go, to put an end to this, and was tragically killed before she could do so. We have to do this for her."

North Sea, off the coast of Sweden

Bridget held the phone close but away from her ear as Brody Gallagher, her new head of security, explained what they had found. He was already at the retreat in Gothenburg, Sweden having secured and prepared it for Bridget who was just arriving on the research vessel RV *Bjørn Østberg*. He would meet her in a few hours.

"Ms. Drummond, authorities have uncovered nothing regarding the death of Williams or your escape. The inmate that killed Williams had served twenty percent of a hundred-twelve-year sentence for several murders and was immediately killed by prison security. The warden of Ste-Anne-des-Plaines Institution is mouthing off that we paid him off, but he can't prove it."

"Any news on the location of Ms. Ricci and soldier boy?"

"We hacked various sources. Neither Jason Sykes nor Sara Ricci purchased a ticket in their own names, but as you suggested, we monitored the Cadieux MT Jet. It did, in fact, land in Seattle three days after they released Sykes from the hospital. The manifest says there were three passengers, but we have no names or descriptions. The flight plans showed Montreal as its destination and we assumed Gustave Cadieux was hiding them. We just found out the same plane left hours later from Montreal and submitted a new flight plan for Verona, Italy."

"I knew that old bastard would help them. Get feet on the ground there and find out where that little bitch is hiding."

"On it." Gallagher snapped.

Former Director Jeremy Hicks was back at home following his nanobot scare and subsequently, having been saved by Sara's invention. It truly was a small world. Despite protests from his wife, Hicks was back in his office when his phone rang. It was Giles Taylor, his old college roommate, and current Assistant Director for the SIS.

"Jeremy, you are well?"

"Yes, Giles. Looks like we both owe a debt of gratitude to Dr. Ricci. Funny how things work isn't it?"

"It is indeed and hence the reason for this call. Jeremy, this is a personal call, not on behalf of the SIS."

"I understand."

"I have some new information."

"You have located Drummond?"

"Not yet, but we might be closer. If you recall, much of our case against Drummond hinged on getting the security chief, Williams, to talk. She knew this and had him killed. We have no proof, but this is a page right out of the Drummonds playbook. That said, Williams apparently knew his boss well enough to know she would sell him out and yesterday at 15:00 hours, MI5 received a package that they suspect was released on his death. Inside were exceptional details on this entire set of crimes, and we have shared this with the RCMP."

"And this recent evidence can convict her?"

"If we find her, she'll never leave prison either in Canada or here."

"But nothing in the package points to her location?"

"Perhaps. We knew she had a residence in Scotland, a villa in Madagascar, a condo in Nova Scotia and a flat in London, and have searched them all to no avail. With this new information from Williams, we just learned she also has a retreat in Gothenburg, Sweden and in the Maldives. I have sent agents to both locations to determine if she is there."

"And your plans if she is?"

"I find myself at odds with my government, but my office is officially only trying to locate her while they put together the legal case. Drummonds' team broke her out because they realized the Canadians had her dead to rights. She will most certainly be gone with the wind soon, if not already."

"Hence the reason for this personal call."

"Exactly. I very well may get sacked, but bloody hell, this Drummond nonsense must stop. One last piece of intel. A drone over the Sweden location just confirmed heat signatures of a female and six large males. She is there."

"I understand and think I know what to do with this information."

"I thought you might. Good luck." As Taylor signed off.

Hicks hung up and immediately called Richard Chase.

Jason's burner phone rang, and knowing it was his dad, he connected. The Versilant team had created burner phones that worked in Europe and mimicked an untraceable cellular number in Washington. This allowed them a cell phone and hot spot that could not be easily discovered and if it was, it would look like the call was coming from Seattle, not Limone sul Garda, Italy.

"Dad, any news?"

"Yes. Is everyone safe?"

"Yes, we're good. Mr. Ricci is unsettled, but that is to be expected. He's not used to being on this side of the action."

"I can only imagine. Keep him safe. Okay, here is what I have. Between Canada and the United Kingdom, they both want a piece of this, but none have issued approval to go after her. By the time they do, she will have already made her move. I got intel they own two properties, previously unknown. One is in Sweden and the other is a small island in the Maldives Islands. A drone with heat signatures just confirmed she is in Sweden."

"Are you saying we should go after her?"

"Nobody else is likely to do it. This is not sanctioned, so the plan is to apprehend her. Richard Chase is assisting, but I need you and Rachael. The SIS is giving us intel they shouldn't, so we're taking that as they are helping us do this for them. I just have to get hold of Director Taylor at

SIS to see if he can provide us with Drummond, a way out of the country, as a contingency if one of us is down."

"Okay. I'm in, but who protects Sara?"

"I have a plan. We'll talk again."

Richard Chase returned a call to Jeremy Hicks who answered on the first ring and asked, "What's the plan?"

"We have a team of six and we'll be ready as early as tomorrow. We don't need help in or out of the country. But we might need help to get Drummond out of the country if we arrest her or, god forbid, any of us are wounded."

"Okay, I understand what you're saying, but I'm not sure how I can help you."

"You and Taylor have history. I was hoping you could call him for me?"

"Shit." Hicks said aloud.

"Director, I understand I'm asking a lot. If the price is too high, I get it. Just think about it."

"Is this a good number for you?"

"Yes."

"I'll call you back," and Hicks hung up the phone.

Giles Taylor picked up his personal cell phone to answer a call from Hicks who said quickly, "Is this a good time?"

"I have a few minutes." Taylor replied as Hicks told him they had assembled a team outside of government to get Drummond and what help was required. Taylor listened but did not answer immediately before he said, "I'll call you back."

Although Hicks assumed he was considering the blow back, Taylor called an ally within the SIS Operations units. They met and discussed, off the record, the requested help, and it was felt that a team of two could be there to intercept the US team to help with a prisoner or wounded. There would be no official mention of this. Taylor called Hicks back and gave him the details and Hicks, in turn, gave the information to Richard Chase.

59

Gothenburg, Sweden

Bridget poured a glass of Rombauer Chardonnay and sat down with security chief Gallagher in the safety of the Gothenburg house. The rest of the security team was in the other room or out, covering the ten-acre grounds.

"So, any information?"

"Ms. Drummond, we need to consider getting to Kaani Palm Beach. There is a chance this location is compromised."

"But the Maldives residence isn't ready for us."

"I understand, but if not there, then Madagascar."

"Not yet. Give me another week."

"It is not advisable."

"I have already decided. What is the status of Dr. Ricci?"

"After they arrived at the airport in Verona, a party matching their description boarded a hotel bus that ferries across Lake Garda to a boutique hotel called the Hotel Camilla. The owner is a friend of Gustave Cadieux. I have a man there now to get confirmation."

"Once you do, I want them gone. Do you understand? No slipups. Her and her boyfriend must die."

"I'll get a team."

"No, you have to do this. I may not have many more chances."

"Ms. Drummond, I cannot provide security to you here from Italy."

"I understand, but the team here will protect me."

"Very well. We'll leave once we have confirmation." Frustrated, Gallagher knew he couldn't change her mind, so he went to plan for Italy and prepare the team for action here. If they really knew she was here, they would come. He just didn't know who or when.

In Italy, Jason had packed, and the hotel had arranged for a driver to get him to the airport. The plan was for him to meet his sister Rachael and his dad and three others at the Dülmen Army base in Germany where a plane would take them over the compound in Sweden. This would be their extraction as well, unless they needed the help of the SIS. Then they would leave via the Bardufoss Air Station in Norway.

Sara gave him a hug and said softly, "I can't tell you what a bad idea this is. If you're there, who is protecting me?"

"Sara, I know your dad is freaking out, but we have a plan for this, right? All will work out, I promise. You and I need Drummond out of our lives, and nobody else is going to do it before they hide her away for good."

"I know all that but..." Jason gave her another hug and kissed her and then grabbed his bag. As he got to the door, he turned and said, "I love you."

Sara smiled and said, "I love you, too. Please be safe for me."

"I will," and he left, happy he had finally got the nerve to say what he felt. And that she said it back. Things were looking up. Sara went next door to hang with her dad and, within the hour, they ordered dinner to his room. They were taking precautions, but not enough. A man at the pool bar used his camera to scan the lower-level rooms and snapped a picture of Sara looking out of the window. They had found her.

Brody Gallagher and two others arrived in Limone sul Garda at two in the morning and stayed at a leased villa for two nights. The next morning, two of them surveyed the hotel and were able to gain access under the foundation of her unit undetected. They had observed Sara Ricci going into that room and her father was in the room next to hers. They had not located the third person who Gallagher assumed was Jason Sykes, but with just two rooms registered, this would work, as Jason was likely with her. The team planted enough explosives to take out the room above.

The team under her building was done and already back at their villa. At 1:00 a.m., Sara Ricci would die.

Army rangers train for many conditions and circumstances, but they are experts at parachuting into location. Any location. Harley and Rachael had done these jumps hundreds of times. Jason and Richard Chase, while trained, were not as proficient. The C-130H3 flew over the Drummond compound from Germany and they exited the plane at 10,000 feet. Their preference would have been to exit much lower, but the risk of plane detection was too high. It was nearing 12:00 a.m., as the six parachutes headed into the woods of the compound, aiming for an area to the right of an outbuilding, possibly a garage. It was not an easy target given the high trees that surrounded it, but thankfully, they all feathered to a graceful landing, silently gathered their chutes, and went into the darkness behind the building.

Three of the six had infrared headgear, and Richard noticed a single sentry was patrolling the ten-acre grounds and was coming their way. He might have heard the plane in the still of the night. He motioned for one commando to intercept the sentry who silently headed toward him and dispatched him with a knife without a sound. As they regrouped and headed toward the house, they located signs of electronic surveillance.

In Limone sul Garda, the night calm was disrupted when Gallagher detonated the plastic explosives under room 104. As he watched from a safe distance, it was just seconds before they reduced the room to rubble, slightly damaging the unit above and to the left. There was a video taken of the event which he sent to Drummond and waited until the police and fire units arrived. Several hours later, two body bags were being removed from the approximate location of Sara Ricci and her boyfriend, Jason Sykes. He took a shot of that as well. His work done, he mouthed a goodbye as he and his team jumped into a car and headed for the airport.

He needed to get back to Sweden, unaware that an Interpol agent had been watching them from afar.

60

Gothenburg, Sweden

Harley led the assault team to the house. The main house was one story, although the master bedroom was on the second floor and the entire roof of each was a terrace. The ten-acre site was heavily forested, with vegetation on the outer edges of the property, while they had sculpted the inner portion to bare ground. Outside the property were high block walls and no homes or buildings within a kilometer.

Using infrared headgear, Harley and Jason disarmed three trip wires and created a bypass on two point-to-point lasers. They had no idea if this was all the surveillance they would encounter, but as yet, no one was up to greet them. As they neared the door of the modern designed home, they noted the terrace on each level. Harley, Richard, and one of Richard's men stayed low on the ground floor. Jason and Rachael went to the terrace atop the second floor via an architectural feature, a steel column added for aesthetics. Another of Richard's men went up to the terrace on the top of the first silently using the same column.

Inside, everyone was asleep except for a young recruit named Pablo Garcia, who laid silently, thinking he had heard the unmistakable sound of a prop plane earlier. He almost allowed himself to doze, but suddenly, he heard another sound. This was coming from the roof, a quiet, but out-of-place sound. He was sure of it. He slowly reached for his Heckler & Koch HK MP5 and walked over to the computer that ran the surveillance system. Nothing seemed abnormal, but the GPS monitor on the sentry showed him unmoving. He looked away from the screen and listened intently, but there was no sound. Had he dreamed it?

One of his mates awoke and asked if all was well. Softly, he replied that the system looked good, but the sentry was not moving, and he swore he heard something. Garcia told him to be on alert and he walked upstairs to the room where Bridget was asleep. He didn't knock, he just walked in and hoped she had clothes on. Bridget, to his surprise, was awake as he put his finger to his mouth as if to say, *quiet*. With the MP5 in front of him, he took in the room and gazed at the windows. There was no movement outside. Bridget looked at him and pointed up. He nodded and whispered, "I'll check it out. Please do not leave this room."

Bridget nodded, but had no intention of staying put. She was dressed in leggings and a long sleeve t-shirt as she pulled herself out of bed and pulled a SIG Sauer P238 Nitron Micro Compact Pistol out of the nightstand. There was not a sound and for a moment, she also thought this was a false alarm. Richard, wearing night vision, saw that two men were moving one downstairs and one was now in the upstairs bedroom.

Richard watched the man head to the rooftop terrace of the second-floor bedroom and saw the form of a woman. He clicked his comm twice to alert Jason. Jason waited patiently as the security man, Garcia, headed his way. As he moved closer to Jason, Rachael dispatched him with a silent but well-placed knife, holding his body upright. Jason came out of hiding and they both laid his body down without a sound.

On the first floor, Richard remained on one side and Harley was on the other, giving them complete access to the glass walls of the house. Harley signaled to one of their two commandos to take out the rear door. It was locked, but a liquid explosive injected with a small syringe opened it with ease as the commando rushed in with Harley. There was a single shot in their direction from the one security that awoke with Garcia, but the commando and Harley quickly left. They quickly used their silenced weapons to take out two, followed by the third. The security team had been eliminated as they headed upstairs to apprehend Drummond.

Bridget crouched in the stairwell that led to the upper terrace and tried to listen for Garcia. She had heard a commotion downstairs and, not hearing Garcia now; she went up. In her mind, higher was better. She opened the door to the outside quietly and slowly. She expected to see

Garcia, but there was no sound and nobody there. The SIG in front of her, Bridget walked in the cold to the edge of the terrace and looked down. Nothing. She did not see, but heard a sound as Rachael flew from behind a large plant and kicked Bridget with everything she had. Bridget flew parallel to the edge of the roof, crashing into a chaise lounge, falling silent for a moment until her breath came back, but wisely held onto her SIG. With fury, she rose as Rachael, anticipating her move, released a throwing knife so hard it went into Bridget's shoulder all the way to the hilt of the specially made knife; about three inches. Bridget screamed and went down, but managed to get a shot off in Rachael's direction.

Jason, at the other end of the roof, walked stealthily towards the north end when he heard Bridget's wail. Rachael must have gotten her good. He leaned in to assess the situation. Rachael was in a sitting position, which was odd. Twenty feet in front of her was Drummond, barely visible behind an outdoor sofa. Behind Jason, Harley had come to the roof and had Drummond trained in his infrared sight. Knowing she was armed; he needed a head shot to drop her before she could use her weapon. She was no soldier, but she clearly knew how to use a gun.

Jason was now close to his sister, and she was wounded in her upper left thigh. She had packed the wound with a plastic puddy to slow the bleeding and wrapped a tourniquet above the wound. She saw him and gave him a thumb up to signify that she was okay.

Bridget was still behind the sofa and called out, "Well, well. Looks like one of us is going to die tonight. Since soldier boy is without his beloved Sara, I will target you, little sister."

"Hey, Drummond, you sure about that? Do you have a picture of the body?" Jason said with confidence.

Surprised at the reaction, Bridget laughed and said, "As a matter of fact, I do."

"No, you don't. You have a picture of a body bag. Think of how I could know that if I'm here talking to you."

Bridget winced at the pain in her shoulder, but took in the words. "Ah, so clever, soldier boy. Maybe I'll kill you after all."

Jason said back, "And one of us will kill you."

"Maybe. But I have a way of surviving." Bridget tossed back with a sickening laugh.

Harley, still watching and waiting, had his sight fixed on where he thought her head was. He thought of shooting right through the sofa but needed to confirm that was where her head was. If he just nicked her, Rachael was dead. *Come on, just lift your head an inch,* he willed her.

In that second, sensing she was coming up to shoot he pulled the trigger. But Bridget didn't just raise her head, she actually jumped up into a shooting stance at that same moment, as Harley's round tore through her neck. As she rose, she had pulled her trigger, which allowed a second shot toward Rachael as the force of Harley's round hit her and spun her completely around as she fell. Bridget instinctively reached for her platinum vial around her neck, but it wasn't there. Her luck had run out.

Jason had sensed her action and dove in front of Rachael as both shots were fired. He hit the ground and rolled in an awkward somersault, slamming into the floor of the terrace. Harley quickly came over to Racheal. "Kid, you okay?"

She responded in pain, "Dad, I'm hit, but okay. Help Jason."

Harley had been so focused on the shot to Bridget through his sight, he had not seen Jason jump in front of her and roll to the side. He turned rapidly, seeing Jason's prone body down hard on the roof. Richard was already with him and as Harley rushed over, he saw Richard's face. Every soldier knows that look. He leaned down to Jason's face. "Jason, son, hang in there. We're going to get you out of here. Mission accomplished." Harley teared up and looked at Richard, then back to Rachael. No one said a word. They understood the situation.

Harley leaned down to Jason again. He had been hit in the back of his head and was unconscious. Harley pulled a wrap from his tactical vest and placed in on his head to slow the bleeding. He silently placed his hand on his shoulder.

Richard had gone over to check Rachael when, a minute later, Harley had regrouped. That's what rangers did. He and Richard placed Rachael's leg into a pneumatic cast that immobilized her leg, and two commandos brought her downstairs and to the edge of the long driveway. Harley and Richard did the same for Jason with a larger device to secure his head and shoulders. They lowered him downstairs and carried him out. The two agents from SIS were there as expected and took Rachael to an awaiting van, followed by Jason. Harley and Richard returned to the house and brought out the body of Bridget Drummond. They all left together to get to the transport the SIS had arranged, and a clean-up crew would attend to the house and the bodies of the downed security men.

The Airbus A400M transport was flying over the North Sea, and the SIS commander had been on the phone with Giles Taylor. Giles was in a tough spot. He wanted to help this team anyway he could, but the government had not sanctioned this. And as much as he wanted it known that Drummond was dead, to disclose that meant revealing the raid on Swedish soil by Americans, which, of course, he would not do. Had they been able to arrest her, possibly, but given how the event had unfolded, there was no chance? He told the commander what needed to happen and hung up.

A medic was on board tending to Rachael and Jason. Rachael might never run the same, but she would be fine. Jason was a different story. They were doing all they could to stabilize him and hoping to hell he lasted until they landed. He remained unconscious with a gunshot wound to the head.

As the SIS commander came back to the rear of the aircraft, he sat next to Harley and Richard Chase. "Sir," looking at Harley, "We have to divert to Germany to offload the wounded and Drummond's body. We cannot land directly in the UK."

Richard understood, as did Harley, who stood and said, looking over at Jason and said to the medic, "Do you think he'll make it that far?"

"Sir, he in unconscious and I suspect in a coma. Although critical, he is stable for now. There is little more I can do here."

"Can he last two hours?"

"He is presently stable, but two hours?'

Harley nodded and walked over to Rachael. "How are you, kid?"

"I heard Dad. I'll hang in there. What about Jason? I feel so bad. He jumped in front of me and took the hit. He saved my life."

Harley, unaware that was how it went down, put his hand on her shoulder and looked over at him and sighed. "He was always soft for you, protected you like a prized possession when you were kids." Harley stood, looked at Rachael, and said, "Rachael, this was my error. I should have trusted my instincts and just fired. She was right where I thought she was and had I done so, none of this would have happened." Shaking his head, he stood and went over to Jason, kneeled down, and placed his hand on Jason's shoulder. "Hang in there, Jason, the world is not done with you yet."

61

Limone sul Garda

They had warned Sara to stay away from the windows, but she couldn't sleep, and curiosity got the better of her. She desperately wanted to think this wasn't for real. That their movement to a safe house was unwarranted. Staying hidden behind the sheer curtains, she looked across the expanse from her new room to the Hotel Camilla. Not expecting anything to happen, an explosion occurred a minute after 1:00 a.m., involuntarily making her jump back. Giovanni jumped off the sofa where he had dozed off and grabbed her, instinctively pulling her down, but they were so far away, it was a meaningless gesture. It was just a natural reaction.

Too far away to see detail, it appeared her former room was gutted, and gray smoke bellowed out of the hole left by the explosion as sirens in the distance came closer. Sara rose and stared at the smoke, knowing she should be dead. She had thought the plan created by Harley Sykes and an Interpol agent was silly, but now she was grateful although this was confirmation. They really were trying to kill her again.

She instinctively grabbed her phone to call Jason, but remembered the mission in Sweden was probably going on right then. She hoped they arrested that bitch, but at the same time, she was scared.

Morning came suddenly and for a moment, all seemed normal when Sara jumped up and realized there had been no word from Jason or anyone on the Swedish team. She ran over and grabbed her phone, but there were no messages, although her dad heard her stirring next door and came over to her room and knocked. Seeing it was him, she let him in. "Dad, do you have any news from the team?"

"No, my special girl. It is a complex situation, so I think perhaps a little more time."

Sara tried Jason's phone again, but nothing. She then tried Harley Sykes. but same, nothing. Not even to voicemail. Desperate, she called Richard Chase. The call went through, but there was no answer. Four hours went by before Sara called Richard Chase again, but still no answer.

Giovanni tried to get her to relax. He had spoken to Gustave, who had already been alerted to the bombing by the hotel owner. Although Gustave had offered to pay for all damages, the explosion would strain their friendship for some time. Damage to the hotel was repairable. Damage to the hotel's reputation was another matter. After Giovanni hung up, he tried to get Sara to return to Milan, but she was headstrong about staying there until she knew what happened to the raid team.

Without breakfast, lunch or dinner, day became night and at 11:00 p.m., Sara's phone rang, twenty-two hours after they had launched the mission. Twenty-two hours after she had survived another attempt on her life. Sara answered immediately and put the phone on speaker for her dad.

"Sara, it's Richard Chase. Are you safe?"

"Yes. They tried to kill me just as you said, but we are safe. We have been so worried. How did everything go? When will you return?"

"Sara, the mission was a success… but there were complications."

"What do you mean? What complications?"

"We encountered heavy resistance, but considering our circumstances, normal channels of help were not available."

"Richard, I don't understand. Please, just tell me. You arrested her, right?"

"We tried, but she had other ideas. She's dead."

"But your voice is heavy. Something else happened?"

"Rachael was hit. When Drummond tried a second attempt to kill her, Jason dove in front of her just as Harley shot Drummond. She got off a shot as she fell back. Rachael was spared, but Jason… Jason took the hit."

Sara was crying and between sobs, said, "Is he dead?"

"No. He's in a coma and they're trying to reduce the swelling in his brain."

Giovanni asked, "He was shot in the head?"

"Unfortunately, yes. Thankfully, the bullet didn't enter the brain, but the impact was severe, and it fractured his skull and bounced off. After extraction, they diverted us to a US hospital in Germany because of our mission status. He has been unconscious since he was shot."

"What do the doctors say?"

"I don't have those details. I am told that normally he should regain consciousness in a week or two."

Sara turned to her dad. "When can I see him?"

"Sara, I'm so sorry, but that is not possible. He is at a military hospital only because Harley and the SIS pulled a few favors, but the reason he is there, and his identity, are sealed. He is anonymous for obvious reason, and that has to remain the case. Without this cover, all of us would certainly be arrested if details of the raid got out. He is in excellent hands, but he'll have to improve and transfer to a public hospital for any of us to see him." Sara sobbed and lowered her head in defeat at hearing his words.

Giovanni asked, "But his sister or father can get us information, correct?"

"Mr. Ricci, Rachael is there recovering from her gunshot wound, and, like Jason, is also anonymous. Harley is there, at least for now, and he can give us updates. He cannot see them, but he can talk to the medical staff as they think these are his recruits from a secret mission. In an hour, you'll receive a text from me to each of you. Open the file and allow it to embed onto your device. This technology will allow you all to message each other securely."

Chase ended with, "Sara, I'm so very sorry. We're all praying for good news?" Sara had already shut down and withdrew as Giovanni thanked Richard and hung up the phone.

All Sara could think of was that even in death, Bridget Drummond had found a way to hurt her.

Landstuhl Regional Medical Center, at Wilson Barracks, in Landstuhl, Germany, was one of the largest and one of only two of US hospitals in a foreign country. Opened in 1955, it rose to prominence in the war on terrorism, although it has been since downgraded to a level II trauma center on the decline of US service persons in the Middle East. The facility has a hundred beds, of which four were in a small, top security area. Jason was there.

Dr. Bruce Chambal, the lead surgeon, was talking with a neurologist. Earlier in the week, they had continued medication to reduce the intercranial pressure, but it was not working. They then had installed a drain to remove fluid, but very little was removed, and he had ordered an MRI.

Looking at the MRI, Chambal said, "Here in this area, you see the swelling. I think there is no doubt we'll have to perform a craniectomy."

"I would have to agree. With limited response to other forms of treatment, I would like to leave the bone skull bone off for at least twenty-four hours. This is a young guy in great shape, but we have to get the swelling down right now to avoid permanent disabilities. As it is, I'm not sure what we are dealing with."

"Okay, let's prep him, we have consent."

Rachel had been in the same ward with Jason on arrival, but was moved once she stabilized. She had asked if she could see Jason prior to his surgery, but they wouldn't let her. Guilt devastated her, as she still believed she had caused this, which was not true. Harley knew she felt this way, but also knew Rachael had to figure this out for herself. There was nothing you could say to make it better.

The surgery itself was complicated, but something they had done many times. The area of swelling was relatively small and the piece of skull they removed was less than two inches square. They told Harley the skull opening would remain uncovered for twenty-four hours, and then they would reattach the bone.

Harley was in a special room when Dr. Bruce Chambal came in. Harley knew him from the past and shook his hand. Chambal did not know the two wounded were related to him, just that they were his recruits on a secret mission.

"Dr. Chambal, it's been a while. How did it go?"

"It went well, sir." He discussed the procedure and said, "We'll know if it worked in 24 hours."

"So, the prognosis is good?"

"It's too early to tell. He doesn't appear to have any permanent loss of brain function as yet, but we have to get the swelling down."

"Okay, thanks." Harley didn't say it, but he was worried about his son.

Epilogue

Giovanni took Sara back to the Milan the next day. Milan was Sara's childhood home, and he hoped the familiarity and safety would help her, but it was hard to say with any certainty, if that was possible. He had called Dr. Ferrera at Sara's request to remove her from the teaching assignment at Sapienza University in Rome. While Dr. Ferrera was disappointed, he understood, shocked by the events in Limone sul Garda and that once again, she had met another violent crime.

Sara had not left the apartment awaiting word on Jason's condition. Not even for a run. Gone was her infectious desire to learn and her capacity to keep information. Also gone was her ambitious 7:50 running pace goal. She seemed to be a shell of her former self.

Giovanni received a message from Harley a few days later, and bless his stone heart, he attached a picture of Jason. His rugged face was shallow as he lay on an inclined bed, IVs, and tubes everywhere, his head wrapped in gauze. When he showed the picture to Sara, she cried; it was a vision of both horror and beauty.

In London, solicitors for MDE Enterprises were battling every side of the legal spectrum. Shareholders were suing, employees were suing, board members were fighting, and, unlike Maximillian Drummond, who had a plan for everything, Bridget had not foreseen her demise. She had vanished from the face of the earth, and they were no closer to finding her than when they started following her prison break. Various police agencies had searched all residences again, and found nothing. And, of course, they never would.

All intelligence communities, except for SIS, surmised that after breaking out of prison, Bridget Drummond had gone into hiding. Although MI5 had frozen all cash accounts, it was assumed she still had access to billions. In London, there was a standing succession plan for MDE Enterprises in the case of an emergency, which would place a senior board member into the role of Acting CEO.

It is difficult for any public company to weather the storm brought by a CEO involved in a serious criminal activity, but to have it happen twice in a year was unprecedented. To appease large shareholders, the board approved a resolution that no insider would become CEO. They would hire an outsider and there was even talk that the entire senior management team should be cleansed throughout the corporation, leaving no one associated with the former leaders.

In the meantime, the stock of MDE Enterprises had fallen almost forty percent, as shareholders showed their complete lack of confidence in the company's management. London investment companies were circling the wagons and eventually, someone would purchase MDE Enterprises for cents on the dollar.

Two days passed when Sara and Giovanni received a message from Harley Sykes telling them they had successfully reduced the swelling in Jason's brain, and they had reattached the skull piece without incident. He was still in a coma, and they suspected he would come out of it soon. I was now ten days since the raid. Sara went out on the terrace, cold from the late afternoon dusk. Sitting with a glass of wine, she was numb, and Giovanni let her be. He knew his special girl and as much as it pained him; she needed to be alone. He had never seen her this despondent.

In Germany, Dr. Chambal read Jason's chart and looked at his patient a week later. As if he meant to answer him, Jason stirred for a moment and Chambal waved to the nurse as she and two others rushed into the room. Chambal approached Jason, whose eyes were open for the first time in two weeks. He looked at the Chambal but did not speak. Chambal asked, "Soldier, can you hear me?"

Jason looked at him and nodded rather than answer verbally. Chambal then asked, "Do you know where you are?"

Jason shook his head and mouthed a whispered, "No."

"You are at a military hospital in Germany. Do you recall any of the events that brought you here?"

"No."

"Do you know your name and rank?"

Jason thought of the question but shook his head. "I don't think so. I'm a soldier?"

"Yes, you're in the United States Army."

"I think I used to be in the army, but that was a long time ago."

"You and another soldier were brought here from a secret field assignment. You don't recall that?"

"No."

"Where were you born?"

"Fort Benning, Georgia."

"How old are you?"

He paused for a moment and said, "I was born in 1983?"

"So, you're 35 years old?"

Jason seemed confused and said nothing. Chambal frowned and stood, unsure what was happening. Jason's eyes were darting over the entire room, taking it all in. Jason knew this was a hospital and recognized some of the medical equipment, but regarding himself, the edges were fuzzy, and he wasn't sure who he was or why he was here. Another doctor entered the room and Dr. Chambal introduced him.

"Soldier, this is Dr. Umar Aamir. He's a neurologist?"

"Why don't you refer to me by my given name?"

"You were on a secret mission and there is no record of your name here at the hospital. Do you know your name? Please don't say it, I just want to know if you recall it."

Jason shook his head affirmative and replied, "I think so, but I can't seem to hold on to the thought." Dr. Aamir did a series of tests over a twenty-minute period and asked Jason several questions from different periods of time. At least once, possibly twice, during the exchange, Jason experienced slight tremors. Dr. Aamir observed him during these seizures but said or did nothing. His only comment to Dr. Chambal was to monitor him. His opinion was the memory loss was temporary, but this soldier should not be experiencing seizures. This was a concern.

Dr. Chambal met with Harley Sykes hours later and tried to explain. "Sir, the male recruit has come out of his coma, and his vitals suggest a healthy man. His scans reveal some brain damage, and we are trying to assess what that means for him. At this moment he appears has some kind of post-traumatic amnesia. A neurologist has seen him, and he has what they call neurological amnesia. He knows of his past and can recall what occurred since he awoke from the coma, so he does not have anterograde amnesia, the inability to form fresh memories. He could not, however, recall the events of any near-term memories. Although we asked him to not reveal it, he could recall his name with some effort. He says he works for DARPA, but doesn't recall his mission or why he is here."

"Have you seen this before?"

"Yes, and no. It is normal to not recall anything immediately after the event that caused the trauma, meaning it is normal to not recall getting shot. It is rare, however, to see what appears to be retrograde amnesia, the inability to recall events that happened in the days, weeks or even months before he was injured."

"How far back can't he remember?"

"We don't know him or his circumstance well enough to answer, but it appears to be several months if not a year."

"So, he could regain his memory, or he might not?"

"I don't know and must defer to the neurologist, but usually, it will reappear."

"Otherwise, he is fine?"

"Physically, yes, but during some tests with Dr. Aamir, the neurologist, the soldier had a series of small seizures. While not severe, they should not have happened at all. This is a concern."

"So, he'll require extensive tests?"

"Yes. He will have to undergo a series of tests to determine if this is linked to stimulation in the injury's area or if this is a temporary or permanent disorder that occurs at random."

"He is secure here until that happens?"

"Yes, sir, we have him."

"So, are we talking weeks or months?"

"I cannot answer that. Ever brain injury is unique, and although I have not seen many cases of amnesia, I have seen a few. It is usually days and weeks rather than months and years, despite what the television shows have led us to believe. Further neurological tests might offer more insight. Again, we are less concerned about the memory loss than the seizures."

"When can the other soldier leave?"

"Within a day."

"Keep me informed. It is my intention to take the other recruit back to the States and I'll await your word."

"We'll be in touch. Your soldier is in expert hands." Harley, never one for emotion, outwardly was stoic, but inside, he was very concerned for Jason.

Two days later, it was midafternoon as Giovanni looked at Sara, sitting once again on the terrace in silence. She would return to Rome in a few days, hoping to speak with a psychologist who Dr. Ferrera had suggested. Part of him was happy for her, knowing that moving on was the best thing, but he was sad at the same time. It had been nice to have her here despite the circumstance.

Sara's phone rang, and she glanced at it but ignored it. Giovanni brought her a plate of antipasto and glanced at the number before the screen went dark. It was her former thesis chair and mentor from MIT, Dr. Adrian Zimbrean, and he asked, "That was Dr. Zimbrean, no? Why are you avoiding him?"

"I'm not really." Sara said, but then added, "Well, maybe a little."

"My special girl, he thinks the world of you and is no doubt concerned."

"I know it's awful of me to close him out, of all people." She sighed as she reached over and picked up her phone and called him. He answered quickly, "Sara. Thank you for calling me back. I have been thinking of you. Are you well?"

"Hello Dr. Zimbrean, thanks for the concern. I'm okay, it's just a painful waiting game. You know me when I can't fix something."

He sensed the reserved tone and replied, "It is a fine quality, Sara. I certainly wish Jason a quick recovery. I also spoke to Dr. Ferrera and know that you withdrew from the teaching assignment at Sapienza. What are your plans?" Giovanni had walked inside to let her have some privacy, but was still listening. He was so worried about her.

"I have none. I'm in limbo, not knowing how he is or how he will be. It seems selfish to make any plans." Sara replied.

"Yes, I can imagine that is how it seems although it is not logical."

"What does that mean?" Sara said in a snippy tone.

"Sara, please, I didn't mean to appear insensitive, but Jason's recovery is up to Jason, his God, and his medical staff. It could be weeks, months, or longer. Your mental health and your ability to accept him and devote yourself to his recovery can only happen if you are also ready and recovered. I have only known you for five years, but during that time, you have always healed yourself through your work. I just assumed this time was no different."

Sara said nothing, but heard him and understood what he was saying. And he was right. Dr. Zimbrean was always right. "I guess I had not thought of that. My PhD was my carrot, and I always just went towards it. Now I don't know what to do."

"Perhaps I can help. I have heard of an opportunity in Iceland being sponsored by MIT in partnership with the University of Iceland in Reykjavik. It is yours for the asking if you can get away." Sara, on hearing the location of Iceland, perked up a little, and it surprised Giovanni when she sat up properly and asked, "What is the project?"

"A few years ago, a student at the University of Iceland noticed data from core samples in permafrost contained higher concentrations of magnetism than those lower or higher. As I understand this, the team will review the original dataset, consider additional samples and develop a hypothesis they can take back to their universities to solve."

There was a pause as Sara looked at her dad, now in the kitchen, and glanced around the terrace and replied, "Dr. Zimbrean, I'm really not sure of my availability at the moment. How much time do I have to decide?"

"The teams have actually been there for a few weeks, but they require a site leader, and that is where I thought you could help. I'm afraid they would require a decision this week at the latest."

Sara sighed, wishing she had more time. She thought of Jason and glanced at her dad, who looked anxious, likely because he knew she would say no. She was about ready to say her goodbyes when she felt a strange sensation. It was like the feeling you get when you know you're right. A feeling of confidence.

She smiled, looked at her dad, and gave Jason a silent kiss before saying, "Dr. Zimbrean. Send me the paperwork. I'm in!"

Eager to enter her professional life, Sara Ricci returns in *Deadly Discovery*. When she aligns herself with a group out of Istanbul attempting to create a space-based energy system, trouble finds her once again.

Deadly Dissertation (Book 1) - PhD hopeful, Sara Ricci is at MIT when a Scottish Industrialist learns of her thesis and desires the science for himself. He wants her work, government agencies want him, and Sara simply wants to stay alive.

Deadly by Design (Book 2) - Nearing the end of her PhD journey, Sara Ricci helps a close friend on a project to create medical nanobots. Unaware that a person intent on revenge is orchestrating an elaborate scheme to destroy them all.

Deadly Discovery (Book 3) - Dr. Sara Ricci accepts an assignment to create a power source from space. While she and the team fight to succeed, a Russian oligarch looking for payback puts them and their project in grave danger.

Deadly Dilemma (Book 4) - A simply phone call places Sara Ricci in a game of high stakes espionage. As she tries to find the truth, a French billionaire does everything he can to make sure she fails.

Deadly Diplomacy (Book 5, coming July 2023) - Sara Ricci has thought little of her great-great-grandfather until a doomsday weapon is created with secrets said to come from him. As Sara tries to uncover the secret, she and her friends become targets of death.

Made in the USA
Las Vegas, NV
26 July 2023

75283540R00193